Reading Madame Bovary

AMANDA LOHREY

Reading Madame Bovary

Black Inc.

Published by Black Inc.,
an imprint of Schwartz Media Pty Ltd
37–39 Langridge Street
Collingwood VIC 3066 Australia
email: enquiries@blackincbooks.com
http://www.blackincbooks.com

The National Library of Australia Cataloguing-in-Publication entry:

Lohrey, Amanda

Reading Madame Bovary / Amanda Lohrey.

9781863954907 (pbk.)

Short stories

A823.3

Book design by Thomas Deverall
Typeset by Duncan Blachford

Printed in Australia by Griffin Press

CONTENTS

For Jan McKemmish

1950–2007

Primates

Isadora

That's me. Isadora Kay Munz. My mother called me Isadora because she greatly admired Isadora Duncan. A free woman, she used to say, I wanted to name you after a free woman. What's a free woman? I wondered then, and still I haven't figured it out. I hated the name, Isadora, and the fact that my family called me Izzie. When I reached sixteen I announced to everyone that hereafter I wanted to be called Jackie (after Jackie Onassis, whom I greatly admired) but soon the borrowed glamour of that wore thin. When I made out my first job application I signed myself I. Kay Munz and I've been Kay ever since.

From time to time my mother will bring the subject up with reproach. I gave you a distinguished name, she'll say, and you have made yourself ordinary.

I fall back on my schoolgirl Latin. *Alis volat propriis*: she flies with her own wings.

The house

The house is in Strathfield, Sydney, Australia, The Southern Hemisphere, The World, The Universe. It is a medium-sized Victorian terrace, six metres wide. Too dark, like all terraces, and with an immense mortgage that weighs on our brains like the hunch on a hunchback. We've been here six years and still we are unable to afford the repairs that would restore it to some level of gentrified grace and comfort. The walls and ceilings are flaking near the cornices, there's a brown damp patch in the corner of the dining-room ceiling, the bathroom still has the pink bath and the baby-blue tiles that our predecessor, a Portuguese bricklayer and cement contractor, got as a bargain deal.

Every night I dream about houses; some of them vast and palatial where I wander from room to room, others small and cramped and Dickensian. Sometimes the roof is missing, sometimes it's a wall. Sometimes there are no doors or windows. Sometimes a great crack opens in the foundations. Sometimes a bright light floods the house and I am happy.

The list

I begin each day by reading the list I have made the night before. Sometimes this is the first thing I do in the morning after I sit up in bed. Here is a list of things I might do in one day. Every day the items change but never the length of the list.

- defrost meat in morning for dinner in evening
- make school lunches

- put on load of washing
- give dog flea tablet
- sign permission note for school excursion and fold into envelope with seven dollars in change
- change Rebecca's dental appointment
- buy white cardboard for Ben's school project
- buy replacement air filter
- buy and post birthday card for George
- buy stamps from slot machine, fresh ham for school lunches, ditto apples
- pick Ben up from aftercare
- hear Ben's reading practice
- wash mosquito nets in ti-tree oil
- cook dinner

And then there's my job. All of the above is just maintenance.

Sex

But I remember whole days spent in the pursuit of sex, not the act itself, but the preparation and anticipation. A date (single) or assignation (married) in the evening; shopping for a satin and lace chemise, a bodystocking, revealing enough to titillate but not absurd enough (red heart-shaped net with black lace, too ridiculous) to make us both laugh (inwardly), to bring on that fatal self-consciousness which is death to ecstasy – which is loss of self, or loss of all but a small corner, one blind focal point of self. The lingerie was not for him: I wanted something new for each new occasion, a new charge, no old associations. This was the flood of sexuality that motherhood dammed. Or dispersed. Men don't know how to handle this in the women they live with – they resist it when what they should do is enter into it; become the father as sexual object. A man who is good with a child takes on a new and subtle, but potent, sexual charge for the mother of the child. If only they knew.

The brothel

It's 8.10 on a Monday morning and as usual I am at the station waiting for my train, waiting for it to throttle to the platform with its loose, dusty rattle.

They are filthy, these Sydney trains – never wear white to work on public transport – but once I am seated my mind tends to wander. This morning I find that suddenly I am reliving a recent fantasy, the one about the brothel. Some time ago I read about a male brothel in Paris. Yes, a male brothel. Those films about respectable housewives who secretly want to be prostitutes make me laugh. That's a male fantasy! Women want to go to brothels alright, but as customers, not workers. In the weekend papers I read about this brothel, and dozing on the couch in the sunroom I drifted into a prolonged fantasy. What would it be like, this place? How would it work? The best thing about it would be its evanescence: easy come (sic), easy go. And now I find I'm reliving this fantasy, on the morning commute of all places.

Burwood!

The harsh nasal burr of the PA system breaks into my reverie like a buzz-saw hitting a brick. But in the overall scheme of things it's a minor distraction. I see a large house, in the eastern suburbs maybe; or it could be a nondescript building in the city, an old office complex, three floors rented out; or a former private hotel of small apartments. I go in, and look through a one-way mirror at some young men playing cards in the parlour. They sit with their shirt-sleeves rolled to the elbow and my eyes caress their tanned forearms, their elegant necks and cropped heads and you can smell them, through the walls, their salty, spicy smell, and I hesitate, and then point, silently.

Croydon!

(The chainsaw again.) The woman on the desk (yes, it's still a madam – cosier, I think) nods, presses a buzzer beneath the desk, ushers you soundlessly out the back through the swinging, ranch-style doors and along a corridor carpeted in ice-blue. She produces a discreet single key and unlocks your apartment door. Inside there is subdued lighting, comfortable white couches, simple mirrors. He comes in, says hello, you say your name, he looks at home in the apartment, relaxed, like a woman, he asks if you'd like a drink, a cocktail, you say yes though you never drink cocktails but you want to watch him mix it. He pours things into a simple silver shaker, his gestures are spare and practised, he hands you your glass and sits opposite you, crossing his legs, one arm along the back of the couch and your eyes are drawn to the golden hair on his tanned forearm. There's something about that forearm that's full of promise.

Ashfield!

His dark hair falls onto his forehead, casual, but he hasn't taken too much trouble with his appearance; he says he's been to the market that morning and found some wonderful barramundi. You wonder if you should believe him, if all the shopping is done by someone else, but you decide it doesn't matter. 'After another martini we'll have dinner,' he says. 'Okay?' You smile, you don't say anything. You gaze out of the window at the lights of the city. You begin to submerge in that feeling of anticipation, of novelty, of alarm, of imminent revelation, although, in the end, it won't matter what it's like, in the end you may not even reach the sex, you may simply eat and eat and eat from his superbly delicate and thoughtful meal, and drink from his champagne, and fall asleep on his couch with your head in his lap and his mesmerising male smell in your face …

Newtown!

You look up, over to the corner. The table's set, but not fussily. He brings in a platter of fillets (he knows you hate fossicking among the bones) in a fine light sauce. He says, 'I didn't think we'd need an entrée – it's too hot tonight.' You are soothed by his judgement, his ease, his conviction. You wonder what this superbly laid-back male has conjured for dessert, your sweet tooth. You shut out the thought of cheese cake

Redfern!

a *faux pas* that could flatten your erotic impulses, deflate your pneumatic balloon, dry up your brimming juices. You are momentarily uneasy at the thought of a fruit sorbet; too light, too unimaginative. You feel a warm, expansive ease in your belly and you cannot tell, or care, if it's your stomach or your womb expanding; you feel the blood flowing; the surge down *there*. There is no moment when it begins to flow, just that sublime gush of recognition when you become aware, when you acknowledge to yourself that the sluices are open. Juicing …

Central!

What do you talk about? You don't want to think about that, words can wreck a fantasy, words can wreck any erotic encounter, he might say something stupid and look suddenly goatish, or worse, say something melancholy, waiting for you to mother him. You make your responses warm but brief to discourage conversation. He suggests you have dessert and coffee on the couch; you think this is a wonderful idea, you tell him you want no coffee because you know it focuses the mind and clarity of thought is the last thing you want now, you move across, sink in the luxurious cushions stuffed with raw wool, not too firm, not too soft, and wait. He brings in the sabayon with raspberry sauce and sits beside you. Bliss, a proper pudding plate of fine white porcelain, a proper spoon, nothing dinky or parfait-like. There is something manly about this spoon, something unspeakably strong and streamlined and fine

Town Hall!

and you are almost at the high point of seduction when the PA blares

Wynyard!

Here you are. Here *I* am in the gritty underworld of my terminus, a dark, musty hole of litter and dust and broken bottles and shit in corners; a place where men solicit rough trade in the public

7

lavatories or, in one famous case, a judge exposed himself to commuters in the stairwell. Up the long, grubby escalator I glide and out into the diesel fumes of lower George Street. And the seduction moment is lost and I am in work mode and all I can think about is how you would pay afterwards. Cash, of course. In those other brothels, the ones for men, you pay before; you deploy your charmless credit card on the formica desk of the madam. Here, you bring cash. One-hundred-dollar notes, drawn especially; those notes that are too impractical for shopping. You fold them in a roll and ease them into the hip pocket of his pants, which hang on the large wooden knob of the door. Slipping that wad into his pants is your final, final pleasure.

You are a woman who likes to pay for it. No emotional investment, no protecting the investment over time (what is time, here?), no ego, yours or his, a total disregard of face; no cherished defences, nursing of sore spots, no ghosts, no vulnerability. Paid civility, the freedom of the cash contract. The free joy of the cash nexus is greatly underrated and we could do with more of it. If we paid parents and children to carry out their family rights and duties we might have less trauma. In the cash transaction we are equals – you are helping me by providing a service. I am helping you to make a living. No murky devious world of manipulation, obligation and superego – should, must, ought to. Duty.

I have heard of a brothel in Paris in the 1890s that had a hundred rooms. In each room a different fantasy: a Samoan hut, a Victorian train carriage, a beggar's archway under the bridge, a dark alley with trash cans (real or fake? How often would they empty them? Would it smell? The smell of fish bones and rotting banana? Would the smell be essential?). I think this a marvellous idea but

8

wonder at the pitfalls. The man would have to have such confidence, such easy wit and physical charm to carry off, unselfconsciously, his costume – his grass skirt, his dirty overcoat, his blue serge uniform and peaked cap. I shared this fantasy with my husband, Frank. Most likely, said Frank, most likely the women would just laugh at him.

I decide to save this fantasy for Diana.

The huntress

Diana is my best friend. She is a senior librarian at TAFE, buxom and blonde and with a great interest in goddesses. She was christened Maureen and changed her name when she turned thirty. To her surprise, everyone took to it straight away, perhaps because it clearly suited her. She was a Diana at heart, a huntress.

Diana is a trivialist. A student of trivia. Not, as she points out, a trivialiser – on the contrary – but one who ascribes the proper importance to the common, the ordinary, the everyday, the familiar, the trite. One who studies the popular, the vernacular, the vulgate. Like a good librarian she is familiar with her reference works and quotes, from the OED, the English author O.W. Holmes, 1883. *You speak trivially, but not unwisely.*

Diana recently enrolled in a goddess workshop. She subscribes to a magazine called *Crone Chronicles* and another called *Sage-Woman*. She read a book entitled *Megatrends for Women* and was deeply affected by the chapter 'The Goddess Reawakening'.

For someone into crystals *et al* Diana is surprisingly hardheaded; ruthless even. When we are discussing sex one day she says, 'Sometimes I think that sex itself is insignificant.'

I stare at her in disbelief. I know of no-one who has had so many lovers.

She corrects herself. 'That is not entirely true. It is significant, like food, only when we have none. Once we are enjoying sex it becomes insignificant; a mere pre-condition, like eating and shitting, to the rest of life. It is a spasm of fleeting and short-lived sensation that helps to regulate the nervous system and dispel accumulated tension, anxiety, etc, etc.'

'This is a very unspiritual view,' I say, deadpan. 'Not very Tantric.' I am mocking her.

I tell her I could not disagree more strongly. When you have a sexual relationship with someone, they have a piece of you. They enter you not sexually – phallically – but electrically (your field). Their vibrations enter your body and disturb your vibrations, sending all your atoms into disarray. After a while you recover – your atoms re-arrange themselves into their old patterns but they bear the imprint of the invader, like lung lesions after TB, or war wounds – an erotic branding iron. And sometimes, with a deep, painful infatuation, sex isn't even necessary for this to take place.

Until I had children I was prone to infatuation. Probably still am, although now I pull back from the brink before I am close enough even to gaze at the view. Why? Because children have radar. They sense the moment when they have ceased to live at the centre of your attention. They sense the alien intruder. An insidious vertigo begins to pollute their consciousness; they reel inwardly. I would not take them there. I would not put them at risk.

Still, unruly desire is always present, always roiling in the substratum.

My dream

I'm in a modest suburban house. There's a small swimming pool out the back that takes up almost all the yard. It's surrounded by a strip of concrete and a high wooden fence on four sides.

The house is full of people.

I go out on my own and look into the pool. At the bottom is a huge, thick snake, cut into several pieces, and three enormous fish like elongated skates.

While I'm watching, one of the creatures emerges from the water and attaches itself to the fence by suction.

I'm mystified. What is it?

At first it looks like a huge, dark turtle but as it slowly inches its way up the fence I realise it's a monstrous flounder. As its blunt nose reaches the top of the high fence it leaps into the air and hovers, horizontal, above me, three metres of dark, streamlined flesh. Slimy, and gleaming like a giant placenta.

Suddenly it soars over the fence into the pool in the yard behind and I hear a thunderous, rasping splash! I see the water rise up on all sides above the height of the fence.

'I'll be back,' I say to the beast. 'I will return later.'

I go inside and say to the others: 'Am I imagining this or are there monstrous fish out there in that pool?' They seem unmoved.

I wake.

Fate

Diana is superstitious. She consults astrologers and clairvoyants. I find this surprising in someone whose IT skills are in advance of just about anyone I know (barring experts). Boolean logic isn't everything, she says.

Diana makes raids into the outer suburbs, looking for clues. Once, when the kids were interstate with my parents and Frank was at a conference in Adelaide, we spent an hysterical weekend together. On the Saturday afternoon we drove out west to see Diana's latest discovery, a woman with second sight. Diana believes there are wise women in unlikely places and this one was a Mrs. Cluny who lived out in the sticks at Bankstown. Diana had rung and made an appointment for three o'clock and when we finally managed to locate the street we were surprised to find a small weatherboard cottage built in the '30s with a rickety fence and bare, scrubby garden. We walked to the back of the house, as instructed, where there was a shabby grey veranda and a white sulphur-crested cockatoo in an iron cage that looked at us and said nothing.

Diana knocked on the door.

No-one came.

She knocked again, and after a minute the door opened a foot or so and the grey head of a woman in her early sixties appeared and said abruptly: 'You're early. I've got someone with me. Wait on the veranda.' And the door was closed again.

After ten minutes a middle-aged man, dressed like a business-man, opened the door, nodded to us and headed down the pathway towards the gate. Diana looked at me knowingly. 'Probably came to ask about his shares,' she said. With a wave of her hand Mrs. Cluny beckoned us in. She was a short, fat woman who seemed to float about in a cloud of flesh. In her movements there was a certain refinement, delicacy even, though she was blunt in her speech and drab in her dress. In her mouth was a cigarette that gave off a strong, acrid smell.

We followed her into a kind of musty parlour at the front where she indicated a fraying couch opposite her own armchair. On the small wooden coffee table between us was a chipped saucer full of ash and cigarette butts, and next to that a packet of Woodbines.

So this is a psychic, I thought. Where is the velvet turban with the crescent moon? The fringed shawl? The Turkish slippers?

Mrs. Cluny asked for a personal object and Diana unbuckled her watch and handed it over. The woman closed her eyes, adjusted her wide bottom in the chair and began to rub the leather band of the watch between her thumb and forefinger, up and down, up and down, mesmerically, as if it were Aladdin's lamp.

'If I see anything dark, do you want to know?' she asked.

'Dark?'

'Yeah, dark. Like death.' This was followed by a long drag on the cigarette.

'I don't know.'

'Make up your mind.'

'Um … yes. Yes, okay. But I've come about something in particular.' I looked at Diana and realised how nervous she was. This was serious. 'Can I ask questions?'

Mrs. Cluny nodded.

'I keep having this dream, a recurring dream about a baby.' And she gave Mrs. Cluny a semi-coherent account of what seemed to me a cluster of mundane events made significant only by the appearance of a baby surrounded by a white light.

For a long time Mrs. Cluny said nothing, just kept rubbing the watchband, up and down, up and down. Then she said, still with her eyes closed, still fingering the fine strap of leather: 'You're not dreaming about babies, you're dreaming about your spirit self.'

'What's that? You mean, like the soul?'

'Whatever you like to call it.'

Oh, no, I thought, oh, no, I shouldn't have come. Not this. Next she'll be talking about past lives.

There was a silence and then she added, 'You'll see it one day.'

'You mean in the dream?'

'No, you'll see the baby.'

What baby? There was no real baby.

'You'll see that baby again, just before you die.'

Diana was speechless. And then she surprised me. 'When am I going to die?' she asked.

Mrs. Cluny closed her eyes, and went on fingering the watch-band. 'I don't see your death at all clear.' She paused. 'That's the way it is. Sometimes I see it clear with people, sometimes I don't. You've got a kind of cloud coming toward you. It could be your death, but it could be something else. In any case,' she added, 'it won't be for a while yet.'

Then she sat, very composed, with her hands on her lap. She put Diana's watch down on the table beside her, a signal that the interview was over. She would 'see' no more that day.

Diana fumbled in her purse until she located her cheque book.

'I only take cash,' said Mrs. Cluny.

On the drive home Diana was uncharacteristically quiet and a little unnerved.

'She didn't really tell you anything much,' I ventured.

'Hmmmm,' she said, biting her lip and staring ahead at the white line. Every now and then her eyes would flutter in an odd way. 'I should have asked her what she meant by *a while*,' she said. She was in a funk.

Back in the city we went to The Malaya for a bowl of blinding hot laksa and then on to a Bette Midler movie to restore our morale. By the time we got back to Diana's place she had snapped out of it.

Despite her weakness for the consumerised supernatural (tarot festivals, crystal workshops, astrology on the net) and what Frank derides as a certain credulousness, Diana can be very funny. She, too, is absorbed in lists, though not of the kind that plague me. Hers are a diverting game of mapping the world through trivia, and often over coffee we compile them together or, rather, she goes off on a riff and I throw in the odd contribution. Here is the latest one, recalled from memory. Knowing me, I've probably forgotten the best bits: I'll have to check with her later.

The narcissist's bedside table versus the non-narcissist's bedside table
THE NON-NARCISSIST:
- K-Y jelly
- toilet lanolin
- tissues
- anti-histamine tablets
- Body Shop moisturiser
- reading glasses
- detective novel or the *Women's Weekly*
- contraceptive pills
- small asymmetrical plaster vase made by offspring in Grade Two art class
- twenty-dollar alarm clock with tinny beep

- bedside lamp: cheap Taiwanese knock-off of a Milanese design

THE NARCISSIST:

- pink ceramic oil burner with ylang-ylang aromatic oil
- vibrator in purple velvet case with silver draw-string
- Almond and patchouli massage oil
- The *I Ching* or Liz Greene's *Astrology for Lovers*, Stephen Coulter's *The Empathic Friend (and Where to Find Them)* or Jack Kornfield's *A Path with Heart*
- Magazines: *Marie Claire*, *Vanity Fair* and, if of a certain age, *Vogue*
- Estée Lauder night cream and eye gel
- buff stick for nails
- black silk eye mask for when partner is inconsiderately reading
- mobile phone for late-night calls when depressed
- bedside lamp: (under forty) cheap Taiwanese knock-off of a Milanese design or (over forty) Laura Ashley with pale-blue flowers on the base and a pleated shade in satin cream

The beautiful object

There is a joy in money, and we are all too refined to speak of it directly. We say, 'What fine linen, what a lovely bowl, what nice shoes.' I'm not materialistic, we tell ourselves, it's just that I love beauty.

Yesterday, I took an extended lunchtime and went to David Jones. I go there often. Frank says it's my temple.

Leaving aside all the deep and meaningful contributions of my career path (more of that later), my job means that I can walk into David Jones and buy two pairs of shoes at the one time. Not that I do this very often – in fact I've done it twice in the last ten years. The point is: if I want to, I can. Something my mother could never do, or her mother before her. And if my shoes are good, I feel powerful, so that no matter how badly things go in other spheres, there is some part of me – the shoe part – that can't be humiliated.

Shopping can turn into mania. Some people buy on impulse. Not me. I am a member of the school of exhaustive research. Come the new season I cannot buy one pair of shoes until I look at every pair of shoes in the city. I must survey the field. I must not make a mistake. It's my professional training. I have a reputation at work for being thorough. I am.

I can't understand Frank. When he goes shopping he buys the first thing he sees that he likes and goes home. Don't tell me it's a male trait because my sister is the same.

I have to conduct a complete reconnoitre, a thorough evaluation of available resources. I cannot go home at night haunted by the nagging thought that something better might have been just around the corner.

Yesterday I went to buy a lipstick. I tried one colour on my bottom lip, one on the top, choosing from the testers.

'I'll just leave these on and see how they look outside in the natural light,' I said to the sales assistant, a girl with short, spiky blonde hair and heavy blue eyeshadow, expertly applied. 'The colours are so misleading under these lights.' She murmured her discreet assent.

'Do they really last?' I asked, with the knowing scepticism of the practised, indeed, jaded buyer.

'They're a drier formula,' she intoned, with all the solemn aplomb of a research scientist explaining the latest breakthrough in genetic engineering, and then she streaked, first, an orange-pink frosted and then a scarlet slash on the back of her hand, just above the thumb – which is where they always do it. Where I do it. Where all women do it. Why there? Is there a lipstick-testing gene in all females? *One Perfect Coral, Mister Melon, Rio Mango, Sherry Pepper*, and a new range with names like *Lust, Vanity, Ambition*. Before I know it, I've spent ninety dollars on two lipsticks.

I pay with one of my credit cards.

Our credit cards are precious. They sustain morale. Every time I hear someone on the radio droning on about the perils of credit, I turn it off. Once I found a credit card in the gutter on Glebe Point Road. When its owner came to pick it up she brought me a cutting of African violet, taken from her own garden and earthed in a small decorative pot to express her relief and gratitude. Her son had broken his arm that day but she had taken the time to show her appreciation.

Credit cards are our life-blood.

I work at keeping the African violet alive.

The zoo

Let me tell you about work. I call it the zoo.

I am a project officer in the Human Resources section of a medium-sized company that does (mostly) outsourced work for government agencies. I won't say who or what: somebody might sue. My director is a young man called Winton, a psychologist by training with an MBA and an infatuation with all things Japanese, especially their approach to corporate management and decision-making. He goes to ikebana classes. I am fond of Winton, and it's probably because he's such an unpredictable blend of the fey and the fly. He's short and stocky with fair curly hair, square practical hands and rimless glasses, and is so improbable a blend of corporate style and winsomeness that it can be disconcerting. He is quietly spoken with a reserve that is neither stiff nor shy but is a kind of charm in itself.

Today is a hat day in the office and Winton is wearing a smart Tyrolean number with a feather.

'Only Winton,' I say.

'I'm amazed that it's not Japanese,' says Christina, tartly. Christina Montiades is Winton's chief antagonist. Christina is the office cynic, a big woman with a deep, hearty laugh. *Cynic: an autocrat in search of a vision.* She is an SCW (Single Career Woman) and a workaholic (she has a life coach). Christina perches on her ergonomic stool typing away at the keyboard with a long, thin pencil set firmly between her teeth. She keeps it there, on the advice of her dentist, to prevent her unconsciously grinding her molars into a paste. This morning Christina is wearing a navy-blue baseball cap with the Southern Cross of the Eureka Flag on the front. She is an ardent advocate for a republic.

I am wearing Ben's Sydney Swans beanie, which rather suits me (red is my colour), but by general acclamation the prize goes to Martin who is wearing an understated grey felt effort, a kind of soft turban. Immensely smart.

'I got it on my trip to Tashkent,' he says. 'It's what the Taliban wear. I also bought an embroidered cap but it's a bit gay.'

'I wouldn't worry about that,' says Christina. 'This *is* Sydney.'

'You can't wear a Taliban hat,' says Winton. 'It's in poor taste.'

'Grow up,' says Martin.

We are dangerously on the edge of politics which, mostly, we manage to avoid.

It was Winton's idea to have a hat day because this week we begin yet another restructure. First off, we have to draft a strategic plan, which will mean redundancies, and Winton thinks we might all get a bit tense.

Stratagem: a manoeuvre in war; a plan for deceiving an enemy; an instance of clever generalship; in figurative speech, any ploy to gain an advantage; a trick or scheme.

We are scheduled to meet in the afternoon in the conference room on the twenty-first floor, the one that's painted grey and has white Venetian blinds. It's about as sterile as it could be, and perhaps that's why we get nowhere. Winton has just returned from a special management conference on how to develop a vision statement for the next three years. But first, he says, you have to have a vision before you can have a vision statement.

'What,' asks Martin, 'is the difference between a vision and an objective?'

'It's the difference between a mechanical and an organic, relational model.'

'In plain English, Winton.'

'I'll have more to say about that at this afternoon's meeting.'

Winton has been reading a book on management called *Theory Z* and he's at pains to explain it to us. It's all about how to adapt Japanese management practices – with special reference to *teamwork* – to Western management hierarchies. He has scanned pages into his workstation and emailed them to every member of the office.

The gist of these is that 'hierarchies' and 'bureaucracies' are out and 'clans' are in, viz: *The Theory Behind the Theory Z Organisation.* 'The difference between a *hierarchy* – or *bureaucracy* – and Type Z is that Z organisations have achieved a high state of consistency in their internal culture. They are most aptly described as *clans* in that they are intimate associations of people engaged in economic activity but tied together through a variety of bonds. *Clans* are distinct from *hierarchies*, and from *markets*, which are the other two fundamental social mechanisms through which transactions between individuals can be governed.' AND 'Type Z companies succeed both as human social systems and as economic producers. A Z company seldom undertakes any explicit attempts at team building. Instead, it first creates a culture to foster interpersonal subtlety and intimacy, and these conditions encourage cohesive work groups.'

I can't help wondering how this squares with what a young mining executive told me at a dinner recently, that anyone in the same job for more than four years is a loser who's going nowhere. 'If he's any good,' he said (note the 'he'), 'he'll be bored after four years or headhunted by someone else.' Winton has been in this job for five years. I should tell him he is in danger of becoming a loser.

Winton wants us to begin our vision statement by coming up with a definition of our work ethic (a *clan* ethic, presumably).

'I've read your material, Winton,' says Christina, 'and it strikes me as just another form of groupism. I know these models, full of love and kindness but with a thin line operating between consensus and coercion.'

'The most efficient working bodies are like clans. Look at the Google corp.'

'You mean packs of nerds who go jogging together in their knee-length running shorts.'

'There's a place for everyone,' he says, 'and if not, you retrain them. This is how the Japanese do it: they always find a niche for you. You work for the company all your life, give them total loyalty, and they find a place for you.'

'But they own you. It's all about creating the corporate personality. You become an automaton.'

'Yes, Christina, but don't you see, it works for them, it works.' He looks pointedly over the rim of his Armani glasses.

Later, Christina will take me aside (her strong grip on my arm) and say that Winton just loves the group thing, the bonding thing.

'It's stronger in some men than the sex drive,' she says.

The afternoon drags on and we wallow in abstractions. Sitting to my right is Lisa, picking at the rim of her styrofoam cup, flicking the crumbs onto the floor and making, in her fastidious way, a mess. Lisa is an administrative assistant, all of twenty-six, with two degrees and a mop of curly black hair. She is tall and thin and neurasthenic. She smiles and laughs too much, in a kind of brittle, high-strung way. She is the youngest and possibly the cleverest person in the office. Except perhaps for Kelvin, our programmer. Kelvin is into minor forms of self-mutilation. During meetings he has been known to trim the cuticles of his nails with a razor blade.

After three hours of squabbling and getting nowhere, we rise from our chairs and head back to our stations.

'That went well,' says Winton dryly as we go down together in the lift. He sighs. I hate it when Winton sighs. I want to console him.

'It's that room. Next time we should meet somewhere nice, outside the building. Bring a fresh perspective to it, try and enjoy ourselves.' We need to get out of the office, I say, to somewhere our heads can clear and we can – just maybe – get out of old patterns of thinking and knee-jerk responses to traditional antagonists. We should go somewhere to have our sense of possibility enhanced, our sense of wonder replenished.

'Where?'

I tell him I hear there's a great conference centre at the zoo (the real one), with a glassed-in meeting room that looks out onto a pool in a rain-forest setting.

'Book it,' he says. 'It's a great idea.'

'Does this make me a Z person?'

Winton smiles, wanly.

Domesticity

Are all pleasures corrupted by domesticity, except the pleasure(s) of domesticity itself?

The moment I leave work it's like some kind of whirlwind. The office is a space capsule, sealed in, airless, quiet; you're unreachable, no-one from the family can get at you emotionally; there is only work that can be done, and I do it. My work has a manageable limited-ness to it, unlike the family, whose demands go on and on and on and you could have ninety hours a day and it still wouldn't be enough.

I get off the train, walk to the butcher on the corner who stays open late, buy some chops for tea because that'll mean a quick meal, jog to the little fruit-and-veg man (it's late and Frank has to eat early tonight to get to his martial arts class), buy some French beans (it's the only green thing Ben will eat) and some melon (a quick dessert). Then I remember I've forgotten the anti-itch cream for their mosquito bites from the weekend camping and I've got to double-back to the chemist behind the train line; I get there and he has just closed and I swear and some schoolboys look up from under their boaters and smirk and I'm doing my high-heel jog back across to the station and down those interminable steps painted with slogans – 'Drugs Kill' – and a fat busker echoing in the tunnel, *'Knock, knock, knockin' on heaven's door'*, and this is the fourth time today that I've been through this filthy tunnel.

When I get home there isn't time to read the mail. I dump my shopping on the bench and switch the hot plates on – still with my handbag over my arm – because they take an age to warm up on this old stove. And I think of when I used to cook an interesting meal nearly every night, only now I haven't the time and the kids wouldn't eat it anyway ('Yuk, not curry!') and I spend two hours cooking something mediocre that nobody likes and then feel let down, and on bad nights hate myself for not making more of an effort, for not being innovative and surprising, and Frank doesn't like pasta and Ben can't eat dairy foods because of his allergies but the only dessert he likes is ice-cream which he can't have, except the tofu variety which he hates ('Yuk'), and some nights I just give up. They can have a toasted bacon sandwich and a banana or go to bed hungry.

I think of my grandmother, Audrey, who worked cleaning floors for six days and on Sunday cooked the household to a standstill. I used to watch her at the stove, a bad-tempered fairy godmother, conjuring up clouds of cholesterol. Eggs and bacon and fried bread for breakfast, hot jam tarts for morning tea (puff pastry loaded with butter, I'd watch her cut the rich yellow knobs into the dough and then roll out the layers), roast lamb and baked everything for lunch with steamed sultana pudding or suet jam roll with cream *and* custard. After lunch I'd feel so full, so terribly heavy that, even though only nine years old, I would have to go and lie down in the spare room until, around 3.30, I'd be summoned for afternoon tea. Scones and sponge cake, and sardines on toast ... We'd catch the train home before tea proper; God knows what they ate then. Audrey all day at the oven and the pine bench by the sink, little and plump with short dark hair and a perpetual frown of concentration. She lived to be seventy, my grandfather until eighty-one. How is this possible? Was cholesterol different then? On our Sundays my children seem to eat nothing at all. If I won't weaken and give them pies and chips and pizza they sulk into an unholy fast. And the fat man in the dirty echoing tunnel sings '*wasting away – wasting away*'. Huh! When they were little I'd lie awake at night and work through, in my head, what they'd eaten for the day. Especially Rebecca. Half a green apple here, a quarter of toast there, some butter on a spoon, a knob of raw carrot, a small bowl of plain white rice. Would she make it into the next morning? Would she survive the week? Now I'm too jaded for this evening review: they're still here, even if they do bring home their lunchboxes with more or less what I put in them, except for the fact that their sandwiches look as if they've been drop-kicked around the schoolyard and the pieces reassembled for my benefit ('Why can't we buy our lunch?'). And then there are those nights when Frank looks dolefully at his grilled fish, sans sauce of any kind. We used to have ginger and chilli, his eyes say, and fennel and coriander. We used to have lamb with apricots and sour cream and roasted almonds ('Yuk!' the children cry). I can't bear his reproaches, my eyes stare back at his. 'Cook yourself,' they say. But Frank is more or less unreconstructed – sausages and chops are his entire repertoire, and then under protest. I made the mistake of trying to impress him with my culinary arts before we were married and I've been paying for it ever since.

Frank helps me clear away. There's something Edwardian about his gesture of lifting the tablecloth off, opening the back door and flicking the cloth outwards to loosen the crumbs. It's one of his unfailing gestures after a meal. Tonight he's in a hurry, stuffing his white Kung Fu outfit into his old Puma kit bag as he strides out the door. I call to Rebecca to come and take her herbal remedy for her eczema. I call three, four times, I am exasperated, I storm into her bedroom to find her, for once, quietly drawing a map; some homework. She looks up at me, calmly.

'Yes, mother,' she says, with grey, insolent eyes.

By eight I seem to have been in perpetual motion and still not to have done the washing-up. The dishwasher is broken and yet to be fixed. Frank does the washing-up on the nights that he's home but these are increasingly few. (I have exempted the children from washing-up in term time on condition they do a minimum of one hour's homework.) A working woman must be ruthless about the house: where have I heard this?

Frank is anally retentive. The washing up must be done immediately after dinner or he becomes anxious. I like to sit over the table and relax, and talk, but Frank takes your plate away while you are still chewing on the last bite. This is the driven trivia of marriage; it is the insupportable resentment of the anal-retentive male who must have petty order, petty control. What would happen if we left the dishes overnight? The cockroaches and the ants would scamper across the mucky plates, copulate in cups and shit on spoons. So what? In the morning the house would still be standing; the trains would still pull into the station; Frank would not be lying in the bath with his throat cut.

I cannot stand his grim, frantic tidying up. It's not as if he could just *do* it. No, he has to do it as a wordless judgement on me; his martyred reproach. Frankly, Frank, it would be a turn-on for me to go to bed with the dreck of dinner strewn across the kitchen. Frankly, Frank, this would say abandon; this would say relinquishing of control, Frank; kiss of death to the superego, Frank; mess, cockroaches, cunt, spit and dribble, nipple in mouth and hair in teeth. Who wants to fuck with the glare of a clinical kitchen in their head? Frank?

Not me.

Afterwards, I don't know what to do. I could iron. I should bake a cake for school lunches. Instead, I sit at the table and flick through *Business Review Weekly* and *Vanity Fair*. I like to read at the kitchen table, don't ask me why. My mother used to like to take a nap on the kitchen floor, on the large rectangular brown mat she had in the centre of the room by the pine table. It was a sunny kitchen, warm, the hard surface was good for her back, she said. She'd take a cushion from the chairs, for her head, and lie for forty minutes, placed so that the sun came in through the window and warmed her back, and she'd doze, half in dream, half in reverie. Sometimes when I came home from school I'd find her there, in a ladylike version of the foetal position, eyes closed, hands placed just so, sometimes still in her apron. 'If you're tired, Mum, why don't you lie on the bed?' I asked once. 'Because then you go into a deep sleep,' she replied, 'and that's when you get bad dreams. In the late afternoon.'

It's just after nine when Frank gets in. He looks brighter; this martial exercise always seems to perk him up. He's a big man. When he was young, when I first met him, he had a buoyancy around the chest which I found irresistible. Now, often, he looks tired around the chest, caving in. Do you study men's bodies? I do. Why not? They study ours. Frank pats my hair, something he does when he's in a good mood; casts a quick glance at the sink (trying to look and see if the washing-up is done in a way that doesn't look as if he's looking and I won't notice), takes in the clean sink, and reverts to what is on his mind from his class.

'Grant thinks I should take another test,' he says.

'Another test' is the next step to the black belt.

'I'm going to bed,' he says. 'You going to be long?'

I look up from my *Vanity Fair*. 'Not long.'

Frank hates to go to sleep alone. He likes me to come to bed at the same time as him, which annoys me. Another way of keeping me under control, colonising my time. Nevertheless I tend to drift in there, not long after him. I marvel at how quickly and cleanly he can go to bed. One minute he's dressed and up; the next he's in bed, looking as if he's been there an hour. I have to check the doors and windows, check the kids, take off my make-up, shave my legs, retouch my toenails, remember at the last minute to get the meat and bread rolls out of the freezer for the next day. Something, always something …

Outside, the thick, sticky air is beginning to move. That ominous and stirring wind that ushers in a thunderstorm is blowing into our claustrophobic little courtyard. I hear the loud splat of the first heavy drops against the roof and look out the window at that weird exciting glow; rosy, energising. The sky is a warm charcoal grey and then suddenly the lightning, the startling, forked flash above the trees. It makes me want to rush out onto the veranda and be a part of it. There is something so cosy, so enlivening and optimistic about a thunderstorm. I can't think why they use it as a frightening backdrop in horror movies. On a hot, humid night it's a wet and fiery joy. It makes me feel connected to the earth.

Soon I will have the satisfaction of lying in bed in the heavy rain, in a house I own and that I work to pay off. I will feel the solid walls around me; the warm, mellow street light through the window; the new guttering that I know won't leak; the dog on the mat, sighing; my king-size bed, my Guatemalan throw-over, my photos of the children. And I will be lulled by the steady clatter of the rain on the tin roof, the whispering drip from the guttering.

Frank is propped up in bed, naked. The hair on his chest is still dark. I wonder when it will go grey and whether it will still turn me on. His neck is just a shade too thick, which looks all wrong in a shirt and suit but good when he's like this, a torso framed by the sheet, just him and the sheet. Swaddled in the sheets. Frank the big baby. He is twisting the hair on his chest into dark tendrils and anxiously reciting aloud the names of his martial arts moves.

After I've settled in between the sheets he hands me a printed sheet. 'Test me out,' he says.

We work to the bottom of the list. 'C'mon,' I say. 'Give it a rest.' This isn't how I imagined foreplay would be, ten years on, conducted in Chinese. He's such a worrier; he knows it all backwards. The pointless repetition.

'I'm tense,' he says. 'Bite me. Bite my back.' He lies on his stomach and I lean over him and make a circle of bites around one shoulder. 'Harder,' he says. 'Give me pain.' I see the little red marks of my teeth, up close. He exhales, heavily. Stretches his arm out and pats me on the knee. 'Good girl.'

Lights out, and we both lie, silently, wondering if we'll go on with it. It's around this time that Ben wakes: he's psychic. We know that if we start, soon we'll hear him cry out with bad dreams. Our parents fuck and we have bad dreams. Our parents don't fuck and we have bad dreams. We, the parents, remember only the bad dreams that intervene. With every lewd, sly, suggestive initiating gesture we hesitate; we wait for the demons to activate. For me it's particularly off-putting; not so much for Frank (testosterone has tunnel vision) but for me, if the children stir, or murmur in the dark, it's the end. And of course, I can't make a noise. How many lovers' cries are strangled by the thought of the nursery and the light sleepers under ten?

Frank sighs. 'Have you made a booking?' he asks. His voice is low and hoarse in the dark. He is tired.

'No,' I whisper. 'I'll do it tomorrow.' I switch on the light.

'Damn,' he says, for a multitude of reasons, and I switch it off. Then I fumble in my handbag which I keep always by my bed, in case of burglary, and feel for my notebook. My notebook is stoked with lists. Lists are the fretwork of my day, how I hold my life together. I draw out my list for tomorrow and in the dark I scrawl, at the bottom of the page: *Ring Russell Hotel.*

Dream

I have a dream about my son, Ben. He is seven years old, a difficult age. I dream that he is shrinking. I'm looking after him and he's growing smaller and smaller and I'm running around in a panic, but he just keeps shrinking and then, finally, he's only a few inches high. But it's alright. He looks up into my face and smiles. He forgives me. It's alright because he always forgives me.

When I wake I think back to when the children were toddlers, when I was at home and I would walk them over to the playground and the bright yellow swings. I remember those hot, still afternoons when there was a strange calm in the park.

I remember my daughter in the backyard, on the trampoline. I remember standing in the kitchen, chopping Chinese cabbage on the board; pale green and white frills under my German cleaver. I feel that someone is watching me. I look up and out the window. My daughter is jumping on the trampoline, looking back at me. She jumps and jumps and turns and falls to her knees and bounces up onto her feet and turns and looks over at me, then turns again, and jumps, her legs wide and high in a scissor jump, and looks back. I wave. Just as I wave, she turns away. Her look fluctuates with each jump, each turn, each bounce and spring. There is something in her look that is perplexed, angry, self-contained, blithe, pre-occupied, a half-smile. My little dancer: remote, buoyant; up, down; up, down; up, down.

Jump, turn away.

Jump. Wave. Turn away.

Around four in the morning, Ben wakes again. He cries out. I get up.

'What's the matter?' I ask, sitting on the edge of his bed.

'I had a bad dream.'

'What about?'

'I dreamed I was in the supermarket, or somewhere like that, shopping, and I looked around and couldn't find you and I went outside and in the street there were all these women who looked like you from the back, they were wearing coats like yours and had black hair and I called out 'Mum!' but when one of them turned around she had a witch's face.'

I hold his hand and press the inside of the palm, gently, at regular intervals, until I can hear his light snoring.

Roald Dahl has a lot to answer for.

And now I am wide awake. I go out into the kitchen to read but there's nothing there and in desperation I reach for the remote control left lying on the table and switch on the small black portable television that sits atop the fridge. There's a sudden blare of sound as hastily I adjust the volume to barely audible. The ABC is showing a documentary on famine in Ethiopia. It reminds me of when I was having breast-feeding problems with Rebecca and I was sitting up, night after night, trying to get her onto the nipple, and feeling sorry for myself. One night, as she nuzzled beside my ample breast, I watched a similar programme in which a young woman stared out at me with black, despairing eyes. Her breasts were grey and shrivelled and the emaciated baby in her arms was dying.

I looked down at my sleeping child. I stopped feeling sorry for myself.

I am a First World Person.

Who are we?

Last night after work I passed three beggars on my way to Wynyard Station. One of them sat on the edge of the footpath, right on the corner as the peak-hour traffic crawled behind him, just inches from his stained army surplus pants, held up with string. His head hung down, he did not look up, he did not make eye contact. He held a piece of cardboard, on which he had written:

Please give
I am starving

I was in a hurry. I walked on towards my train, just as I had hurried past the other two beggars who also squatted on the grey bitumen at knee height to the throng of passing commuters. Why didn't I stop and empty my pockets? Why didn't we all stop and beat our breasts and cry, 'Who will look after these men?'

In bed last night I couldn't sleep. 'We are so self-absorbed,' I whispered to Frank. 'We don't do anything to help anyone. What do we do? We rush around, but what do we *do*, really?'

Frank was drowsy. 'I coach the under-10 football team,' he murmured. 'I'm doing my bit to keep manliness alive.'

'Don't be flippant.'

'Go to sleep, Kay.'

Go to sleep Kay. Go to sleep Kay.

I can't sleep.

Who are we? I think. Why are we here?

Why did I walk past three beggars? Not one, Frank, but three. Like everyone else, I walked on.

Core values

One evening Rebecca announces at the dinner table (for once, no-one is at a class and we are all eating together) that she has been elected delegate from her class to a special student forum. The forum has been set up so that the students can join the staff in drawing up a new behaviour code of Core Values.

'What values?' Frank asks.

'Core values.'

'Core?'

'Yes, core.'

'What does that mean?'

Bec rolls her eyes like he's a moron. 'You know,' she says.

At the special parents' meeting (Frank is away) I learn that the school has embarked on revising its discipline code in the interests of Quality Assurance. Students and pupils both are being asked to draw up a list of Core Values such as Truth, Honesty, Responsibility, Kindness and so on.

Some parents oppose the idea, though they are strangely inarticulate in their efforts to say why. One woman laughs and says: 'In my day the bishop came in and gave us a pep talk.' This sounds so witheringly archaic that we all feel uncomfortably out of step.

A week later I ask Bec how her work with core values is coming along. 'Okay,' she says, with quiet aplomb. 'Anna Stuart Jay gave a talk today in assembly.' Anna Stuart Jay is the school captain.

'What did she say?'

'She said someone had called one of the Koori girls a black tart on the bus the other day. And when she was reported she said she hadn't done it when she had, so she violated the core values of Truth and Honesty.'

'You mean, she lied.'

'That's what I said.'

'No, you didn't ...' I check myself. She is eleven years old. Lately it seems that I am always nagging her about something. I will take this up with the principal. Wait until I tell Frank – Frank the purist about language. He will sigh and shake his head.

And he does.

One weekend he comes back from the DVD store with an old copy of *The Ten Commandments*.

'These kids, Kay, know nothing.'

'Charlton Heston?'

'At least it's something.'

So we all sit down on a Saturday evening and watch *The Ten Commandments*. The dialogue is impossibly stilted and portentous and the Pharaoh given to crossing his arms and scowling: '*I'll have you torn into so many pieces even the vultures won't find them.*' Bec's friend, Jessica, is staying over for the weekend and the girls watch it in fits and starts, staggering around in parodic imitation of the Pharaoh and droning: '*So it is written, so it shall be done.*'

I am struck by something I missed when I watched this movie as a student. Then I had found it hysterically and deliciously camp. Now I am aware of something else: the whole epic is a saga of slaughtered children.

A vengeful God. Not mine.

The doll

Did I mention the chest pains? Lately I've begun to feel a painful, squeezing tightness in my chest. I hold my breath, I assume it's indigestion (another hasty meal), I try to burp discreetly, there is no relief, the pain squeezes and I'm afraid. Not me, I think, not me.

I mention the pains to Frank. He frowns. 'Have a check-up,' he says.

I mention the pains to Diana. 'I'm not surprised!' She almost spits in disgust. 'You're always rushing around like a mad thing. You do too much. You're stressed, you need to do relaxation. You should take up yoga or something.'

Yoga. It's not a bad idea. But where would I fit it in? On some days I am so tired I lose the desire to please anyone. I am on the edge of martyrdom.

I remember a friend saying of his children: 'You forget you've got them. You come into the kitchen in the morning to make toast and you're pottering around and suddenly there they are and you have this small moment of shock. Like: Oh, yes, of course, the kids.'

I looked at him incredulously. Only a man could think this way. 'I never forget I've got them,' I said. Not adding, 'They inhabit my dreams like wild, surreal flowers.'

Tonight the pain in my chest is bad – scary – and I can't sleep.

I get up and I go into the spare room and I lie with the doll.

The doll is my shameful secret. I am forty years old and I have a doll. The doll is one of those soft ones, made of cloth. It lies on the bed in the spare room. At the window of this room there are lace curtains so that it is never pitch dark in here, not even around three in the morning when I push open the door and look in. I've been lying on my bed in the humid dark of our room, my feet hot and tense so that I push them out from under the doona into the cool air. I can't sleep, and after that long space of passing beyond resistance, I ease out from under the doona and creep from the room. It's important that Frank doesn't hear me, that he doesn't get up, come encroaching on me, even in the dark, breathing his hostile fatigue and saying, 'What's up? Why are you up again?' as if he must have a sleeping eye, a sleeping ear in radar mode; some control over my being, in the house, even in his sleep.

I push open the door of the spare room and it makes its scuffing swish noise of wood scraping against carpet. I wait for Frank to stir. He doesn't.

In the spare room, on the bed, is the doll.

When I first looked at these dolls, one Christmas in Myer, stacked in a boxed and cellophaned pile, I was shocked at their ugliness, their boofheadedness, their daring deviation from a century of sweet doll faces. I searched for several minutes for one that was less offensive; appealing if not pretty (none of them were pretty). Eventually I chose her, in the blood-red cotton dress with the white flowers, her woolly tufts of hair, oatmeal blonde, and her absurdly puckered-in, tucked-in, sucked-in mouth, a deep fold beneath her tiny nose; and painted green eyes, round like road signs. Potato face, and a soft, unresistant cloth body and big white plastic shoes. She came with a birth certificate and a name. I opened the envelope. 'Aurora'. Potato head Aurora! Rebecca wouldn't be able even to say it.

She grew on me. Her chubby, undemanding plainness, her soft body, were no reproach. The palms of her hands are streaked with pink where Rebecca painted them with nail polish (not content to stop at the nails). Her toes are grubby. Here she lies, on the bed, in the spare room, the way dolls lie; wide-eyed, stiff-backed and expectant; not lying at all but somehow in a horizontal standing-up state.

Ben stirs. I hear him coughing, the rattle in his chest. 'Mum!' he cries, a sharp, loud, commanding cry. I leave the door of the spare room and tip-toe to his bed. He's asleep, twitching his nose, rubbing it urgently, something in the humid room invading his mucous membranes, the dust mites dancing in his nostrils, his wide-open but barred window letting in the gases from the late-night traffic. Ben hears me in the night; even in his sleep he senses my presence near his bed, which is why I have learned not to go into his room, late, after he is asleep, but to trust in fate (though it's not in my nature to) or to look in briefly from the door.

In the middle of the night I must occupy my territory warily, caught between two male colonisers. I am a scout treading a stealthy path between two poles of fierce demanding energy.

Night after night Ben has woken like this. I begin to resent it. That anyone should claim my nights now is unbearable. I feel estranged from him and his restlessness. His insistent possession of me seems akin to Frank's petulance; their unspoken resentment, their desire for that something more I'm not giving – all this has made me feel lonely. Un-nourished. I could say 'uncared' for, but no, since 'care' is a form of possession (he had 'care' of the land). No special moments for me lately, other than the ones I give myself.

I return to Aurora. She is propped up on the bed, arms splayed out, painted eyes wide. I lift the thin cotton bedspread and climb under it. I hold her to me, high against my chest, the mild prickle of her woolly hair against my chin, my hand on her padded arm that lays across my breast, my other arm resting against her small padded bottom (stuffed and sewn). How full she feels, a soft, full firmness that nestles into the sadness around my heart.

How comforting it is to have a soft, inanimate object in my arms; a cushion even, but this, better still. I know I ought to feel silly but I don't: the desire for comfort needs no defence. I wouldn't care who surprised me here with this doll, though defiance is not what I feel. What I feel is sadness.

Sadness isn't a word I would have used once. Too pedestrian, too worn with mundane use. I'd have waited for a special word.

In the hospital I lay for hours and hours, and slept, floating in an anaesthetised daze. An old, shabby hospital, it seemed to be gummed together with glue and cardboard. It was intimate, informal; they left me alone. I lay in my bed with a sensation of smiling, drifting sleep; effortless benign sleep that went on and on. And I didn't want to go home.

Frank drove me home. My mother was waiting for me, looking for signs, waiting for tears. Finally, just before bed, holding her glass of warm milk in one hand, her knitting in the other, she asked me if I was upset about the abortion.

I thought about my great-grandmother, opening her womb with a crochet hook, not once but seventeen times. On the seventeenth time and at the age of thirty-six she got septicaemia and was close to death. Her mother made her promise never to do it again.

The gynaecologist had silver hair, was handsome in a soft way, usually called distinguished. His rooms were brown and dull. It was a very male room. Drear, unadorned, spare.

Spare: kept in reserve, being in excess of present need; frugal, meagre, scanty or scant as in the amount of fullness.

I remember saying, 'I'm very tired. Often my husband's work takes him away during the week. I couldn't face another one (so soon),' and thinking, I couldn't bear to spend my days in this room. Is he such a dull man? How does he bear to come into this brown room every day? From the plain green operating theatre to this dull brown room.

In the spare room I think about my lost, aborted daughter (I had an intuition it would be another girl). She would be two and a half now, she would sleep in Ben's room in the second of the twin beds. She would run alongside me on the cracked path, catch the toe of her shoes, trip, and bawl, ungainly with outrage. This is sentimental, as is my sadness, as is the doughy-headed doll I lie with under the bedspread.

Sentimental: mawkishly tender.

My grandmother, Audrey, used to say: 'I am a sentimental person and I'm not ashamed of it.'

Mawkish: sickly, nauseating.

Morning sickness: the first pre-emptive strike, the warning that things will never be the same again, that the mother must get used to her body belonging to another …

How to describe that sudden transformation of the moment when you learn that, once again, you have life within you? I was appalled; surprised at myself; and yet I felt as if a light had come on inside my body. I walked to the station, looking in shop windows, and everything seemed vibrant and humming. I walked home, it was winter, there was hardly anything in the garden and I searched intently for something to put into a vase; three blue hydrangeas and a red leafy shrub and some piebald creeper, and I cut them and arranged them in a pewter vase and sat them on the kitchen table and felt my body triumphant again.

This is a musty house, there is mould in the corner of this room, I can smell it, soon I will sneeze, Frank will hear me. I press my nose into her grubby nylon arm.

I am forty, and my fertility is dying.

How can I tell you about the feeling of loneliness that a woman can have in a house with a man and two children sleeping around her? In other rooms. They are pre-occupied, on their own stubborn trajectory; they are dreaming their own dreams. That's why I'm here, with the doll. The doll has no dreams.

The doll is for me.

I can cuddle her now and in the morning I can put her aside. I paid for her. I own her. I bought her for Rebecca but Rebecca never took to her. Other dolls, but not this one.

I want a man who's a doll. Without memory, without motivation. That's what men have. They have prostitutes who don't speak or tell of their dreams or oppress them with their yearning.

My darling little one. Why did I abort you? I aborted you because your father didn't want you ('Honestly, Kay, two children is enough') and I wasn't strong enough to raise you on my own.

On nights like this I could kill Frank.

Frank's strong points

I must concentrate on Frank's strong points.

Like his surly and sharp-tongued mother, Frank is a good gardener. It pains him to have only a small courtyard at the rear of the house. He wants to retire to the south coast and plant a large native garden; hakea and bottlebrush, she-oak and the feathery silver-blue of the Cootamundra wattle (his favourite tree). He says that when work is getting him down and he can't sleep at night he lies in the dark and plans this garden in his head. It is the secret map of his desire: lush and spiky, blossoming with red and golden hues and overt with flagrant and noisy birds. Frank is carrying this little Garden of Eden around in his head.

Frank's father died when he was eleven, in a car accident. Sometimes I think this may not have been altogether a bad thing since his mother says his father was a tyrant (she, on the other hand, is not a reliable source). Still, I have observed other men and their fraught relationship with Oedipus, and for once I wonder if she might not be right.

This reminds me of a brief relationship I had with a young soldier, an electrifying encounter of the kind you read about in silly romance novels. At the airport, in the crush, he walked up to me and said: 'Remember me? We queued together at the city terminal when we booked our tickets' (this was before online booking). I looked up and barely recognised him: he was in jeans then and now he was in the uniform of an officer in the army. He could only have been my age, twenty-three. He took me firmly by the elbow and ushered me to the counter: 'Can you put this young lady in a seat next to me?' he said. Not bad for a second lieutenant. Lots of front.

On the plane he held my hand possessively, as if he'd known me for a long time, as if he had plans for me. We drank whiskey and looked away from the cellophane sandwiches. Neither of us could eat. After we'd talked for a while I realised I knew his brother. 'You know my brother?' he asked, and something black flickered across his face. 'My father always preferred my brother to me,' he said. His eyes were angry and hurt. 'When I finished my degree I joined the public service but that didn't work out and now ...' he looked down at his khaki lapels and smiled. I hadn't realised how attractive a uniform was, in all its subtle greens. The tie was especially nice, a soft smoky rainforest green. He ordered another two whiskeys and ice.

I was hot, sweaty. My head was dizzy. I had a dim awareness of being swept off my feet. I tried half-heartedly to armour myself with irony; he's practising at being masterful I told myself. But this didn't work. He gave off voltage like a human powerhouse, exuding a force-field of sensual pain. I was in a daze. His wounded, urgent need was overwhelming. 'My father is supposed to be meeting me at the airport,' he said, his eyes hot and cloudy. 'I'll bet he doesn't come.'

He knew I wasn't stopping over for more than an hour and would be taking up a connecting flight. He called the flight attendant and asked her to book me onto a later one. He was being masterful. I didn't argue, I was still in a daze.

We spent an hour in the pale-blue airport lounge talking in senseless, unmemorable phrases, broken off from time to time as he jumped up and strode away, in his authoritative peaked cap, to look for his father. I was by this time erotically lost to him. After several sorties his eyes had blackened and his skin was flushed. 'I knew it,' he said. 'I knew he wouldn't come.' Something heavy in my chest thudded and fell away into space. We altered my flight yet again. Limply I stood by a line of phone booths while he rang his father. The phone didn't answer. He waited for it to ring out and then he rang a hotel in the city and booked a room. We took a cab, saying almost nothing to one another by now. In our hotel room, it was the old Southern Cross, we made love all afternoon. We took no precautions. I thought he might cry after he came the first time but he didn't. His briefcase stood propped absurdly by the door, his soldier's jacket draped across a chair. My chest felt as if a leaden rose had grown within it to fill a cavity I had until then been unaware of. It anchored me to the bed; only my hips were light and floated above me.

In a limbo of dim light and buckled sheets he lay on his back, his pink chest rising and falling. 'You're beautiful,' he said. He held my hand. 'I knew he wouldn't come,' he said. 'In a minute, now, I'll ring his number again ...'

One thing I had learned by the time I was thirty: men never get over their fathers.

Some of us live, some of us die

When I was twenty-six, I was hospitalised with pneumonia. It was a ghastly time in my life and I've never been as unhappy since. I was in a destructive love affair and it was killing me. That's why I got sick. For a brief time, propped up in my hospital bed, I thought: Let me die.

How pathetic. Not long after, something happened that made me ashamed of this morbidity.

It began with a bout of pleurisy. My GP examined me and said it would go away. There were too many antibiotics dispensed now and he did not think they were called for in this instance. Not that I blame him, Dr. Richard Wesley-Cameron: tall, slim, handsome, English, mellifluous vowels, a certain edgy manner. Always a little hurried, harassed even, but willing to make home visits, he had come to my flat at around seven on a very dark mid-winter's evening, and found me scarcely able to move from the pain in my chest.

I was in a destructive love affair and it was killing me.

I heard him drive up the long avenue of dark elms that lined the driveway and it was an effort for me to get up from the bed and open the door. A double door, a double lock. I sat tentatively on the edge of the bed in my pink cotton nightdress and black shawl while he examined me. 'You have pneumonia,' he said. 'You live alone here?'

'Yes.'

It was late when the taxi delivered me to the private hospital on the hill overlooking the city. Inside there was an institutional hush. The lights had been dimmed, the corridors were empty. In the front office I registered with a young nurse; the receptionist had long gone home. Then I was led to a room on the second floor, a single room with a high bed. It was after midnight. My suitcase stood unpacked in the corner. I hoisted myself, gasping with pain, onto the high bed and sat upright, my back against four firm pillows, and I sat like this for a long time. No-one came. Outside I could hear the distant traffic, the wind in the trees.

Finally a nurse arrived, stocky and middle-aged. 'You should be lying down,' she snapped.

'I can't lie down,' I snapped back. 'That's why I'm here.'

When I awoke from the warm, drifting sleep brought on by sedatives, a man was standing by my bed. He introduced himself to me as Victor Parish, a cardiac physician, and then he sat on the

45

chair beside my bed. 'The type of pneumonia you have,' he said, 'is called pericarditis. The pericardium is a membranous sac enveloping the heart. It's the covering of the heart, the heart's capsule. When it becomes inflamed, usually through a bacterial infection, friction arises and that's the pain you are experiencing now. When I listen to your heart I can hear these friction sounds.'

How clear he is, I thought, how lucid.

'It's nothing to worry about,' he said. 'All you need to do is rest.'

For three days I slept through the afternoons in a sleep I have never experienced before or since, a blissful, restorative trance. Dozing in and out of consciousness, floating, light. For three days I slept like this and it seemed as if, each time I awoke, Dr. Parish was sitting by my bed. One afternoon I dreamed that the sac around my heart had swelled up like a balloon and was carrying me off up into the sky. It was not an alarming dream. No danger. Only the sensation of flight, of drifting upwards.

Would it be possible, I wondered, to drift up into death?

Every day he came to see me. Each day he would sit by my bed. Each day it seemed as if he were there a long time, though he was probably present only ten minutes, at most. Dr. Parish, or Mr. Parish, in the protocols of his profession; my heart's rescuer. He was not handsome like Wesley-Cameron but short and plump and bald, with rimless glasses and a quality of immense stillness. He sat with me by the window and looked out. Was he with me only five minutes? It seemed like thirty … an hour … endless. He had golden, freckled hands that lay composed on his lap, and sometimes he gazed out through the glass of the hospital window, as if he had nothing better to do than sit with me. There was something of the sunlight about him, something fair, though he was in late middle-age and solid. Short, corpulent and balding. But definitely of the light. Just to see him made me feel better. Just to have him sit by me, exuding his immense, unfathomable calm. His warm serenity assured me of the inevitability of my survival.

Just a few months after I recovered I read in the papers that his son had been murdered – lured into a park by a mystery phone call and beaten to death. He was my age. From the photograph on the front page I could see that he resembled his father. In the newspaper report, his girlfriend described him as 'a ray of sunshine'.

I was not a ray of sunshine and yet I had lived. What justice was there in the cosmos when the father should nurse a young woman like me back to health while his own son was taken from him? I said something along these lines to my boss, a kind woman who took an interest in my welfare and found me crying in the staff toilets. 'You mustn't brood on this,' she said. 'Some people live, and some people die. And there's no rhyme or reason. It's a mystery.'

It's a mystery, but it haunted me then and it haunts me now.

The day after I got out of hospital I stood on the bus and trembled all the way home, aware that I was, for a time, an inhabitant of some privileged no-man's-land; some body in transit between a receding fragility and a re-emergent strength.

Mr. Parish, you are not forgotten. You are here in the lining of my pericardium, in this heart that is still beating, and I wish you were here now.

Back at the zoo ...

At my desk I find that someone has left a stack of new brochures on my keyboard.

* Genderless Negotiation Skills for Women
* Preparing and Delivering Perfect Presentations
* How to Handle Employees with Attitude Problems
* How to Become Successful Taught by People Who Are (The Seminar of a Lifetime)
* Empowering Your Employees to Reach Peak Performance
* Getting Everything Done – How to Avoid and Overcome the 'Top 10 Time Thieves'
* Designing Corporate Culture – How to Convert Vicious Cycles to Virtuous Cycles. 'Management is not about command and control but designing and managing the culture of a place. If you create a good culture you release energy that's latent in the group. Many managers focus too much on tasks and not on the culture that would help the tasks to get done.'

I know where these have come from. Winton has put them there. I file the brochures away under *Miscellaneous*.

This is how I spend my lunch hours. I spend my lunch hours paying bills, shopping for kids' clothes, replacing lost lunch-boxes, looking for Hallowe'en hats, collecting dry-cleaning, buying Happy Anniversary or Get Well Soon cards. Jogging – half-walking half-running – up Hunter Street in my high heels, trying to pack two hours into an hour, eating standing up at the yoghurt and fruit-salad bar in the crowded basement of Centre-point, resenting those languid men who take ten-minute lunch breaks or skip lunch altogether to beef up their flex time until they can have an afternoon windsurfing or walking their grey-hounds!

This reminds me. The pains in my chest are getting worse. I am beginning to feel a creeping panic.

Frank says, 'Have you got pain in the arm?'

'No, I haven't. Why?'

'It's a sign of heart trouble,' he says. 'Otherwise, it's probably stress or indigestion. You do bolt your food down, Kay.'

'That's because I'm always in a hurry, or being interrupted.'

I ring up Diana. 'Have you found me that yoga class?' I ask. Or perhaps I just need a night at the Russell Hotel.

Romance offshore

The first time.

The first time that Frank and I sought solace in a private hotel we skipped dinner. The women's magazines tell you that going out to a quiet, intimate dinner is an 'opportunity to talk to your partner'. The last thing we wanted to do that night was talk to one another.

We parked high above the Rocks on Miller's Point, under the plane trees and beside the historic sandstone terraces. Then we walked down the steep hill and under the stone archway beside the steep bank cut out of rock. Instinctively, we walked slightly apart, as if we did not quite know one another.

I wanted to have a cocktail in the coldly modern and impersonal harbourside Hilton, in the bland and soulless mezzanine bar full of cane chairs. There was a moment on this impersonal balcony when I thought our stratagem wouldn't work. I looked out over the black-and-white floor tiles and the long vases filled with bird of paradise stems. Frank seemed stilted, a little awkward, a little withdrawn. I felt separate from him. I didn't want to know his worries. To have solicited his confidences at that point would have been fatal. Empathy is fatal to sex. That kind of sex. Hotel sex.

Next we strolled down to a rowdy wine bar, almost next door to our destination. The bar was a better class of pick-up joint. There was beer on the floor; it was noisy. Here I had a moment of restlessness, an impulse to take control, to say 'It's noisy here, let's go to the hotel,' but I resisted. I wanted to prolong the moment, to be passive, and floating, free of time. Free of my relentless schedule. It had to be a timeless moment. This is what being young is about, every moment is like every other moment, which is why sex is so good when you're young. It's not true to say that it gets better as you get older. For childless narcissists, maybe, for everyone else it gets tired, gets *fitted in*. When you're nineteen it expands to fill the time available; it swarms over everything, a haze over every page of every book, a certain kind of humid light in your dreams, a sense of possibility. Now, in our assignation, Frank and I had to *make* our sense of possibility, to artificially generate that haze.

In the bar I gazed out the window, beyond any of the bodies there. Through the red bubble-glass in the window I could see the quay, the red, bubbling water.

At last he took my elbow in a firm grip and looked in the direction of the door. It was a look that in another context might have been risible but it was right for this moment. I left my half-drunk glass of red wine – lipstick-rimmed, inconsequential, a token – behind on the table, a glass-topped table with puddles of beer slops and flecks of dried cappuccino froth. I liked the word, *froth*. Froth was a word for that moment. A carnal word. It suggested a prick off the leash. His. A frivolous, unaccountable cunt. Mine.

On another night I might have taken an interest in the waiter behind the bar – lean and dark, in an expensive white shirt and wearing that cool look of hostile distraction that young men assume behind bar counters – but not that night, that night I was looking nowhere special, looking only within my own body heat; an unfocused, erotic blindness.

We went up a narrow staircase painted grey and yellow to a small, discreet reception desk and then into the room. It was an old room with a high ceiling in panels of ornately moulded tin. I stood beneath the whirring ceiling-fan and the light breeze caught at my hair. The walls, and almost everything else in the room, were in shades of smoky pink, an insinuating pink, the colour of tumescence, except for the brass bed, in black and gold. There was an old iron fire-grate surrounded by mosaic tiles and on the mantel two vases stuffed with masses of fake smoky pink-and-white orchids, and between them a Picasso print of a barefoot girl, her back turned, stroking some weird headless animal, suggestive of a greyish-black dog, her hand resting on its phallic neck. A large cedar mirror opposite the bed, an old oak wardrobe in the French style, an armoire. A deliberate style of louche luxury.

Outside was noise, and traffic. Drunks singing in the pub on the corner spilled out onto the footpath in the warm night air, while trains thundered past at window height, the glass rattling, shaking, vibrating in spasms, the bridge looming from a corner of the quay.

Frank sank to his knees and groaned softly. I was taken by surprise. He'd never done this before. He hitched my skirt up and

I bent at the knees, he lifted his arms to push my top up over my breasts. A second train rumbled past the window, high up, on its track towards the bridge. I saw its red lights flicker through the slatted blinds, and I knew it was going to work, it was going to be one of the good nights in our life together; sublimely intimate, sublimely impersonal.

We arrived home at midnight, in a satiated trance. But it was a strategy, and a world, of diminishing returns, and each time the charge grew weaker. The second time, there were no rooms available at The Russell and I bit my lip in disappointment, like a child. Someone at work had suggested a small boutique hotel in Kings Cross. The room was large and painted in pale blue, pale apricot and a dull cream. There were blue floral curtains and a grey-white marble fireplace. Genteel.

I showered, a long, hot shower on the nape of my neck, which was aching from a day at my console writing a report. I forgot to put on the packaged shower cap in the basket on the bathroom ledge and soon my hair was wet. I wrapped the inevitable white hotel towel around me and climbed onto the bed, still in my tube of towel. Frank unwrapped me, turning me over on my stomach. I curled the white pillow up under my breasts. When we had sub-sided we began to talk again. He said how having time to talk like this was as big a luxury as our love-making. I was thinking how different it was from last time at The Russell – less urgent, less intense. There we had hardly spoken a word to one another all night. Here we were like old friends. Laid-back, conversational, affectionate. We dressed, and drove home.

The third time it was January, the height of the tourist season, and the only hotel we could get into at short notice was a new one behind the Rocks, in Ultimo, called The Lawson. It was a catalogue hotel designed for Malaysian and Hong Kong tourists. On the walls of our room were framed reproduction caricatures of the writer Henry Lawson. Here he was leaning on a walking cane and holding his pipe. Here was a black-and-white drawing of a drunken man splayed on the back of a frenzied galloping horse. Over the settee was a large print of the facsimile cover of *On the Track* with two bushmen humping their swags. Here they were, Kay and Frank, sitting up on the bed, fully clothed, except for their shoes, sipping bourbons and ice and discussing the absurd prints on the wall. It was cosy, it was anodyne, it was just like home. We decided it was only going to work at The Russell and if we couldn't get the room we wanted we wouldn't go at all.

The primate in his cage

On the morning of our conference at the zoo – this time, the real one – we all feel a bit skittish. Like kids on an outing. I have chartered a mini-bus to take us there and have my directions from the functions manager, Cecile. 'You can't miss the convention centre,' she said over the phone. 'You just follow the arrow marked *Primates*.'

The conference centre is, in fact, bang in the middle of the primates section and we are booked into the Flamingo Room, a huge hexagonal space with a vaulted ceiling like a church, and three whole walls of glass so that you can look out at the animals in their dense tropical garden, their rock pool and their high enclosure of wire netting. Among all this is a three-metre bamboo wall and a fretwork of ropes for the primates to swing from.

'What sort of primates have we got here?' asks Martin jocularly. Even he is in a good mood.

Winton peers at the plaque beside the glass wall and reads aloud. 'Black Gibbon: *Hylobates concolor*,' he reads. 'A small arboreal ape known for its suspensory behaviour.'

'What does that mean?'

'It means … hang on … it means that the black gibbon throws itself from tree to tree over gaps of ten metres or more using its arms.' He squints and reads on, half muttering to himself, '… adult black male is around 6.3 kilograms … the pelage of the male is black with white whiskers …'

We leave him to it and look for coffee. Winton always has to be across the detail. Eventually he joins us at the urn. 'I hope this isn't going to be too distracting,' he says. 'The pool is nice, and the rainforest, but I'm not sure about the arboreal apes.'

There are two tables in the room and the first decision is this. Will we sit at the round table or the oblong? We decide on the round, 'for equality'. There's some discreet shuffling so that almost everyone is skewed to one side and can look directly out onto the black gibbons who have begun, languidly, to cavort among the trees. Two adults and their children. The female is a kind of albino, a light yellow colour, but it's not she who is the show-off in the group. It's her old man who is hell-bent on impressing us and he now begins his warm-up. It's as if he knows he has an audience. We've been warned not to go out onto the terrace and look at them, or wave, or talk to them, because, said Cecile, they are very territorial and they make a shrieking noise to warn people off.

We settle into our chairs and our agenda papers and get down to drafting our vision statement. The first hour is long. At some point I hear a terrific racket and look up. Lisa has defied the guide-lines and gone out onto the terrace to look at the black gibbons, has slipped out through the glass doors on her way back from the loo. The gibbons have begun to shriek.

Christina fumes. 'Tell Lisa, for God's sake, to come inside and stop provoking the beasts!'

Kelvin gets up and joins Lisa, who has retreated to the inside of the window, from where she continues to look out onto the cage, and they are both giggling. After a minute or so they begin to wave their arms in imitation of the gibbons, as if they are doing some dumb tribal dance.

Winton sighs. 'People, can we stay in our seats here?'

Lisa and Kelvin are called back to their places at the table.

During the lunch-break we stroll around the narrow paths of the primates area. We have bundled the sandwiches provided by the caterers into some paper napkins and carried them outside to eat in the sun. Winton is pensive as he walks beside me. 'You know, Kay, this isn't easy for me either, and it doesn't help to be working with a group of piss-takers.' He looks so childlike that, as usual, I feel the need to console him.

'They're just tired,' I say. 'The re-structuring has been hard on them. That's why I suggested we get out of the office. It will all come together this afternoon, you wait and see.'

But when we resume our seats the troops seem not restless but over-relaxed. Some are dozy, others have cast off their work mode altogether and are frisky. Instead of taking our ape friends for granted they are even more distracted by them and look up admiringly at the male, who is ready to perform for us once more. With manic energy he swings, and swings again, from his immensely long, furry arms, hurtling himself almost in free fall from one side of his luxurious cage to the other, like a trapeze artist on speed.

'It's hard not to watch,' says Kelvin, lazing back in his chair with his arms folded behind his head. 'To ignore him would be like you were sitting behind a great artist but not bothering to look at the canvas.' I'm impressed by this: it's the most empathetic thing I've heard our programmer say. Winton just sighs.

But by mid-afternoon, in the tea-break, we are all drawn to the window, even Winton.

'*Hylobates concolor* has psyched us out,' I say, and Winton gives his resigned little smile, and gazes across to that agile black ape who is flinging himself into space with a driven, rhythmic leaping that is utterly mesmerising, from bare tree limb to bare tree limb. So we stand and gawp, poised with cups in hand. There is no sign now of the mother and the young ones, who appear to have taken their rest in the dense foliage, leaving the big black male to strut his stuff, to uphold the honour of the species before these tired and jaded humans down below. He is the supreme acrobat, flying above the carefully planted rainforest, grinning all the while. Occasionally he pauses for one second, but always at an unex-pected moment, as if moving to some unpredictable syncopation. How daring he looks, yet how insouciant. His flying self, his fling-ing arms, seem too sudden, too unthinking and uncalculated to be sure of reaching his mark, and as he approaches the intricate wire-netting wall at what looks like all the wrong angles, and at reckless speed, you think that this time he won't make it. Your breath catches. This time he'll fall. But no, he hits the wire netting lightly, at an impossible angle, full on, like a limp carcass, a sugar bag thrown against a wall that doesn't ricochet off but adheres, and he looks up and around, but only for a moment, still grinning. See, he says, I can do this, this is nothing, but I'm not trying to impress you, who are *you*? What do I care? And he's off again. On and on and on, barely pausing, each swing twice as far, twice as wide as you anticipate. You calculate, in a blink, the width of his swing, and each time it's far wider than common sense would think possible. Absurdly, recklessly wide: *out of all proportion*, you think.

'Bravo!' cries Winton. 'Bravo! Encore!'

And suddenly we are moved, moved by this inexhaustible display of poise to break into a round of spontaneous applause. Here he is, in his cage, locked in, a mere beast, and yet he is the epitome of transcendental élan. He makes our vision statement seem lame.

In future we will refer to this conference as Black Gibbon Day. Winton will refer to the vision statement as the Black Gibbon vision statement. It's the only honour we have to bestow on him.

The mystery

There is a mystery at the heart of my day, a mystery at the heart of the mundane. Take yesterday. It was one of those days when I woke up in a fog of negativity. One of those days when everything seems repetitive and dull. My job is stale: I am going nowhere. The heavens are vast and I am a small, insignificant speck of dust. What is the point of all this, you think? If it were not for the children, why would anyone bother to get out of bed? I tell Frank I have a headache and he will have to organise the children and I stay in my fog beneath the blankets until the house is empty. When I drag myself out of bed I am late for work. And yet, mysteriously, without even my noticing it, once I settle at my desk, my work goes well for the day, almost as if I am not in charge of it and someone else is doing it for me. That evening, without planning or forethought, I cook a particularly good meal. Somewhere in the course of my day a current of animal well-being has risen in me, like a sap. In the morning I was ready to abandon hope, to succumb to ennui, and by evening I am an artist in the kitchen. How does this witless transformation occur? When it happens it seems independent of my thoughts, independent of my will. It just is. But what is this 'it' and where does it come from? Is it the same current that animates the black gibbon, that keeps him swinging extravagantly about his luxurious cage?

Fluctuat nec mergitur: *we are tossed by the waves but we do not sink.*

I think back to my brothel fantasy. It is, in truth, a rare one for I no longer fantasise. It's age. I am forty, I am myself at last. I have arrived, chosen, worked out, drifted into who I am. When I was young I daydreamed all the time. Now I no longer need the daydream, those future scenarios of Kay as X or living in Y. It's healthy, I suppose, but I miss the electric charge of a fantasy life. I still occasionally daydream, but rarely, and this is not age, or maturation itself, but what age brings: the children, schedules, no free time to just sit. What I really want is not to fantasise but to have time to daydream. Daydreaming is not fantasy – it's not imagining yourself in a new situation. Daydreaming is freeforming narrative. You let all the facts of your past and present drift across the screen of your consciousness, like a diorama, and you form and re-form them in varying stories – as heroine, as failure, as navigator, as warrior, as magistrate, as woman, as mother

– and you surrender to its dreamy, excitational, trance-like state; ecstatic with the free flow, the sense of the story of your past, the wonderful form and drama of it, of having lived, completely, no matter how stressfully, your own plot.

And what follows is a state of calm elation, of the dissolution of time, of being in the present moment, like an animal washed up onto some paradisiacal shore. Somewhere at the heart of the day-dream is a mysterious source of bliss.

One day I'll learn how to go there and stay within it forever. I know that I will not be able to take my children with me, but they will remember me, and that is enough.

Benigno numine: *by the favour of the heavens.*

Reading *Madame Bovary*

It was the end of her final year in law and as a graduation present her aunt gave her the money to go trekking in Nepal. But she didn't like it there: too cold, too steep, too dirty. She found she didn't do well at high altitudes and in any case she had never liked camping. She liked comfort and above all she needed to be warm. She hated the feel of dirt under her nails, of small stones beneath her ground sheet and the sense of zipped enclosure within the fuggy padding of a sleeping bag. Nor did she like being in a group of backpacking Americans and Germans who had endless banal discussions about the best kind of walking boots or the merits of brand-name packs – or worse, sat around the campfire singing so-called 'Rainbow' songs or offering up recollections in sacramental tones of their own feats of abseiling. The nadir was reached when they drifted into tedious and shallow raves about Tibetan Buddhism. Nirvana? It was all just dirt and squalor to her.

Just three weeks after leaving Sydney she arrived, broke, in Amsterdam. There she hooked up with an English guy called Tom, who corralled her in a dark corner of a bar on the Zuyderzee. Before long they were bunkered in on the top floor of his cousin's apartment overlooking one of the canals, and she found herself just a touch smitten. Tom was one of those big hunky men she had a weakness for. It was a particular kind of body she craved, almost independently of the person who inhabited it. He might be infuriatingly taciturn – an enigma – and bloody hard to talk to but with a body like that it didn't matter. You could let it smother you until the breath stifled in your chest or you could fight back with abandon and get into a good heaving sexual scrap with just enough spite to sharpen the senses.

Tom invited her to return to London with him and she said yes. Though he appeared to be one of those stolid Englishmen who are unable to express their feelings it was clear that he was serious.

Within four weeks of having met they were crossing the English Channel. Almost immediately she found a job as a receptionist for a computer firm in Camden Town and moved into Tom's flat, half of a bare-fronted, red-brick terrace in the East End, a block away from where he taught maths at the local high school. The school was a grim place, more like a gaol, with high wire fences, asphalt yards and bricks the colour of soot. The buildings even had wire mesh along the upper-storey walkways that made them look like cages. Sometimes on her morning walk to the tube station she would glance across at the school and thank God she didn't have to work there.

One night Tom came home and told her that soon he would be going away. Every year the school had an Easter holiday pro-gramme for some of the most deprived and disturbed kids and he had volunteered to go along. At first she was piqued at this. Easter was her birthday, which meant he wouldn't be there to celebrate it, and when she told him he apologised solemnly and said he was very sorry but it was too late: he had volunteered before they met and he couldn't let the others down now. He and two other teachers, husband and wife, were to take some of the worst cases from Tom's year (they were mostly twelve, though some were thirteen) on a ten-day trip along the old industrial canals of the English midlands. The husband and wife had been before and knew the ropes and they would be in charge of one boat and Tom would command the other. An unspoken invitation hovered in the air.

She ignored it. For one thing she had no experience with kids, she didn't even like them. Shut up on a barge with a mob of rampaging feral children didn't sound like a holiday to her, more like *Lord of the Flies* on water.

Then, just two weeks before they were due to embark, the married couple had a death in the family and dropped out. One of the boats would have to be cancelled but it was still possible for Tom to take a party of children on the other, though it would be unwise for him to go alone. He asked Kirsten if she would come with him, and in a moment of post-coital weakness she said yes – and almost instantly began to have misgivings.

But Tom was affectingly grateful, saying over and over again that it would be fine, it would be fine. It would be great, in fact. She'd see a bit of the English countryside and it might even be, well, you know, idyllic: punting along the glassy waterways in the mellow afternoon light, rolling green hills in the distance, trim hedges on either side, picturesque locks left over from the industrial revolution. And as for the boats themselves, she really must see them, they were marvellously decorated, all painted up in bright colours with romantic landscapes on the sides and elaborate scrollwork along the transom. 'Like gypsy caravans,' he said. 'A lost art.' He made it sound romantic.

Undaunted by lack of experience (he had, after all, been on a canal holiday as a child), Tom borrowed a stack of books from the municipal library. Every night he pored over maps of old canal routes (the locals referred to a canal as 'the cut') and studied diagrams of the many different types of lock and their iron workings until he could sketch the most common of them without reference to the originals. Sometimes he would read aloud to her. 'A lock is an assemblage, a kit of parts, and no two locks are ever alike.' Then he would look up with one of his deadpan stares. 'Are you listening?' he would ask.

'I'm enthralled,' she'd reply.

'A typical old-style lock is a rectangular chamber of brick or stone, finished with flat stone copings. The heavy gates are balanced by wooden beams which also act as levers. Each gate is anchored by a collar and turned on a cast-iron pin in a pot. The whole thing is held in place by water pressure with hand-worked paddle gear mounted on a gate or on a stand set in the ground nearby. Sometimes the gates are of steel and occasionally cast iron. They are usually black with beam ends picked out in white. The use of paint, tar and whitewash preserves the gates and makes them visible in grey weather or the dark.'

'Really?' she would say. 'How fascinating.'

But it was the boats he had fallen in love with. These low barges were known as narrow-boats and they harked back to the 1760s. Far from being dour they were covered in bright patterns that were positively gaudy, carnivalesque even. The highlight was always one idealised scene on the starboard side, which might be a cottage beside a pond but more likely a Bohemian castle set high above a mountain lake, some luridly crimson Shangri-La sunset flaming behind the turrets, and the whole scene encircled by an outer wreath of yellow and pink roses entwined in dark-green ivy. The overall effect was of a floating sideshow, crude but somehow enlivening, a diorama of the utopian.

*

Each day Tom grew more and more enthused while she, Kirsten, began to feel a secret, queasy reluctance. It was an English spring. She had been warned that it could be cold and there was no heating on the boats. It would almost certainly be wet. She began to meditate on excuses she might give for opting out, but could think of none that she wouldn't be ashamed to utter.

In the end what swayed her was the photograph.

She found it in one of the books that Tom had brought home from the library, a large picture book about barges in the nineteenth century. Right at the end was a photograph that they both found peculiarly affecting, an old sepia print, dated around 1870, of a barge with the strange name of *Gort*. The boat was taken in long shot and the figure of a woman could be seen standing at the stern. In the long shot the woman was a faint image, like an apparition, but in the enlarged detail she was as solid and material, as mundane and domestic as any woman could be. This was the bargemaster's young wife and behind her you could see the small wooden cabin that was her home and into which, astonishingly, she had crammed all her possessions. The curved wall at the back was hung with small pictures in ornate frames, while on a narrow wooden shelf to one side there was a lace doily, a teapot, a brass oil lamp and tiny porcelain ornaments. *Often*, said the caption, *the living areas of these boats were like small shrines*, and here at the centre of her dark, domesticated hollow stood the young wife, a kind of low-life industrial Madonna, her head compressed with tight ring-lets, her body encased in a dress of drab grey serge that fell into a wide Victorian skirt, as wide almost as the door of the cabin. And in her arms she was holding a baby.

This baby was wrapped in a funnel of white swaddling clothes so that only its face was visible, and in this face – was it an effect of the sepia? – only the eyes could be discerned, just a few grainy markings, a shadow here, a smudge there, but somehow the effect was uncanny. The baby looked not as if it were being held in its mother's arms but as if it were hovering there, like a ghost.

Kirsten had stared at this image for some time, gazing at it with a kind of horror mixed with pity. It was unbelievable that anyone could live in that dark, confined space, never mind make a home of it for a baby. Day after day, on the grey water, so flat and oily in its man-made channels; so dense with a sense of enclosure, of brick and tar and charcoal and smoke.

But what moved her was this. In the accompanying text it said that despite growing up on the canals, hardly any of the canal chil-dren ever learned to swim. Drowned children were registered in parish records and when canal children perished the name of the boat would be entered in the parish register as the child's home. It shocked her, the idea that anyone would keep a child on the water and not teach it how to swim. But then for most of the year the water was freezing, and according to the text it was more than likely that the child's parents were themselves unable to swim.

She had set the book aside and pondered this. She could not remember a time when she had been unable to swim.

The canal

They boarded the boat at four o'clock in the afternoon. The day was cold, the sky overcast, the canal so narrow she felt she could reach over and touch the sides. As for the boat – ah, what bleak irony! – the boat was indescribably drab; bare, shabby, with no colour or decoration save for a faded red heart that had been daubed on the sliding hatch of the cabin. And even that was cracked and beginning to flake.

As their car pulled alongside the mooring ramp, Tom stared at the boat in glum disbelief. For a moment he could scarcely conceal his disappointment, then pursed his lips and said nothing.

Soon the kids would be arriving in their chartered bus.

Tom climbed on board first and offered her his hand. Looking down to the decrepit transom, floating on a slick of oily water, she hesitated – and for a split second lost her footing and had to lunge across the gap. Above her loomed the grey hump of the cabin roof, its black tin funnel looking thin and worn, curiously fragile against a low charcoal sky.

Rain was beginning to fall as they entered the long cabin that took up almost the entire length of the barge, and she could see immediately why they had once gone by the name of narrow boats. At one end was a stack of bunks and at the other a primitive kitchen, with a table and benches in the middle. Tom set about inspecting the sleeping bunks while she stood haplessly in the cooking area, surrounded by wet patches on the floor where the roof leaked. When she looked up she found herself staring at a motley of pots on the kitchen shelf, all made of battered aluminium with scarcely a flat bottom between them.

The brochure had described the barge as having been converted into a comfortable holiday boat. The brochure, clearly, had lied.

'Where's the lavatory?' she asked, and Tom nodded curtly in the direction of the bow where a narrow door had been cut into a wall. The door was ill-fitting and he had to wrench at the handle to get it open. Inside was a pokey little closet with a dead rat behind the cistern.

The place was a floating slum.

Worse was to come. Tom opened the cabin door and she climbed out after him. Together they edged their way along the narrow deck towards the stern and already there was a heavy weight in the pit of her stomach. What am I doing here? she thought. She was trembling from the cold. It was freezing. Could this possibly be spring?

When they reached the bargemaster's cabin at the rear they found a dark little hollow of a shelter, curved like a big scallop shell and made of planked wood. Inside it was completely bare and smelled of damp. They had to stoop to enter the cabin – being tall, neither of them could stand up straight in it – and once inside they bumped awkwardly against one another as they dumped their gear onto the floor. Then they looked around them, aghast. Or at least, she was. Tom, as usual, was impassive.

'This is awful,' she said.

Tom turned away and she could see that he was angry; disappointed with the boat, yes, but angry with her for not pretending to a stoicism she didn't feel. He stood for a moment at the open door, watching the grey drizzle fall while she kicked at the flap of her pack. She felt like kicking *him*.

Morosely they began to unpack, although there was nowhere to put anything, not even a narrow shelf (so much for the 'small shrine'). She set down her torch beside the pillow and arranged her shampoo and face-cream packs so that they stood upright and ordered in the corner. Then they heard the bus pull in. Here they come, she thought; the hordes. Tom was waiting in silence for her to finish her adjustments, and when everything was in place she followed him back along the narrow deck towards the main cabin.

Just as they reached the door the kids began to clamber aboard, and they at least seemed happy enough: most of them were on the first holiday of their life. They scuttled about in jeans and parkas, looking ragged and half drowned, hair plastered against their foreheads by the rain. Tom marshalled them inside the main cabin and made a brief speech of welcome. Then he introduced them to Kirsten, who was trying not to stare at the damp patches on the floor where the roof dripped water onto the rotting wood. The children (they were no longer children but not quite adolescent) looked giddy with disorientation and glanced at her as if she were one of the fixtures. It had been a long coach trip and a few of them began to crowd around Tom, asking if there was anything to eat. He shrugged and looked uncharacteristically at a loss. Meanwhile the others were milling around the cabin, and around her; shiny, bedraggled, strange. I can't bear this, she thought, and turned her back on them. In one quick, unobtrusive movement she opened the cabin door, climbed out onto the deck and retreated to the stern, back into the bargemaster's cabin. Back into the bat cave.

There she sat on the air mattress, in the dark, in a stupefied state. Fuck, fuck, fuck! In five days it would be her birthday, and she was going to spend it in this hole! She had been looking forward to a club in the city, dressing up, going out with friends; a night of drunken abandon. And here on this rotting hulk she couldn't even have a joint to console herself; Tom had made her promise not to bring any dope, and *he* didn't smoke it even at home because he was allergic. Allergic! Sullenly, in the dark, she sat and stewed on her bleak feeling of being trapped, gnawing at her nails in bitterness and frustration. How could she have ended up here, on this miserable strip of water? This claustrophobic cupboard. This floating purgatory. What on earth would she do for ten days?

It was some time before Tom appeared at the door of the cave, carrying a plate of food which he offered, wordlessly. She took it.

All the next day she sulked in her dank little cabin, reading the one book she had brought with her which, at this rate, was only going to last her until evening. Some French novel, set in the nineteenth century. *Madame Bovary*. She was not the type to read much but she thought she'd better bring something and found this in a carton of books Tom had bought at the local flea market. One of the best books ever written, it said on the cover, but they all say that. If only it weren't so cold – she had never known this kind of cold before, the kind that got into your bones and made you feel as if all your organs were shrinking and your kidneys were two dull stones dragging in your lower back … and it was worse here in the bat cave, because she had to keep the door open. To close it was like being sealed in a wooden tomb.

After a while she lay the book aside and dozed, as if in sleep she could somehow escape the boat, but when she opened her eyes in the dim cabin it was still there, an ugly hulk gliding along the flat, grey water. Every now and then she could feel the bump of the barge as it knocked against the walls of the canal. Outside was a world of stained brick and smoke but at least, for a while, she could immerse herself in the shimmering haze of the French provinces, *where the sky is blue and the leaves still, where the heather is in bloom, where there are patches of violet beneath the bushes of russet and gold, where rooks caw softly among the heavy overhang of oak-trees* ... From time to time the shouts of the children penetrated her narrative fog; the sound of their boots clumping on the deck, their cries as they leapt onto the grassy bank and tugged at the ropes, or ran to see who could be first to grasp the turning wheel of the lock. At odd moments she could hear them close, just a damp timber-width away, remonstrating in a quiet fury.

'Geez, you're a stupid cunt, Sean.'

Madame Bovary. Quite a good read, better than she had expected. And in its way – a way that would make her smile later when she recalled it – it was the right book at the right time. Because there was a particular moment about four-fifths of the way through the novel – she was almost to the end of it – when suddenly she recognised this absurd, selfish, narcissistic woman, Emma Bovary. This drivelling romantic sensualist pining for the glittering life of the cosmopolitan centres. It was her! It was her, Kirsten, here on this hideous boat with these clamouring children whom she could not escape. And she felt a sudden surge of shame at her behaviour; her moodiness, her remoteness, her seething discomfort.

All afternoon the boat meandered on, gliding its way along the narrow canal. It was late afternoon and beyond the bargemaster's cabin where she had read all day in a half-light she could sense the grey English day deepening into its evening gloom. She read on for another half hour, until the final page, and then she put the book aside.

What am I to do now? she asked herself, and the answer came back to her, soundlessly. She got up and stepped from the bat cave onto the deck. Outside it was dark, save for the bright light from the main cabin which illumined the drab water.

The children scarcely registered her entry, though Tom did, looking suddenly alarmed, as if he suspected she might be about to throw a tantrum.

For a moment she stood there, taking in the scene. The kids appeared to be in the early stages of preparing dinner. There was a mysterious pale powder, a sickly mustard-green colour, spilled across the wooden table and in patches on the floor, and she realised, after a perplexed moment, that this was packet soup out of some giant caterer's pack, a large circular tin that stood by the sink and was labelled 'Asparagus'. The floor was still wet from the leaks in the roof and the powder had begun to congeal into little clots and stick to the boots of the kids whom Tom had rostered on for cooking. One of them, a girl, was measuring water from the pump into a battered old aluminium soup pot, and even this she was doing clumsily, somehow managing to spill even more water onto an already damp floor. Kirsten looked at this child, fumbling with her ladle, and realised there was no escape, nowhere to go, no way to leave the boat.

'Here, let me do that,' she said.

Over the next hour she marshalled them into some kind of order, giving them the simple jobs they could manage, like peeling things, setting the table, opening cans. The entire store of food for the trip had been bought by the absent husband and wife who had made the journey in previous years. To Kirsten it was almost unrecognisable junk but she read the instructions on the back of everything and because she could cook it wasn't hard to figure out what to do with the base ingredients, even something so indescribably repulsive as a packet of Trix lard, a little square of paste-coloured suet encased in a garish foil wrapper. By seven she and the team under her supervision had prepared a three-course meal and belatedly they sat down at the long wooden table to packet asparagus soup with sliced white bread and margarine, sausages and mashed potato with tinned peas and tinned carrots followed by a huge jam tart with pastry made from the lard and thick, sticky 'jam' from a caterer's tin in which no trace of fruit could be discerned. Oh, yes, and custard made from a bright yellow powder. The children ate with gusto and declared it one of the best meals they had ever had. She could scarcely believe this, but sitting with them and listening to their jeering, good-humoured jokes, watching them scoff and guffaw and poke one another, she found herself ambushed by a faint flush of well-being, somewhere around the first bite of jam tart – which, considering its origins, was better than might have been expected.

Later, in the bat cave, as they snuggled into the double sleeping bag, Tom turned his back on her and went instantly to sleep. Fair enough. She thought she might be rewarded with a word of praise, of mere acknowledgement even, or failing that, some kind of embrace. But no. Over the washing-up she had looked at him, sitting at the long wooden table, wearily playing blind poker with a group of them and trying to keep up with the boasting and the rowdy banter, but he was dog-tired, pale with exhaustion from the effort of the first day and the workings of a lock system he'd never before set eyes on. At nine-thirty he had risen and enforced a strict curfew, and because the kids were tired they had offered only token resistance.

She, of course, was wide-awake, having lounged all day in her cabin.

The next morning she got up at six-thirty and supervised the breakfast team. Soon her hair hung in damp tendrils from the rising steam, and the smell of hot bacon fat clung to her clothes. The plates were no sooner empty than the kids bolted outside, out into the grey English light. All morning a drizzling rain fell across their faces and the day seemed endless, but by eleven she was mustering the lunch team and before long it was dinner again. Tom supervised the working of the canals and operating the locks; she ran the kitchen with the kids on roster and they cooked up a storm.

On the morning of the third day they glided into the dock of a small market town, a grim settlement of iron footbridges and tall black chimneys, and she and a party went on a shopping expedition to buy fresh food and an adequate frying pan. With a decent frying pan, she explained, you could cook almost anything, and she found herself drifting deep into a relaxed discourse on the properties of heat and cast iron, and the kids humoured her by feigning interest. It was another dull, chilly morning with a threatening bank of grey cloud in the sky and they pulled their beanies down low over their foreheads so that they looked like a tribe of alien dwarfs. Soon they found a shop that sold cabbages, cauliflower and kale and, to her amazement, a small quantity of zucchini. At another she bought three bottles of chocolate sauce to be hidden away for a special occasion. The kids wanted to know why she bought so many vegetables and she told them it was an Australian custom.

*

One morning, as she stood at the sink bench with her back to them, unwrapping the sliced bread for the breakfast toast, she found herself smiling at the punchline of an obscene joke she was pretending not to have heard, and she realised that in just a few days she had become comfortable with them, and they with her. There were two especially, Yusuf and Ruth, who had become her lieutenants in the kitchen, both able to anticipate and direct the others. Ruth was black, had a wild falsetto voice and amused them all by yapping out an unending stream of profane commentary. She appeared to have no concentration whatsoever but her air of insouciant incompetence proved to be deceptive, for she exuded a natural authority that made the others jump. This meant she could be left in charge of the kitchen, or what passed for one, at least for short spells. Yusuf was a quiet, conscientious boy with sad eyes who worked with intense and methodical concentration, as if the least mistake would see him consigned to Hell. And then there was Terry. Terry was another black kid with whom she had struck up a kind of bantering camaraderie as he made sporadic raids on the kitchen, at Tom's instigation, for supplies for 'outdoors'. He was big for his age, a muscular boy with a swaggering demeanour and a dark glare of ferocity in his eyes which, in another place and at another time, might not be good news. Already, at thirteen, he had been up before a children's magistrate on a charge of grievous bodily harm. But for now he was Tom's lieutenant on the cut. One night Terry confided in her that his surname was Nelson and that his parents, in all seriousness, had christened him 'Admiral'. 'But anyone call me that, Miss, they get a buncha fives.' At some point in his childhood – 'dunno when' – he had re-named himself Terry, and since he refused to answer to anything else the name had stuck. Thereafter she could not help but think of him as The Admiral, and it became a joke between her and Tom, a rare joke for the privacy of the bat cave.

As for the others in her kitchen, these were her foot soldiers. They worked with varying degrees of competence and liked to lose themselves in chopping and stirring or in trying to remember exactly how to set a formal table: 'Which way do the knives go again, Miss?' (meaning, do the blades turn in or out?). They were thirteen and still wearing the last traces of their childhood grace: in another two years – less – they would be fully in the grip of their hormonal demons. But as they worked now over the sink or the chopping boards they breathed in an oasis of calm. The girls gossiped about bands and fashion; the boys talked endlessly of football. They told her about their lives, about their custody arrangements and which parent they got on with best (those who were lucky enough to see both). Some boasted of older brothers with convictions, embroidering the feats of gangs in their area. There was a casual violence in their lives ('Yeah, well, he gets a bit carried away, my dad') which bled into the landscape of their jokey narratives, and they swore at one another with habitual venom. Tom had described them as little bastards in the classroom yet they were prepared to work hard on the locks, scampering from barge to embankment in their earnest efforts to assist him. They seemed almost touchingly determined to get it right, and on those occasions when they mucked up were abashed with contrition. Away from home they were surprisingly generous and forgiving, as if, in that temporary capsule on the water, they could suspend their grievances, pack away their resistances and sail on; enlightened pilgrims who had left their burdens behind in the old country. Of course, they were still in the old country, but they were on the water, and being on the water made it different. From Tom's stories it seemed that in the classroom they were like caged animals; tormentors. Out of it they were gracious, mature, forgiving and funny – but only, she knew, on the boat. Off the boat it would be different – they would be skiving off for cigarettes and alcohol and any drugs they could afford, or steal. But the narrow boat was like a floating desert island. Here on the cut their space was finite, their roles were defined, their options few. And yet they were happy. And why? Because for a short time they formed a community; they belonged to the boat. For ten days they were water gypsies, living with a horizon that was always, but slowly, moving.

Often enough she escaped from the kitchen to amble with them along the tow paths, and when they began to bicker dangerously she would distract them with hair-raising tales from the Australian bush, a landscape they imagined as more perilous than any remote planet and teeming with lethal wildlife. Her shark stories went down particularly well, not that she had ever seen a shark outside of an aquarium – nor did she know anyone who had – and she realised that in her tales she was constructing a mythical landscape, like something from *Gulliver's Travels*, or *The Water Babies*. Some other world that was hot, white and ferocious. She also guessed that this proximity to the monstrous would enhance her mystique, and with it her authority.

Sometimes the scene by the tow path was bucolic, with local boys fishing by the canal, a church spire in the distance or a quaint early pumphouse with dome and Ionic columns, and a water mill beside. In other parts they glided through a landscape of iron bridges and tall brick chimneys; the water stained a metallic orange from mine seepage, the dour Gas Street Basin in Birmingham and, later, the giant cooling towers of a power station flaring into the sky. She liked both landscapes, was entranced by their strangeness: so different from the wide plains and the diamond-white light of home. She even became resigned to the weather, the unexpected beauties of the English gloom. The gates and beams of the locks were painted in tar and white-washed to make them visible in fog. On one misty day their ghostly outlines loomed up ahead with a kind of eerie beauty that made her think of hobgoblins, and later that evening from out of the fog she saw the startling image of an eye painted on the bow of a strange boat, gliding into her vision like some disembodied Cyclops.

Not surprisingly, on the first night of fog the kids wanted to have a séance. At first Tom was dismissive and scoffed at them. Then to her surprise he relented and let them fiddle about with a glass for an hour, but they talked and fidgeted too much to be able to spook themselves, to generate any satisfying frisson. And because he had worked them hard, they were tired. At curfew they collapsed into their bunks with barely a murmur of protest.

Not long after, she and Tom embraced avidly in the gloom, their bodies rocking on the hard floor while the smells from outside wafted in over their skin ... diesel from off the oily water ... fresh-cut grass by the embankment ... the dank, alluring smell of moss along the stone coping. In the early hours of the morning the wind came up so that the narrow boat began to knock against the brick walls of the canal ... and she woke, and listened with a sense almost of enchantment.

On the Wednesday there was some kind of scuffle on the bank between Yusuf and a kid named Joel. She had taken an instinctive dislike to Joel, a weedy little smart alec who sniffed all the time. There was something about him that got under her skin, his ratty little body, his sour, acrid smell, the way his hair stood up in unwashed spikes. He seemed always to be following her around, mimicking her accent and forcing on her his clumsy attentions so that she had to restrain herself from giving him a shove. That morning Joel had spat on Yusuf and the two of them grappled and slipped together all the way down the grass to the edge of the water. Tom had to stop abruptly while halfway through turning the lock and in the act of looking away cut his thumb badly on a piece of loose tin. He swore and shouted at the two boys as he strode toward them, muttering as blood oozed from the gash. She half expected this incident to stir them all up into factional warfare, to render them seething and unmanageable. But no. Abashed at Tom's discomfort, shamed by his stoic patience (wary, as well, of the black look in his eye that underwrote that patience), they tiptoed around for the rest of the day and tried to make it up to him.

Later in the bat cave Kirsten expressed her surprise at this display of contrition. 'I thought they were supposed to be hard cases,' she whispered as they lay on their sleeping bag in the dark.

'They are.' He sighed. 'I think it's the boat. They haven't been half as much trouble as I feared they might be. The boat seems to be having a soothing effect on them.'

Yes, she thought. It was the flow. The endless flow.

'Also,' he added, 'it's their age. In another year, they'll be impossible. Terminal cynicism will have set in.'

'I won't come next year,' she said, laughing.

'Neither will I.'

On Good Friday it was her birthday and, as it happened, Terry's birthday as well. Tom had told the kids and they organised a sur-prise party. Tom bought a cake at the little town where they stopped the day before and they hid it under Ruth's bunk. After dinner – spaghetti bolognese at Terry's request and a Caesar salad (or what passed as one) for her – she and Terry blew the candles out together. There were ten candles, though he was fourteen and she twenty-three. Then the kids presented her with a gift bought from a whip-around of their pocket money. It was a small pyrex casserole dish with blue cornflowers on it because she was 'such an ace chef'. At this point Tom allowed himself an ironic smirk and she knew exactly what he was thinking. Then one of the smallest and, at school, most troublesome of the boys, Patrick, a scrawny boy with protuberant ears, stood up from his bench and leapt onto the table. The cutlery went flying in all directions and a bowl fell to the floor and broke but no-one seemed to care, least of all Tom. With a half smile of anticipation he was looking up at Patrick, who had broken out into a wild patter, a kind of high ululating sound, half yodelling, half keening, as if he were speaking in tongues. In fact he was mocking them, mocking them all in a semi-coherent rant of cruel mimicry. It seemed he had prepared for this moment (with Tom's collusion?) spraying his words over their heads like verbal confetti. And when this went down well he launched into his Elvis impersonations, and he was such a natural, so manically gifted in either mode, that they all surged as one to the edge of hysteria, drunk with laughter. Two of the rowdier boys scruffed one another and began to whoop and bray, while the more self-conscious boys like Yusuf shook quietly and blushed at their own mirth. Kirsten laughed so hard she had a coughing fit, while around her the exuberant girls, led by Ruth, clutched one another and shrieked so piercingly that the drab narrow boat seemed to vibrate into the stillness of the countryside. Even Tom guffawed into his beard.

Curfew was approaching and Kirsten wanted to do something; it was unthinkable that after such a good time they should all just fall into their bunks without ceremony. She stood up and rummaged around for the new frying pan, and the chocolate sauce she had stashed away, and she set about making flapjacks for supper. At the first sight of these the kids swooped on her, and the mixing and the pouring and the frying seemed to take forever, because of course there were so many of them, and they wanted to eat and eat and eat; wanted the night to go on and on until they were comatose with a fullness they rarely felt.

When Patrick's turn came he dipped his fingers into the sauce and daubed his face in brown chocolate streaks, flapping his arms and legs and whooping around the cabin like a lithe little demon.

*

Their last night.

It had been a hard day on the locks and the kids were subdued, almost sombre. 'They know they're going home,' Tom muttered, as he settled into the sleeping bag, 'and they're not looking forward to it.'

Jesus, I am, she thought. She was looking forward to a hot shower. But the kids seemed to be in another space altogether. A few of them were sullen, angry even at the prospect of having to leave the boat.

In the middle of the night she was woken by a tap on the door. Tom was a heavy sleeper. He didn't stir. 'Who is it?' she called in a pronounced whisper.

'It's Ruth, Miss. It's Joel. He's acting all funny.'

When she entered the main cabin she couldn't see the boy at first and shone her torch into the corner behind the table. There was Joel, curled up in a foetal ball on the damp floor, keening in a low, shivering moan.

In a dismissive gesture she patted Ruth on the shoulder and nodded in the direction of the bunks at the far end. Then she moved towards the boy.

'What's the matter, Joel?'

The boy looked through her.

Again she asked, and again, but he would not reply, nor would he respond to her requests that he return to his bunk. Even when she crouched beside him and looked directly into his eyes he continued to stare ahead with a glazed expression, his arms locked around his sides. It occurred to her then that she should wake Tom, that the situation might be beyond her, but Tom had a long drive ahead of him the next day and it was worth at least one more try. So she began quietly, so the others couldn't hear, to talk coaxingly to Joel; about the trip, about what a good time they had all had and how it was a pity to spoil it now, about how, whatever was bothering him, he could talk to Tom in the morning and she was sure that Tom would be able to help in some way. All the while she could feel the chill from the damp floorboards rising up through the soles of her feet, through the thin skein of her thermals and into the small of her back. Her feet were turning numb. Damn this kid, she thought. She would try a more forceful approach and if that didn't work she would have to send Ruth for Tom. Squatting on her haunches she grabbed hold of his arms and attempted awkwardly to raise him to his feet, but with a sudden jerk he twisted to one side and then fell back against the wall of the cabin so that his head made a dull thud against the wood. For a second or two he lay there and then, like a puppet, he sat up as if in shock, with one hand held gingerly to his head.

Kirsten was relieved to see that he was conscious. 'Will you get back into your bunk now, Joel?'

The boy shook his head.

This was too much. 'Ruth!' she hissed. 'Bring me the blankets off his bunk.'

Soon two outstretched arms were handing her a mound of grey blankets, disgusting army-ration serge for those without sleeping bags. She disentangled a blanket from the pile and laid it across Joel.

What now? She couldn't possibly leave him here like this. There was only one thing to do and that was to snuggle into the corner against him and draw the other blanket around her.

The boy made no resistance. Indeed, he had become calm. Before long his breathing slowed and deepened and she knew he was asleep.

Good, she thought, and allowed herself a slow exhaling sigh. Thank you. Thank you, God. It was their very last night and all they had to do was get through it without further mishap. There were so many things that could have gone wrong, and hadn't, and she had played her part well, all things considered, all natural obstacles taken into account ... and with this thought she settled beneath the blanket, her head drooped and she began a slow drifting into sleep, but not before she caught a glimpse of herself as a figure from one of those sentimental prints of the kind that had hung in her great-grandmother's house. 'Young maiden comforts orphan in the night'.

And she felt almost virtuous. She was cold, she was uncomfortable but she had done a good deed.

What woke her was the sound of the splash.

It wasn't loud, but instantly she knew what that sound meant. She opened her eyes and glanced instinctively to her left where Joel had been sleeping, but the corner of the boat was empty. As she flung back the sliding door of the cabin she shouted, 'Tom! Tom!' and glanced hastily up and down the narrow deck. Then she saw him, a shadowy figure flailing in silence by the edge of the lock and seeming to sink before her eyes. 'Tom!' she shouted again, and at the moment of shouting leapt from the deck of the barge.

The icy shock of the water rose up through her blood like voltage.

Later it would seem as if at that moment she were lifted off the deck by some blind force, for she had no sense of agency, of any operation of will. She simply leapt into the black water and grabbed hold of the lump that was rising up to the surface. At first she thought Joel might be unconscious but the minute she grasped hold of him he began to howl and writhe. Fortunately he was puny, but he bit her on the left hand so that for a moment she lost her grip and had to struggle – treading water all the time – to lock her right arm around his skinny neck. And still Joel fought her, lashing out with his feet. It was a full moon, and an eerie lambent glow bathed the canal and surrounding fields in a ghostly sepia gloom. Those few moments when they thrashed around in the dark chill of the English countryside seemed like an eternity until, in a sudden moment of apprehension, she understood that the boy wanted to die.

By this time Tom and the other children were crowding onto the deck. Some of the boys had leapt onto the embankment for a better view and stood shivering in their pyjamas. Tom, meanwhile, was kneeling on the deck, preparing to grab hold of Joel as Kirsten manoeuvred him alongside the barge. Assisted by Terry, he managed to drag the dripping Joel onto the deck and by the time Kirsten had climbed aboard they had wrapped Joel in a blanket. 'Hold onto him,' Tom said to Terry, and a look of grim understanding passed between them. Then, turning in consternation to Kirsten: 'Are you okay?'

It was a feeble question and she resented it. If it hadn't been for him and his bloody excursion she would not now be standing here in a state almost of shock. 'Go to the cabin,' he began, 'use my towel to dry off. I'll deal with Joel and I'll be along in a minute.

I'll get Ruth to make you a hot drink.'

'You can't just leave him there unsupervised.' She was shaking violently.

'True.' He hesitated. 'I'll probably have to sleep in there for the rest of the night. On the floor. But I'll come back to the cabin first.'

Without a word Kirsten returned to the bat cave. Her eyes felt as if they were coated in icy grit and she had a headache from the chill of the water. From the neck down she was numb. Standing, dripping, outside the door, she stripped off and bundled her sodden clothes into a nearby bucket. Inside she towelled herself down as briskly as she could and put on her warmest gear. The torch had disappeared. Too shaky and exhausted to zip the doona up into a sleeping pouch, she wrapped it tight around her and then, almost falling onto the air mattress, she lay there bent in a foetal arc and could not control her trembling.

After a while Ruth appeared with a tin mug and set it down beside Kirsten's head. 'Here you are, Miss,' she said. 'They put Joel to bed in one of the bunks and Sir is lying with him so's he can't move.'

'You'd better go back,' Kirsten whispered. 'I'll be okay.' But when she sat up and took a sip from the mug it was full of a tepid and sickly cocoa that made her gag.

Tom did not return.

In the morning the kids were mute as they packed up their kits and went about cleaning the interior of the main cabin. Joel had been placed under Terry's watchful eye but for the moment he appeared okay; he had eaten some toast for breakfast and would nod when spoken to by Tom. Mostly the kids ignored him, deep in their own reluctance to leave the boat. They had the air of mourners in the wake of a funeral procession. As the barge glided and bumped into the mooring dock they gazed with blank, resigned faces at the big green bus that awaited them. Then, hoisting their packs over their shoulders, they lined up by the cabin door and awaited Tom's command to walk the plank.

Kirsten felt like death. Her head throbbed, her throat was raw, her limbs ached in every muscle and joint and she knew that some bug or virus had ambushed her in the night. All she wanted was to crawl under a blanket but she knew she must stand and say good-bye to the kids. She waved from the open door of the bat cave as Tom stood at the end of the plank and shook hands with each boy and girl as they trooped off, and she saw a gruff male courtliness in her lover that she hadn't seen before … but was too sick to hold this thought for long.

After they had waved the kids off on the bus she fell into Tom's car, aching in every bone. It was clear that Joel must travel back with them and Terry was delegated to the back seat to sit beside him and keep an eye out for sudden moves. Tom was afraid that the boy might open the door and attempt to leap out, but for most of the drive home he seemed almost normal, as if that nocturnal parabola of watery flight had purged him of his demon. At least for now. Kirsten was beyond caring. All the way back to London she drifted in and out of a painful sleep in which it felt as if her body were encased in a rotating drum of fire. Tom, exhausted, drove like a maniac.

*

She spent the next three days in bed.

It was the sickest she had ever been in her life. All day and all night she lay in her track pants and polar-fleece jacket under the thick doona and still she was cold. Her head felt as if it were being compressed by an iron weight while a current of raking pain tormented her back and joints. Her fever it seemed came and went, and came again, and with it a series of dreams so torrid that at times it was hard to tell whether she was dreaming or hallucinating. One late afternoon she dreamed that she was kneeling on top of the main cabin of the narrow boat and banging with her fist on the door, and the door was stuck so that she had to break in through the hatch. And there they all were, the children lying on their bunks like angels, their eyes closed beatifically while through the open hatch poured a torrent of milk so that in their sleep they were force-fed, their skin bathed in rivulets of cream, their eyelids glazed with a thick white coating. Not long after, Tom came home from school and sat by her bed, muttering about Joel who had gone berserk in the playground. Joel? Who was Joel? Then the doctor arrived; a shadowy figure, like an apparition in a cloud of warm pink fog.

On the third day, the fever broke. In the early morning she woke, feeling better. Instinctively she fumbled for the torch, but of course it wasn't there. The book was there, *Madame Bovary*, looking much the worse for wear, mottled and wavy from where hot tea had been spilled on the cover. Poor Emma, she thought, poor Emma. Too young to be the wife and mother of a plain man in a small village; too constrained too early. Thank God that she, Kirsten, wasn't married. She wouldn't marry Tom, and perhaps not anyone. And with that thought, suddenly into her head came the image of a narrow boat, not the boat they had just returned from, which had no name, but the photograph in the book; that strange picture of the *Gort*. There in the gloom she could see the young bargemaster's wife at the door of her dark hollow; could see the tightly wound ringlets that framed her head, the prim white collar, the neat cuffs and the wide serge skirt of dull grey, so wide it skimmed the sides of the doorway. *How on earth had she borne it?* And how solemnly she gazed back at her onlooker, though the seriousness in her eyes was an enigma. How steadily she held herself before the camera, because it took so long to make an exposure then, and it was impossible to hold a smile for long without feeling foolish. And perhaps, after all, she was not inclined. It was unbelievable that anyone could live in that dark, confined space, never mind make a home of it for a child. Day after day, on the drab water, so flat and oily in its man-made channels; so dense with the sense of enclosure, of brick and tar and charcoal and smoke. And in her arms, still, the white swaddled baby, its blank face all but erased save for those eyes like two sepia smudges, staring out in hope.

Kirsten sighed, and turned over onto her flank. Time to let the long night of water-sleep draw in on her, and burying her face she snuggled down deep into her padded cocoon. Now, once again, she could feel the buoyant curve of the narrow boat beneath her, rocking gently to the familiar slop, slop of water against the stern, while outside there hummed the deep stillness of the countryside. And all the while she was moving inwards, floating on a slow tide of surrender, floating towards the turning wheel of the lock. Sleep, she thought, savouring the word … sleep. And drifting off into the limp repose of the convalescent, she wondered if that baby had ever learned to swim.

Ground Zero

All his life he had been restless and discontented, haunted by a fear of boredom. There were various incidents that need not be recounted here, just the stuff of early manhood, but beneath them ran a powerful current of unfocused anger that never left him, even at the best of times. Much of that seemed to fall away once he was married; in the years following his marriage to Zoë it was as if he were on a roll and he experienced one of the most uncomplicated periods of his life. He felt at last that he was maturing, that he was settling equably into early middle age, that the worst of the devil had gone out of him. He had fallen into something called normality. He had grown up.

And then, in the '80s, he descended into hell. Everything at work began to jar, to shudder and crack under the pressure of the recession. Sometimes it was as if pieces of him and everyone else were strewn around the floor and they scarcely had enough energy to pick themselves up, like broken tin men, and put themselves back together again for the evening drive home.

Anger began to fester in him, slow and insidious. In his sleep he ground his teeth and would wake some mornings with his jaw clamped and aching. On the drive home, stuck in traffic, he would bang with a loose fist on the steering wheel of the car, robotically, over and over.

In his twenties he had thrown himself into his work in a gung-ho way and it had not been difficult to cover his tracks during the black periods. But now the future was no longer an ocean of possibility, more like a river where the waterline was lowering in the face of recurrent drought.

He was forty-three and he was stalled. Too often, mostly around three o'clock in the afternoon, he felt as if time was standing still for him. He wondered if he was having a mid-life crisis. For the first time ever he began to question the meaning of his work. He felt his mortgage like a leaky barge, creaking beneath him. There were mornings when he was fuggy; late afternoons when he was brittle. And then a strange thing happened: his ambition began to bore him. He saw that there was just work and more work, the next project and the next, and the one after that. His old ennui returned, only now the feeling was worse. There was no longer The Future to look forward to. He was in it. The Future had arrived, and it was no different, no more satisfying than the rest of his life. It was not the repository of some special meaning, some revelation that was the reward for stamina, for hard work and for being sharp.

The anger rose in him, anger seemingly about nothing.

He began to have night rages. He would wake in the dark with his fists clenched or with that aching jaw. Sometimes he wouldn't even get to sleep; he'd be over-tired and living on his nerves and a problem at work would have him lying awake, bug-eyed in the early morning. He became increasingly sensitive to noise and the least little thing would set him off into a hair-trigger tantrum.

One night, he was disturbed at three in the morning by a shouting match below his window. In that area the streets were alive until sunrise and it was a rare night that he wasn't woken at least once – sometimes, depending on the state of his nerves, into a fury. That night he had thrown open the front door and shouted at two men and a woman who were arguing drunkenly beside the cast-iron fence. One of them had moved, threateningly, to open the gate and that gesture of transgression had sent him over the edge. Indifferent to the fact that he was naked, he'd moved instinctively towards the stranger, ready for whatever might be coming, and gashed his toe on the edge of the brass sweeper that had come away from the front door. He could feel the blood trickling over the nail as he kept his eyes on the man who at that moment was backing off, retreating in an aria of screamed obscenities to cover his loss of face.

Closing the door he turned back for the bedroom, only to find Zoë at the bottom of the stairs, furious. 'You idiot!' she seethed, 'they could have worked you over well and truly! You don't know what they're on or what they're carrying. Or if they'll come back!'

He said nothing. Bandaged his toe. Poured himself a whiskey, and went and sat in the darkness of the living room. The toe throbbed all night.

He knew he was taking it out on Zoë. He withdrew from her emotionally; he fought with her over money; he neglected his share of the chores; he started dropping into the eleven-o'clock sessions at the local movie house, although sometimes he would fall asleep after the movie began and have to be awakened by an usher. Then he would slink home and Zoë would be awake. She would lie on her side and say nothing.

They slept with their backs to one another.

Each day his anger began to bite into him corrosively, like an acid train, stopping at all stations: lungs, heart, liver, spleen, kidneys, and the whole messy labyrinth of his guts.

He was in good health, he had a nice wife, a son he doted on and a good job. Why wasn't he happy?

And then the chest pains began. This is it, he thought, I'm going to be one of those men who drop dead at forty.

He went to his GP, David Wang. 'It could just be stress, Rick,' David said, 'although you do have a bit of a heart murmur. Did you know that?'

No, he didn't.

'It could be nothing to worry about. But then again, you do have chest pain.'

That night in bed he thought: I'm not ready to die.

But what would 'ready' mean?

He was over forty now, and any day death was a possibility. He might need to have a bypass, or a valve replaced. He had heard that any repairs to the heart could be more complicated than a transplant. Surely that couldn't be true? For one thing, the after-effects would be fewer. And what did the murmur sound like? A whisper? A slight rumble in the orthodox rhythm? A click? A trill? Was it some kind of electrical fault? And he drifted into sleep, alive to the thought of that murmur, that whispering sound. What am I panicking about? he thought. All I have is a murmur.

One wet Saturday afternoon he went with his son, Luke, to the university's medical library, bent on doing his own research. But immediately he walked through the door of the Bosch building he was overcome by his old library claustrophobia with its memories of enforced tedium, of the brain in institutional harness. He had always felt an antipathy to books *en masse*; stolid, musty little rectangles of the arcane. Using the keyword 'Murmur' on the medical library data base, he scrolled through a bewildering array of titles: *Clinical Disorders of the Heartbeat/The Disorders of Cardiac Rhythm, Vols I and II, Interpretation of Complex Arrhythmias, Electrosystoles and Allied Arrhythmias, Intraventricular Conduction Disturbances, Frontiers of Cardiac Electrophysiology* and *Ventricular Tachycardia*. Proceeding on the intuitive principle that the right book would jump out at him from the shelves, he strolled through the rows of cardiac books while Luke rode his scooter up and down the parapet outside. The books were more dryly technical than he had anticipated and there seemed to be two hundred varieties of heartbeat, each characteristic of a different syndrome and carrying a different name, not one of which spelled out Dream-disoriented Systems Analysts in Mid-life Panic. And he knew his coming was absurd. After only a few frustrated and increasingly half-hearted minutes his eye was caught by the title of a slim black volume, *Sudden Death of Athletes*, written by a man with the improbable name of Jokl. Taking it from the shelf he slumped into a black vinyl reading chair and read a lurid chapter on 'Collapse Syndromes': hypothermia, effort migraine, mountain sickness and cataplectic loss of muscle tone (athletes collapsing of shock when informed of their win), the Mexico Olympics in '68 proving to be of special interest.

This is absurd, he thought. He stood up, walked outside and whistled for Luke, who was careening down a long path into the trees. On the way home they stopped for pizza and a bag of movies on DVD.

A week later he presented himself for an echocardiogram. It was somewhere around six o'clock on a rainy Thursday evening and there he was, sitting in the antiseptic waiting room of one of those private pathology centres that smell of money and death.

He was the only one there. Waiting to be summoned. Within an hour, he was thinking, everything in my life could change.

It was a heavy old house, a Victorian mansion converted into medical suites with cheap chipboard partitions subdividing what were once grand and gloomy salons. After a time, a statuesque woman appeared and beckoned him over. 'Richard?' she asked.

'Rick. It's Rick.'

'Hi, Rick, I'm Helga.'

Helga was a large Nordic-looking woman in her fifties, solidly built with cropped blonde hair streaked with grey.

'Ever had an echocardiogram before?'

'Never.'

She pointed to a cubicle. 'Strip from the waist up.'

'Shoes?'

'No, you can leave your shoes on.'

For some reason this summoned up the notion, both comic and macabre, of dying with his boots on. Draped in a clinical wrap made of pale-green paper, he opened a padded door and entered a small, dim room where the ultrasound machine was waiting for him, a stolid block of gun-grey metal, six feet at its highest point, with two small video screens at the top. Helga, he realised, was the technician, or rather, the high priestess in charge.

Lying on the high white surgical bed, with his head resting on a small pillow, he felt as if he had been taken up into a spaceship by a benign alien.

He liked Helga. There was a certain warm gravitas about her; in her pale-olive track pants and grey ugg boots, which on anyone else would look shapeless and woolly, Helga looked stylish, like an astronaut in a lab. She had a comfortingly androgynous quality, like a hi-tech angel, a cross between Nordic *hausfrau* and goddess. It was clear she read the heart like an old letter, like the back of a cereal packet; there were no mysteries there for her, but nor was she jaded. There was a quality of concentration, of low-key command: rapid, efficient, absorbed. She worked the machine in the way that competent women cook, with the kind of familiarity and ease of those who've done it all before, but with the relaxed alertness of one who knows that at any minute it could all go wrong, something malignant and fatal could appear, some squiggle or smudge on the screen that could signify a death sentence for the hapless figure prone on the surgical bed. Some fatal flaw, some warp or blockage, or malformation; some enlargement, or tissue damage, or clot, or calcification; some startling arrhythmia like a code that's been scrambled; some electrical fault running malign interference.

Ah, but here was another alien. A man in his sixties came in and introduced himself as Dr. Cullen. He was old, grey, thin and dry-looking and Helga called him 'Doc'.

So there he was, Richard Kavanagh, lying in his green paper gown on a white surgical bed, reclining on his left arm, like a model sitting for a life class. On the wall opposite was a poster in the abstract style, a large red tube with smaller, thinner offshoots at one end. In this room everything was tubes, even the token artwork. Helga, meanwhile, was holding a small tube that looked like one half of a stethoscope and was rubbing one end of it with some gel.

'What's that?' he asked.

'That's the traducer,' she said, and he smiled, because the name itself conjured up trespass and violation. Meanwhile Helga was placing the traducer firmly against his chest, just under the left nipple, pressing hard against his rib cage so that it hurt.

Without fanfare his heart appeared on the top right-hand screen. Just like that.

He was gobsmacked. There it was, in black and white, a slightly blurred image of heaving mass, working away with such ferocious energy that he was in awe. Even more in awe than he had been when he first saw his son's foetal form in utero on the ultrasound screen. In awe of himself? Well, that made a change. Nothing, he thought, prepares you for the experience of seeing your own heart. He continued to gaze at it in frank arousal, almost expecting a round of applause.

Helga, of course, was disinterested. Sitting on her high stool, leaning in towards the machine, she began matter-of-factly to scan the image from different angles and cross sections, adjusting the dials to give close-ups of certain features, like the valves; reading off numbers to Cullen, who sat behind her on a low chair and repeated her observations, muttering comments in corroboration or dissent.

Helga was reeling off the numbers. '27, 28, 47 ... good functioning of the left ventricle ... 28, 40, 8 ... 7, 21 ... A good set of numbers there, Doc,' she said, and winked at Rick, letting him know that she was mocking the words of the economic pundits.

Cullen looked up from his notes and peered at Rick over the top of his half-moon glasses. 'It's all numbers these days, isn't it?' he said dryly.

Rick smiled politely, thinking: It's like watching the Keno machine on TV. This is my life's lottery, my flesh-and-blood poker machine.

Suddenly there was a noise, and he realised with a start that Helga was adjusting the sound dials on the machine and this, now, was the sound of his heart ... whoosh-whoosh! it went, whoosh-whoosh! like a loud, emphatic washing machine. Look at that pump; that manic, heaving pump – rhythmic, implacable – could that really be him? All those times in his life when he had suffered from lassitude, from negativity, from doubt and despair, all that time this heart had been oblivious ... whoosh-whoosh! ... Here it is, he thought, the prosaic soundtrack of my self. Indifferent to the dreary thoughts of my brain, it pumps on regardless. And he was moved. Yes, he had been told about it, had had it described for him, seen other people's hearts on TV in documentaries, but let me tell you, he will say to Zoë that night, it's different when it's yours.

Helga and the Doc were still muttering to one another, swift, matter-of-fact statistics and appraisals. By now, all fear had left him. He wanted to ask a dozen questions but he didn't want to disturb their concentration in case they overlooked some tiny but fatal flaw. So he gazed at the wall opposite his feet, at another print in hazy patterns of blues and greens, soft and soothing. He heard Helga say: '17, 21, 28 ... a murmur there ...'

A murmur! He jerked his head up. This was it. This was the death sentence.

'... but I'd say that was trivial, Doc. I wouldn't say that constituted a prolapse.'

Cullen was gazing up at the screen, his glasses having slid down to the end of his beaky nose. There was a horrible pause, and then he said: 'No, not a prolapse.'

'What does that mean?' asked Rick, sharply.

'Nothing to worry about,' said Helga, still staring up at the screen. 'I'll explain in a minute.'

Then Cullen left the room, unceremoniously, with only a dry nod at Rick who was no longer interesting, who had failed to produce an interesting set of numbers. Helga switched off the machine.

Just like that.

No more heart. Heart put away, back in its rib cage, back in its box.

Helga leaned forward on her stool and adjusted her glasses.

'There *is* a murmur,' she said, 'which is what your GP heard, but it's an innocent murmur.' She said this quickly, so as not to cause him alarm. She called it 'trivial'.

'What does that mean?'

She brought her two index fingers together. 'This is the normal valve' – moving one finger up over the other an almost imperceptible fraction – 'and this is yours. There's just a very slight misfit, if you like, an infinitesimal gap or cusp. A slippage. If bacteria get in through this, into the bloodstream, they like to congregate there and breed.'

He had heard of this condition. He had heard (but didn't like to say) that the bacteria eat away the valve and then you're in big trouble. Yes, he would say it.

'They can damage the valve?'

'It's rare. Very rare. That's why you take antibiotics before dental treatment, just in case.'

'That's it?'

'That's it.'

The verdict: innocent. But still he couldn't quite accept it, still he was holding his breath. 'I just don't understand,' he said, 'how any murmur, any deviation from the norm, can not mean *something*.' How could a murmur be innocent?

At which point Helga put her large reassuring hands on his shoulders. 'There is absolutely nothing,' she said, 'wrong with your heart.'

Back in the cubicle, he put on his clothes. He felt he would like to shake Helga's hand, or kiss her on the cheek, but that would be inappropriate. It was all routine to Helga. Helga saw eight hearts a day.

Outside. He was outside and walking down the winter dark of Macquarie Street, past the Catholic shop with its sombre crucifixes, its painted statues of the Virgin, its gilt candles. He paused for a moment by the window and looked for a statue of the Sacred Heart. There wasn't one. Perhaps it was out of fashion now, that lurid icon of blood and fire. There had been no blood and fire on the machine, just the blurred black-and-white smudges, the rhythmic pulsing, the whoosh-whoosh. And Helga the high priestess.

It was four blocks to the underground car park and he walked them in a kind of alert trance, breathing in the cool, damp smell of rain, taking in the world around him; the all-but-deserted city, the wet road, the traffic lights, the grey drizzle, and all the time in his mind's eye that surging, inexorable mass of muscle and blood, *his* heart.

So long as the heart is doing its work, the murmur may be pardoned for its innocence. He had read that in a book in the Bosch Library and it had lodged in his brain: things may not always be perfect but that doesn't mean they can't do their job.

And it was nothing personal, not something he could take credit for. If they took it out of him and put it in someone else it would go on in exactly the same way; like the rhythm of the universe, like the movement of the tides. And he felt humbled: it did all this work for him, without pause or rest; twenty-four hours a day for forty-three years. Such a long time for a muscle to pump without missing a beat. Suddenly it seemed almost beyond being credible. No wonder they called it the miraculous pump. The cyclonic funnels, surging and throbbing, like mini-storm channels. Relentless – that was the word he was searching for, the quality he was awed by; the sheer *relentlessness* of it. He knew his other organs were working hard but not so dramatically, so noisily, not with the same unabated, day-into-night, night-into-day rhythm. And what he felt was gratitude. He was grateful and he must show his gratitude. He must not take this heart for granted. He must find a way to exercise more. And to relax. He had his heart, and his heart was good to him. Why wasn't he good to his heart?

For some time after the ECG he existed in a state of simple-minded gratitude that was new to him. For a while he felt good, almost invincible. Small pleasures would ambush him; the simplest things. Spring arrived, and he began to feel that the worst of his anger was over.

*

It was a Wednesday morning. He was feeling off-colour and he rang the office to say he had the flu that was on the rampage that spring and he would not be coming into work. Zoë was late and frazzled and sharp-tongued with Luke. He hated it when she spoke to the boy like that, even though, increasingly, this was the way he, Rick, spoke to *her*. It was one of those hateful mornings of family dissonance, though he wouldn't for a minute blame her for what was to come.

'I'll drive him to school,' he said. 'I'll drop you off at the station first and you'll save twenty minutes.'

She shot him a glance, almost of truce. 'Thanks,' she said.

By this time he had lost the knack of patient endurance in peak hour – if ever he'd had it. Cars banked up all down the highway like a line of moronic tin beetles, while the humidity, already rank by 8 a.m., seeped into the car like a noxious gas until he felt he was bumper to bumper in thick cotton wool.

Two blocks before the school he pulled into the kerb by a small park opposite a frantic intersection. Cautioning Luke to be careful crossing the road, he watched as the boy, nervously glancing from side to side, waited for the lights to change and then ambled across the road with his distinctive bobbing walk, his backpack dangling awkwardly from one shoulder.

He waited until Luke had disappeared through the school gates and then he turned the key in the ignition. Then he turned it off again. There was a small convenience store on the corner and he would get the paper and some milk. They were out of milk and he was looking forward to coffee. He walked to the edge of the corner and stepped out onto the kerb. At that moment a flash of white metal swerved with a screech of tyres around the corner on his blind side and almost ran over his foot. The car, a dilapidated hot rod with a gash in the driver's side and a smashed headlight, stalled on the turn into the main road and suddenly he was standing there looking down through the driver's window – it was rolled down as far as it would go – and into the glinting brown eyes of a young man. He leaned in and with his open hand he slapped the man across the face, registering in a split second that the face he was striking was black. The driver was a young Aboriginal guy, twenty-two, twenty-five, maybe, who stared back at him with eyes of molten rage. And next to him, another face, his friend, whose mouth was open in hostile shock, though only for a second, perhaps two, before it widened into a grimace of growling obscenities.

Not that he heard them. Or rather he heard them, but didn't hear them because his attention was focused on the driver, who had flung open the door and was lurching towards him.

For a moment he considered turning to run, but his pride would not allow this. The first blow he felt against his upper right temple. The second caught him on the shoulder. Positioning his feet instinctively to maximise his balance, as he'd been taught in martial-arts class as a boy, he ducked from side to side as the blows came, one after another. Not for a second did he consider fighting back. For one thing, he was in the wrong, and his heart was a black hole of stupefying foolishness, a sunken galleon in his chest, and for another, if he managed to land even one halfway decent punch then the other guy in the passenger's seat would get out and he'd really be done for: there was no way he could beat the two of them, and probably not even this one who was younger and fitter and heavily built. The blows came at him in a rush and any one of them might have smashed his jaw or broken his nose if he hadn't been ducking and weaving so that they glanced off him in jolting grazes and he scarcely felt the lacerations of his skin, the bloody contusions on his scalp. But with the fifth blow he felt the hard bone of knuckle against his skull and he fell to the grass, almost in slow motion, for a moment on his knees and then keeling over, slowly, onto his side, so a green blade of grass was in his eye, the dank earth in his nostrils.

He lay there in a daze, thinking: Here it comes, the boot in the head. But it didn't.

When eventually he sat up, shaking his head slowly from side to side, he looked around him. The hot rod was gone. A woman and her two small daughters were staring at him as if he might bite.

'Are you alright?' the woman asked. 'Do you want me to call the police?'

'No, it's okay,' he said, and his voice came out like empty bellows. He was winded. His mouth tasted of acid bile, his body felt like putty. His heart lurched suddenly, rancorously, into his guts, and with a rising groan he vomited his breakfast onto the grass. He remembers glancing across at the sandstone wall along the high grassy mound on the northern side, and the familiar graffiti in red spray-paint – *FUCK ALL WOGS* – was blurred.

Somehow he drove home. When he got there he made himself a cup of scalding hot tea and put four heaped spoons of sugar in it. Sugar for shock, he remembered. Then he rang his GP, David Wang, who said to come over immediately. David pronounced him mildly concussed and wrote out an authorisation for him to go straight down to the public hospital along the road and get his head X-rayed. He thanked David, said yes he would, wrote out a cheque and didn't bother. He was beginning to feel better; physically, anyway.

David had been outraged on his behalf, had urged him to report the incident to the police. But he knew better. It was his own fault, he had brought this madness on himself, not that he could explain that to David, who prided himself on his counselling skills. He would warn his patient about the classic syndrome of the victim blaming himself, feeling somehow that he had invited attack, that some inadequacy or quintessential unworthiness had marked him out. Everyone knew this sort of spiel by now; it was even in the lifestyle section of the papers. But he knew it wasn't that. It was something else, and it was this. He had looked into the younger man's eyes and seen his own madness, his own ugliness, his own rage and humiliation reflected back at him.

That night he waited until Luke was in bed and then he told Zoë what had happened. 'I got beaten up today,' he said, baldly.

What had he expected? Sympathy? Muted fear? Cool disdain?

She screamed at him. 'You what? You hit a black man, four blocks from an Aboriginal street, in the middle of the city …' her first shriek trailed off in disbelief. *'Are you out of your mind?'*

And before he could respond, could say anything more ('It wasn't in the middle of the city—'), she screamed at him again.

'How could you? *How could you?* There were children there! Young children. And what if Luke had witnessed this, his father being beaten up in broad daylight! As it is, he'll probably hear about it!'

Her face was a grimace of pain. Tears leaked from her eyes. At that moment, he could see, she despised him.

'And what about us? Did you think of us? You could have been seriously hurt, you could have had your face smashed in, you could have had your ribs broken. You ...' her voice cracked and faltered, '... you could have been killed!'

But I wasn't, he was thinking, I wasn't. I was agile and I did okay. But these silent words were just a last gasp of self-defence against a great grey tide of self-pity that was about to engulf him at any minute and he couldn't bear the despair between them for another second. He got up and walked through the open door of the kitchen and out onto the back lawn. In the darkest corner of the garden he sat on the grass, under the platform of Luke's tree house, and put his face on his knees. He could hear the synapses of his brain firing and misfiring, over and over and over until he thought his head might explode.

After a while, he looked up. It was a clear night. The stars blinked down at him.

When he went inside, she was sitting at the kitchen table, waiting for him. She had been crying. 'Sit down,' she said. 'I have something to say to you.'

Here it comes, he thought, my second divorce. He could see Luke asleep in his single bed, and he knew he would do anything not to give him up.

Her voice was low, quavering and grim. 'I can't go on living with your anger,' she said. 'In the last year you've been unbearable.' She spoke hurriedly, as if she could not afford to pause. 'Either you go and see a counsellor and get some sort of therapy, or I'm leaving.'

Therapy, he thought, what was the point of that? He had tried it once in the past and while it had helped, it had not been enough. The vessel was still half empty. He wanted something more, something more than – what? Something more than comfort. But what else was there? What else could any of us offer one another but that?

For most of the next day he slept.

That evening, Luke was at a friend's place, staying for dinner; Luke who could always ground him, could induce him to play-act his best self.

Zoë brought home take-away for dinner and they barely spoke. He jabbed at his food listlessly until the silence got to him and he stood up. 'I'm going to sit outside for a while,' he said.

Out in the shadowy courtyard he felt spacey, disoriented. There was an obscure humming in his head. He sat down, carefully, on the edge of an old deck chair and closing his eyes he began, involuntarily, to relive the events of the previous day. A garish reel of film ran through his head, sometimes speeded up, sometimes in slow motion, until he could bear it no longer and blocked it out in a black dissolve …

When he opened his eyes, everything in the garden seemed exaggeratedly *there*, larger than life but alien. His senses were acute. A mosquito buzzed by his ear and he looked up. It was a warm, scented night and the brightness of the moon ought to have calmed him but his pulse was slippery, his breathing taut and irregular and his heel drummed against the concrete slab. A slow, disengaging cog began to shift and grind in his chest … He looked down, looked up again, blinked … the back of the house was receding from him, the kitchen window panes framing little squares of golden light that seemed to grow smaller and smaller and smaller. He stood up with a start and shook his head. Any minute now he would lose his grip on reality, would tear and splinter into gaping viscera and jagged bone.

Inside the kitchen Zoë was sitting at the table, reading the paper.

He stood in the open doorway. 'I'm going for a walk,' he said. This is it, he thought. I will start to walk, and then I will just keep on walking until I drop.

She nodded, curtly. Then she looked up at him and her eyes were full of a sadness he hadn't seen there before.

'I'll come with you,' she said, and rose purposefully.

And walk they did, he unthinkingly beside his angry wife; aloof, holding his breath, oblivious to the world around him, to the blur of shrimp bushes, of overhanging hibiscus and fraying palm. They walked and walked, looping around the hill and taking the long way back, and somehow the walking began to work its spell, the simple rhythm of striding in step, feet on the ground, arms swinging, withthe black fog in his heart seeping down into the soles of his shoes to be left behind, like an invisible film on the grey asphalt.

*

In the weeks that followed he felt as if he were waiting.

Waiting for what?

And Zoë, too, was waiting.

And then one of his programmers, a man called Carl Kremmer, hanged himself in the basement of the North Sydney offices. The cleaners came in on a Monday morning and found him hanging from an air-conditioning pipe. The irony of this was not lost on Rick. A man had contrived to cut off the flow of air through his body by tying himself with nylon cord to a valve that was there to enable him to breathe more wholesomely, more comfortably, without the extremes of heat or cold, without noise or smog or wind or dust, without frost or mist or airborne pollen.

By the end of the month, the office of human resource management had circulated a memo offering free programmes in stress management – a reward, as Zoë had remarked, tartly, for working late into the night and falling asleep at your workstation.

One of these programmes was a short course in meditation. The memo came accompanied by a glossy brochure extolling 'an age-old technology of the self' and promising a technique that would 'eliminate stress' and enable you to 'maximise your potential'.

Why not? Rick thought. He'd tried everything else, and this at least would placate Zoë, would look as if he were making some kind of effort.

When the forms came back, only two from his team had elected to go. The other was Mark Paradisis. Mark was a young systems analyst, twenty-eight years old and cocksure, a real Mr. Cool whose reddish-brown hair was shaved with a number-one blade and who ran to a series of stylish oversized jackets, collarless shirts and occasional waistcoats that complemented his dark looks. Bumptious and clever, in that narrow-banded way that tech-heads have, he treated Rick with a deference that was part mock, part real, and would circle around him like a teasing child, absurdly deferential one minute, taking stinging liberties the next.

One evening he informed Rick that currently he, Mark, was 'between cars' and since they'd be going straight from work to meditation classes – 'Oops, sorry, stress management' (winking at him) – he thought perhaps Rick could give him a lift, at least to the introductory lecture on the Monday evening. Beyond that, he couldn't, y'know, guarantee that he'd front. 'They might be a bunch of crazies, K, know what I mean? Hippies, cult-struck mind-benders. Whatever.'

When the time came, Rick was glad of the younger man's company. As part of a twosome, he felt less self-conscious. It seemed like more of a game.

The classes began at seven and they drove straight from work, journeying across the bridge in the wake of peak-hour traffic and going by way of Taylor Square to make a pit-stop for souvlaki, which they ate in the parked car. It was hot and dusty, and as they sat looking out the window at the squalor of the square – its rough street trade, its sinister little patch of grassy parkland between the traffic lights, its pungent smells of burnt coffee, rancid frying oil and carbon monoxide – the absurdity of their dinner setting, only minutes away from the meditation centre, made Rick feel perversely cheerful, and he chortled out loud, almost choking on the first bite of dry pide bread.

Mark turned his head sharply. 'What?' he asked.

Rick was still struggling to swallow. 'Nothing,' he coughed, 'nothing at all.'

Mark then began, in between bouts of wolfing down the kibbeh special, to launch into a riff on the mechanics of his mental well-being – which would have been funny, if it hadn't had a certain quality of robotic desperation.

It was like this, he explained: he was not moving forward, he was not making progress in his life. He'd had a few knocks in the last couple of years; been dumped by his girlfriend, got pissed a lot, lost his licence, lost the plot you might say. Then this came up and, well, as he saw it, it was like servicing or reconditioning your car. Things wear down after a while, the engine's not ticking over, there are some clunks in performance – you go to a good mechanic and you get it seen to. So you can move forward, so you can progress. As he saw it, the car you've got may not be much good but it's the only one you've got. You've got to tune it up from time to time, otherwise the wheels will fall off. You won't move forward, you won't progress.

By this time they had finished their hasty supper and Rick had pulled out into Oxford Street. 'How do you know when you've progressed?' he asked, teasingly. He noticed how nervy Mark was, how he couldn't sit still and jiggled one knee up and down like it was on voltage. Hot-wired.

'You look at it this way,' Mark said. 'You check for reality statements. You ask yourself: where am I now compared to where I was? You get feedback from people you work for. They'll tell you: now you score – I don't know – say, eight out of ten, whereas once it was three, four, something like that.'

He remembers thinking: here is Mark, talking as if he were a machine, a machine within a machine; a bright red Honda SL encased in my old silver Fiat. And then Mark said something poetic: 'Y'know, K, I'm annoyed at having my future dictated by my footprints in the sand – places I've been, what I've done in the past, all that.'

'You read that in a book somewhere?'

Mark shrugged, glanced away. 'Yeah, probably.'

At that moment they turned into Underwood Street.

The house they were looking for was an elegant old terrace,

painted in lavender and white. It stood on the brow of the hill looking down to the sweep of the bay and had a big peach-coloured hibiscus bush in bloom by the front door. He remembers it now as one of those stifling summer evenings, the gardens petrified in a humid stillness; remembers how he and Mark paused at the iron gate, struck by the shadowy beauty of the street; the exquisite tracery of the trees in outline against the darkening sky and the rich, orderly beauty of the terraces, unfolding down the hill with the satisfying symmetry of a series of perfect numbers.

The door was ajar so they went in and through to the front salon, a room of elegant proportions fitted out like a corporate office; pale-grey carpet, eight rows of pale-green chairs and a whiteboard positioned in front of a marble fireplace. On the chairs were twenty or so men and women who looked like Mark, mostly in their late twenties or early thirties, stressed-out yuppies in casual but expensive clothes. Instinctively he cast an appraising glance at the women in the room and noted Mark doing the same. Primal instinct.

They sat and looked ahead without speaking, as if they had exhausted their chitchat in the car. Before long a man in his early forties, dressed in a suit, entered the room from the rear and stood by the whiteboard. Smiling at them, he introduced himself as Jack.

Jack was to be their trainer.

Rick liked Jack on sight. In his light-grey suit, pale-blue shirt and yellow tie he presented in every way as a middle-level executive. His skin shone with a tanned glow and this, combined with his balding head and round face gave him the appearance of a corporate buddha. Jack spoke with an almost permanent smile on his lips, as if sharing a joke, but his eyes shone with a warm dark gloss, insinuating that yes, the unfathomable *could* be fathomed.

He began by telling them that meditation was a simple, undemanding process through which the mind effortlessly arrived at the source of consciousness. *The source of consciousness?* Immediately Rick's fickle mind began to play with this, punning on the idea of source – he couldn't get out of his head an image of sauce on the brain; a large brain on a plate with a lurid red sauce poured over it, and then a white sauce, and next a yellow, like thick custard … without this sauce the brain looked remarkably naked, uninteresting even … doughy and grey, like batter left overnight in the fridge that has begun to oxidise … could this be the *organe supérieur*, the *summa cum laude*, the source of all that was bright and beautiful and inspired?

Look how his mind had wandered already! He recollected himself.

Jack was talking about peak performance. 'During meditation the body enters into deep levels of relaxation and rest, a more profound rest than that experienced even in deep sleep. The body becomes attuned to the subtle vibrations of nature, which repair the body and release the creative energies of the human organism …'

Next to him, Mark had fallen asleep, which was not surprising, given that the words had a high degree of abstraction, an airy quality, and that often Mark didn't leave his workstation until after ten at night. And Jack had a soft, soothing voice which exuded warmth. The effect was soporific. He was, Rick could see, a very contained man, though with a surprising tendency to a soft, silent giggling. Nevertheless there was something attractive in his persona that was hard to define, something subtle.

Rick looked around him. Not everyone, it was clear, had a mind as restless as his. Everyone else appeared attentive, and serious. Most of them were younger than he, and as junior executives they were used to paying attention; used to listening for the 'grab', the slogan, the key phrases, the code words, the open sesame.

And now they were here for the mantra. As Mark would say: 'If it works, it's cool.'

In Jack's discourse there seemed, he thought, to be a lot of emphasis on the brain. What about the heart?

As if reading his mind Jack moved on to the subject of 'perfect health' – didn't these people ever use qualifiers? – and heart disease, and how medical research had shown conclusively that meditation regularises blood pressure and lowers cholesterol and stress levels. Indeed, in orthodox terms, this was the area of its greatest success.

Beside him now, Mark had begun, gently, to snore.

Jack's soft, hypnotic tones were such that perhaps they didn't need to learn to meditate; perhaps all they needed was a tape of Jack's voice with one of those piping flutes in the background and the sound of running water. On the way over Mark had told him about the time he worked for a hot new IT company in Palo Alto in California where, during a particularly tense and difficult project, one of the supervisors had had a notion to play a relaxation tape as background in the office, a tape of running water, until all the programmers had shrieked that it was getting on their nerves. Tonight, however, The Voice was working for Mark, who dozed through almost the entire talk, eyes closed, head slumped forward on his chest.

Jack concluded by asking each one of them to say why they had come. And they all said something sensible. They wanted 'better concentration'; they wanted 'to achieve more', to do twice their current workload. They wanted to feel less tense, less tired, less impatient, more calm. No-one said they wanted to maximise their potential. No-one admitted to being fed-up and angry. And no-one talked about 'the mysterious absences at the heart of even the fullest lives', to quote from a book review Rick had idled through in the dentist's surgery only yesterday.

Mark woke up in time to say that he regarded his body as a prime racing machine, and just lately he realised it needed a bit of a tune-up. Rick said he wanted to get more done with less fatigue. What else was he going to say? That he was angry? That as he grew older he was getting angrier? Angry at the universe for failing him? Listening attentively to the reasons the others gave for being there that night, he wondered if they too were dissembling, camouflaging some inner vision of flames – some moment of madness, some visceral ache of yearning – with the managerial workspeak of the brochure, a language they knew how to put on like a suit of armour; like battle fatigues.

The introductory talk finished early, around nine-thirty, and Rick hadn't far to drive his companion who asked to be dropped off at a club in Oxford Street. Refreshed by his nap at the meditation centre, Mark was ready to party on. On their way up the hill Rick teased him about falling asleep and with the disarming ingenuousness of a child, Mark asked for a 'recap' on what he had missed.

'Fill me in, K,' he said. 'What was the gist of it?'

'Some things are too subtle to be rendered into paraphrase.'

Mark threw back his head. 'Seriously?' And then: 'Yeah, yeah, I'll bet.'

God, he was a boy; a slick, smart-arsed boy.

'You'd better stay awake tomorrow night.'

'Yeah, definitely, if you say so, K,' winking at him as he lurched out of the car at the intersection and sauntered off up the neon-lit street.

Driving home, Rick was disconcerted by the fact that even if there had been time, he couldn't have told Mark much of what Jack had said. Was his concentration as shot as all that? Or had it all been too vague, too abstract? He would have to say the evening had been something of an anti-climax: he had expected revelations but none came. Perhaps the first night was a test, and if you persevered and kept coming back, in the end you'd get a pay-off; the magic word, the open sesame.

And you did. Get the magic word, that is. On the second night Jack told them about the *mantra*. The mantra was a special sound. It was like a key in the lock of their inner being, and the insistent chant of it would open them up and put them in touch with—

With what? On this they still weren't clear. Everything Jack said sounded reassuring at the time, but evaporated in your ears within seconds.

For the next two nights the talks continued as before. And each evening Mark sat dozing in a chair beside him, so that Rick had to 'recap' for him on the way home before dropping him off at a club: Zero in Oxford Street, Moscow in Surry Hills, Yada Yada in Leichhardt. Clubs seemed to have a life of twelve months; Rick hadn't heard of any of them. It made him feel old. 'I don't know any of these places,' he said to Mark.

Mark shook his head in mock commiseration. 'This is what happens when you get married, K.'

He found it extraordinarily difficult to summarise what Jack said about anything – like the words were little nodules of polystyrene filler, the sort that come in vast crates as packing around white-goods and spill out of the box when you attempt to extricate the new appliance. You could gag on them. On another night he would find the words rolling around in his mouth like ball bearings: precise, elegant and full of weighty momentum, but cold, smooth and hard to trap.

One night, clearly bored with Rick's struggle to condense 'the message', Mark interrupted his waffling to say: 'Y'know, K, I was really surprised when I saw you had put your name down for this course. You impress me as the strong type. You know,' his mouth curled into a mock grimace: 'Stress? What stress?'

'I *am* the strong type,' Rick said. He was not about to enter into emotional correspondence with a younger man.

And anyway, it was far too difficult to explain, especially to someone like Mark, that lurking somewhere in his consciousness, like a virus in the bloodstream, was a sliver of pain he could neither disgorge nor salve. He could think of some parodic scenario that might make sense to Mark: a virus, say, infecting his programme, or that movie, *The Invisible Man*, where something starts making its way through the pathways of the body, like a microchip afloat in a vast cyclotron.

Was it in the shadowy background of his consciousness? Or at the forefront of his unconscious, whatever *that* was. When he thought of it at all, he tended to think of the unconscious as a level playing field where small, neurotic athletes jostled for the front row – and learning to meditate might enable him to marshal them into some kind of team where all the elements could combine well, could get on cosy terms, could resolve whatever it was that was creating friction between them. The mantra would be the oil in the grease-and-oil change, some soothing balm that would ease them into their right formation, and he would become a cyber programme without glitches; debugged.

The perfect dream of neuroscience.

At last he would be rid of the unresolved yearning that had haunted him all his life; that was so unsettling, like a metaphysical pinprick in every balloon of pleasure; in every activity, actual or potential, virtual or real.

On the fourth night they got it: the mantra. The payoff, the special word, the magical formula.

As usual he and Mark went straight from the office and they were late, and hungry. Mark wanted to stop near Taylor Square and get a falafel.

'We haven't time,' Rick said.

'I'm starving.' He knew that Mark, like many of his team, would have skipped lunch, or shot out for a Mars Bar from the machine in the corridor. The way they worked was crazy. In the glove box, he told Mark, there was a bag of roasted almonds his very practical wife kept for times like these, or when his son, Luke, was hungry. And had he, Mark, remembered to bring the ritual offering? He half expected his young colleague to have forgotten this: the flowers and the fruit. He was touched to find that Mark had remembered, that he had them in a white plastic take-out food container in his backpack.

When they arrived there was an air of quiet expectation. Everyone was sitting on the green meeting-room chairs with their small parcels of flowers and fruit on their knees. Some had bought a large expensive bunch, wrapped in sharp peaks of cellophane and tied with twirling boutique ribbon. Others appeared to have garnered random blossoms from the garden, or purchased something cheap and already wilting about the edges from the fruit stall at the station kiosk.

Rick was first to be initiated.

In a small room at the top of the stairs Jack was waiting, seated in a stylish cane armchair. Against the wall facing the door was a table that looked like some kind of simple altar with a gold silk cloth and a single candle. Jack was dressed, as ever, in his corporate suit and welcomed Rick with his usual glowing smile. Awkwardly, and with both hands, Rick held out the small bouquet of mixed flowers, the apple and banana and the white cotton handkerchief. The ritual gifts, the token of respect. But respect for whom, and for what?

Jack accepted the gifts and placed them casually on the altar. 'This is a very simple procedure,' he began, 'and it won't take long. I'm going to say a prayer in Sanskrit in praise of all gurus, or spiritual teachers, and then I'll give you your mantra.'

Spiritual teachers? What spiritual teachers? Could Jack be classified as a spiritual teacher? Surely not. All through the course Rick had resolutely turned a deaf ear to the more esoteric parts of Jack's discourse; they would hover, like a haze, on the fringes of his perception. He knew the technique was an adaptation of a practice derived from Eastern mysticism, similar to, say, a suburban yoga class, and beyond that he did not wish to venture. It wasn't necessary, as Jack himself had intimated from the outset. But now the presence of the altar, however minimalist, made him feel uncomfortable.

It was a low-key ceremony, simple and precise. The mantra was no recognisable word, just a high-pitched sound, an exhalation of air with the tongue against the bottom teeth. Jack said it, and then he asked Rick to say it. After Rick had repeated it a few times, Jack said 'Good,' and then cautioned him not to repeat it to anyone else, as this would diminish its potency.

Rick nodded but his neck felt stiff. He was not used to being in a room with an altar. He hadn't expected to be inducted into anything spiritual: he thought it was about getting a technique that was scientifically based.

As if reading his mind, Jack said: 'Remember, this is not a religion, you are not being asked to adopt any set of dogmas. Just meditate on your mantra each day, morning and evening, and come back in a week for a checking.'

And that was it. Something of an anti-climax, really. At the back of his mind was the thought that some people, not under corporate sponsorship, were paying hundreds of dollars for this. Could anything that expensive be this simple? Could anything worth having be that simple? Could peace of mind be so simple?

Mark was second last to go in. Outside, Rick waited for him on the veranda, looking out over the dusky roofline of the hill, the purple night sky over Port Jackson Bay.

Eventually Mark emerged, exhaling heavily in a bemused sigh. 'I need a ciggy,' he said. 'Do you mind waiting?'

Like furtive children they moved into the side lane and Mark lit up. He looked around him, up and down the lane, down at his feet, and then up and down the lane again. He seemed edgy.

'So that's it, K,' he said.

'Apparently.'

'The secret word.'

'Yep.'

'Is yours one syllable or two?'

'One.'

Mark seemed reassured by this, as his was two, which meant at the very least that they were not all getting the same mantra. The idea of this was an affront to them both, a possible sign that they were being suckered, not succoured.

'Are you seriously going to do this every morning and every night?' Mark asked.

'I'm going to try. I'll give it three months.'

Something told him that Mark, on the other hand, wouldn't last three days. He seemed unhappy with the outcome; his cock-sureness had fallen away and he was peculiarly sombre, as though he'd been purged of all his wise-cracking. He was as restless, as jittery, as ever but not in his teasing, good-natured way; more irritable, hostile even, curiously offhand.

'I'm starving,' he said, with a sharp intake of breath, and tossed the glowing butt of his cigarette into the bougainvillea that ran like a flame along the side wall. And then, brusquely: 'Do you have to go home? Why don't we go somewhere and eat?'

Rick thought for a minute. 'Why don't you come back to my place?' He had been thinking of bringing Mark home for a while. Zoë would find him amusing.

Mark hesitated, and then, with a kind of shy, haunted look, said, 'No, no, thanks anyway. I'll grab a bite on the way home.' There was something in the way he said it, something in his manner that was worrying. For Rick the little ceremony had been of scarcely any moment – bland, even – but Mark seemed unnerved.

Rick felt protective towards him. 'Let's go to Miro's,' he said, mentioning a bistro only a few streets from where he lived. Mark could get a taxi on from there.

At Miro's they sat on a quilted leather banquette in a dim red light and Mark downed two quick schooners of Guinness. As he drank, he became more and more morose, straying ruefully into a reverie of childhood dreams.

'Y'know, K, all I ever wanted to do was play Rugby League,' he said, crouched over the lip of his glass. 'Not because I wanted to be rich and famous, not that ...' His voice trailed off, and he brooded for a minute. 'Even now, sometimes when I'm watching a game on TV, I get so emotional I could cry. There's something pure about it, you know what I'm saying? Honest. No bullshit. The speed, the strength, the raw courage ... the sight of one man hurtling through the pack like ...' He stopped, lips pursed together, as if stymied by the inadequacy of mere words, '... like a human fucking projectile. All heart, nothing's going to stop him, you can see the veins bulging in his neck, you can see the look he's got in his eyes, and it's a look of ... of ...' He shook his head. '... pure momentum – like an arrow,' and here he raised his right arm in a gliding motion across his face, 'straight ... straight ...' And he shook his head again and gazed out into space, unable to finish the sentence. 'And I cry, I cry just watching it. I admit it.' And again, he crouched over the lip of his glass. 'And that's all I ever wanted to do. Ever.' He said it again, loudly and with drunken emphasis. '*Ever!*' And banged the parquet table that reeked of smoke and beer.

By the end of the night they were both drunk, slouching out of the bar with all the élan of two deflated tyres. He dropped Mark at a cab rank two blocks down the road and hoped that he, Rick, would make the two kilometres home without being breathalysed.

Zoë, thank God, was a heavy sleeper. Stumbling into the bathroom for a pee, his head in a purple-brown fug of Guinness, not to mention the vodka chasers, he stubbed his toe on a broken tile and began to bleed, a thin rivulet of red dripping onto the white tiles. He swore, fumbled in the cabinet for a band-aid and sank heavily onto the lavatory seat to bind his toe. For such a small injury, the pain was acute. Softly, he swore again. So much, he told himself, for meditation.

That night he dreamed that a currawong was pecking out his eyes. Strangely, there was no pain. Around five o'clock he woke in the dark with the mantra spinning in his head.

*

After the first week he asked Mark how it was going.

Mark hesitated. 'Uh … on and off, K, on and off.'

'More off than on?'

'Uh, not exactly. I just don't do it at the usual times. You know, morning and evening.'

Rick didn't pursue it. For one thing he was having his own difficulties. To his surprise he found he couldn't sit still for five minutes, never mind twenty. At his workstation he could sit for what seemed like hours without moving a muscle but without his beautiful backlit colour screen and his Boolean logic, his algebraic grammar, his magical formulae of conditionality – *if this, then this* – he was at the mercy of his chaotic and untidy brain, a jerky and primitive slide-show of trivia. Football fixtures for the coming week, what to buy for Luke's birthday, reminders to get the drier fixed, had he paid his car insurance? – all the endless minutiae of daily life flashed across the inner screen of his brain like balls careening across a billiard table. The minute he settled himself in the stiff-backed dining chair, his scalp would begin to itch, his collar chafe … he would send the mantra spinning into an imaginary space before his eyes like a bowler unleashing a ball, but he could never, as it were, find his length: the mantra-ball would fall to earth with a thud and roll grimly along the turf, or fail to land at all and sail off, disappearing into the clouds while his thoughts, those mad computer-game figures, scuttled about in the ballpark of his neural field in a noisy, short-circuiting clamour, like machine-gun fire ricocheting in a stadium.

Only a few months ago he had been near despair, all but lost to the black dog; now he was like an idiot child struggling to master the first letters of the alphabet. After what seemed like half an hour he would look at his watch and find that five minutes had passed or, on a good day, ten. Where was the timelessness, the loss of self that others spoke of? How come he never made it into the zone, not even for a second?

A week later, at the first group checking on the Monday night, Rick sat and listened to the others, with Mark beside him. Mark had only managed to 'try it' on 'two or three mornings' and couldn't understand why even to contemplate doing it seemed an enormous mental effort. It felt like homework, he said: the mere thought of it triggered an internal resistance.

Rick smiled and patted him on the shoulder, as if it were no big deal really, and all the while he was thinking: *You're not desperate enough.*

All through the first checking Mark fidgeted in his chair as they listened to the brilliant experiences of the others. One man had seen white lights, another had drifted off into an orange haze, someone else had experienced an intense sensation in the middle of her forehead where the third eye lay. With each declaration Mark looked sideways at Rick and rolled his eyes, as if to say: What a bunch of tossers. There's always someone, someone who's had an *experience*. Always the goody-goodies in the class, the point scorers who announce with transparently fake wonder and humility that they've hit the mark, can top whatever you've got to offer, are among the chosen. Always someone whose experiences are bigger and better than yours.

Jack sat quietly, acknowledging each individual response with his customary smiling detachment. When Rick at last spoke up it was as if Jack had been waiting for it, as if the other responses had been too good to be true, and what Rick had to say was real. While Rick laid out the banality of his efforts, Jack nodded sympathetically. 'Firstly,' he said, 'scientific tests show you are always doing better, and going deeper than you think you are. Second, don't ever force it, just witness the thoughts that come up and then let them go, while gently bringing the sound of the mantra back into your head.'

But nothing Jack said served to dispel Rick's scepticism. I'll give it three months, he thought. It seemed, then, like an eternity.

*

A few weeks later his sister came to stay, with his nephew, Justin, who was fifteen. Justin drifted into the study one Sunday morning as Rick was halfway through his meditation practice, sitting up straight-backed in a dining chair he had carried upstairs for that purpose (important to have the spine straight for the breathing to be steady and even, the lungs open and expanded). Rick was there with his eyes closed, hands on knees, assuming the posture, he sometimes thought, of one of those stone pharaohs. He heard Justin come in and said, without opening his eyes, 'I'm meditating.'

Later that morning over breakfast his sister had given him a look of bemused scorn. 'You've gone New Age,' she said.

'I think it's cool,' said Justin.

But, no, it wasn't cool, it wasn't at all cool.

It was impossible.

On one of their Sunday lunches with Zoë's parents, his father-in-law, Joe, said: 'I hear you're meditating, Rick.'

Looking up from his plate he saw Zoë cast a warning look at her father.

'Yeah.'

'You find it relaxes you?'

'Not exactly.'

'From what Zoë said, it sounds to me a bit like playing chess. You lose yourself in the strategy and afterwards you feel surprisingly refreshed.'

Rick laughed. 'Depends on how competitively you play chess.' He knew Joe was intensely competitive and he was hoping to change the subject. Perhaps he would discuss it with Joe later, when he knew what he was doing, but not now when he was at sea. As a novice he could scarcely speak with authority. And there was nothing to say. Nothing was happening. Which was kind of the point. For a while, anyway. As long as he wasn't losing his temper and slapping strangers, the rest could be counted as a plus.

Over the following weeks he maintained his regimen. And then one morning it came to him that he would do this, every day, and that it would work. It would be his cure, and the essence of that cure would be silence, and surrender. But the cure would be a long time coming. He must wait, and for the first time in his life, he must have faith.

Freedom, Order and the
Golden Bead Material

All Frances had ever wanted was for her son to be happy. Happy, successful and safe. Was that too much to ask?

She and Mattie had arrived in San Diego to be reunited with her husband, Tony, then on a year's secondment to one of the city's big research hospitals. Four weeks earlier Tony had flown out of Sydney alone so that he might settle into the job without distraction and have time to look for a house to rent. Frances had been lucky enough to line up a part-time job in a dialysis unit; now all they needed was to locate a good preschool, somewhere safe and nurturing where they could leave four-year-old Mattie for a few hours each day. But already it was causing her sleepless nights. It would have been a big enough issue back home in Sydney, where she knew how to read the signs, but here she was a stranger. They said America would be pretty much like Australia but they were wrong.

The city was expensive and all they could afford to rent was a small box-like house on the edge of an infamous drug-dealing area. Their nights were broken by the wail of sirens and frantic shouts emanating from a block of derelict apartments at the end of their street. In daylight she had to endure the beggars. A three-block walk to the dingy supermarket was an encounter with panhandlers on the sidewalks, some black, some white. She found it easy to ignore the sullen professional who sat cross-legged in her regular spot outside a shop, her shabby hat set down on the pavement, but it was the random and the crazy ones that she found disturbing, the look of desperation in their eyes, their agitation, their twitching bodies and trembling hands. One day she arrived at the supermarket just after a shooting and there was shattered glass and blood spattered across the doors. Once inside she rushed through her shopping in a cold sweat. She resisted this market; the lighting was bad, the paint on the walls was peeling, the assistants were surly and the rows and rows of processed food looked time-worn and lifeless.

Only a few days after this, a young woman with matted red hair attacked her outside a DVD store, landing a wild haymaker punch on her shoulder. The woman's clothes were dirty and her eyes glazed with a black film. Frances could see she was on something and that the effect of the drug rendered her body flaccid; her muscles were slack and her punch lacked force. 'So you don't like Madonna, eh?' the woman screamed and Frances could see that in her assailant's waking nightmare she, Frances, was someone else.

An elderly black man stopped and asked: 'Are you alright?'

'I'm fine,' she said, but she was shaken. When she told Tony that night he was surprisingly detached. 'There's a lot of stuff here we have to get used to,' he said. She could see he was worried that she might not cope, that she might pack up and return home.

Every Thursday she would go to the city library to borrow books and quite often there was a figure in the women's lavatory, huddled on the floor in the corner and completely covered by a ragged brown blanket. The figure, she assumed it was a woman, would sit for hours, keening in the most miserable wail. The first time she encountered her there she went to the librarian on the information desk, a neat little woman who sighed and said: 'Is *she* there again?' After a while, like everyone else, Frances ignored the sobbing figure huddled in the corner. She washed her hands quickly and returned to the shelves.

One afternoon, on the walk home, a tall, slender black woman of around thirty stepped into her path, put out a hand and demanded money. She had a dissipated beauty, a kind of worn elegance in the way she carried herself, but her aura was seething and dark. Unlike many of the street beggars, she stared directly into Frances's eyes, holding her gaze with a look of unalloyed hatred.

Frances froze. She had never been looked at in this way before. Even though she had lived in some tough neighbourhoods back home this was a kind of abjection that was new to her. Hideous and shameful.

'You have to stare ahead into the distance and keep walking,' Tony told her. 'You can't let it get to you.'

In the third week after she and Mattie arrived, Tony took a morning off and they drove to one of the two preschools that had been recommended to them by one of Tony's colleagues. The first of these was The Free School, not far from where they lived. This, they had been told, was a cultural icon. One of the old flagships of '68 and the counterculture, it had been set up to 'shine a new light' (this from the brochure) and to 'enable children to bloom like flowers under a free sun'. Flowers? A free sun? This was hippie talk.

Still, the supervisor of Tony's lab had sent her own daughter there so they were obliged at least to go and look it over.

The main building was a rambling two-storey timber house surrounded by a large garden that was mostly sand and trees. The swings were tall, dangerously so it seemed to Frances, and the adventure play towers were also very high and with low rails. They looked perilous. The place was a mess: sand and toys strewn everywhere, clothes spilling out of lockers or lying on the ground. Some children had stripped down in the warm weather to their underpants and ran gleefully about in pursuit of one another. A small girl tottered around in high heels with a red satin skirt pulled up around her neck and a pink net tutu on her head like a fuzzy halo. Snot ran from her nostrils to her top lip. She looked up at Tony and said: 'I'm a rose.'

On the walls of the main building there were life-size cut-outs of each child pasted on the walls and stuck at crazy angles to one another, with names scrawled across each one. Rhiannon. Skye. Jacob. Jordan. Saba. Lindsay. Out in the playground a cluster of children were at the water trough, drenching themselves and one another.

'Okay, you guys,' shouted one of the teachers, 'I told you to put those aprons on. Now it's time to dry out.'

Frances looked up. A boy was hanging by his ankles from a twenty-foot pole, his blond hair floating down into the air. Her heart bounded with anxiety for him.

'You be careful up there, Max,' bellowed a tall, bearded teacher who introduced himself as Dean. Dean was around forty, a kind of ageing hippie. He wore a bright-red gypsy scarf tied around long hair that drifted in fronds to his waist.

The school administrator, Sadie, was a petite woman with a friendly, no-nonsense manner and a black Afro perm. She wore black stiletto heels, tight black pants and a black leather jacket.

'Our kids have confidence, they're outgoing. They come here; they're fearful, they're timid. Six months later they're climbing the highest scaffolding. They get a lot of colds, it's true, but when they leave, they're tough.' She led them through to the kitchen, where flour lay everywhere. 'Lucy here is making soy pancakes for afternoon tea. We only use wholefoods for snacks. We explain to the children about holistic energies. No sugar, no biscuits or cake in lunches. That's a rule.'

'They have rules here?' hissed Tony. 'Could have fooled me.'

The rooms were in need of painting. There were shelves stuffed with old boxes and the husks of toilet rolls, rags and paint-encrusted yoghurt containers. There were guitars with broken strings hanging from nails above a battered and dusty piano. In the book corner the mat was fraying, the shelves scratched, the books old and tattered (though there were plenty of them). The sofas were battered and stained. The mattresses in the jumping room were piled on one another and scattered with sand. 'Oh, dear,' said Sadie, scarcely missing a beat on the tour, 'they're not supposed to bring sand inside. We'll sweep it up later. Well, listen, you guys just wander around here and look at whatever you want to look at. Talk to the kids. Feel free if you see someone on their own to be that person's best friend for a while. Feel free to make a connection.'

Out in the yard, in the far corner, was a large wooden cage on slats, with a black rabbit inside. In a small fenced-off plot the remains of a carrot patch were in seed, and two white ducks pecked at an empty water trough.

'The children study the animals?' Frances directed this question to Dean, who at that moment was mounting a chipboard and glue project on a trellis table.

'Nah, the novelty wore off on the first day. I don't know why we keep 'em.' He brushed his sticky hands against his jeans. 'Mostly these guys just like to fool around.'

'Do you have any classes?' she asked.

'Sure we do. We have, like, a music class for the little ones and a dance class for anyone who wants to come. Boy, are those dance classes wild! Then there's a yoga class, and sometimes they cook. We've got serrated plastic knives and stuff. No-one's been stabbed yet, eh, guys?' he glanced around at his charges. 'Depends on what the staff feels like doin' that day, y'know. We keep it spontaneous. But the classes are optional. Basically these guys can move from inside space to outside space and back again as they want. Face it, these guys are up for twelve years tied to their desks in school. This is their last chance to be free, right?'

A tousled girl held up her gluey chipboard assemblage, so covered in white paste as to resemble a geometric suet pudding. Dean patted her on the head.

'Wow, Elisha, that's far out!'

In the cramped corner that was the principal's office, Sadie asked if they had looked at any other schools.

'Well,' said Tony, 'we were planning to check out the Montessori school in North Avenue.'

'Oh dear,' Sadie shook her frizzy curls. 'Oh dear. We have all sorts of problems with that. We all believe in early learning but, you know, there is such a thing as too many rules. Too much structure, too soon. We've had kids come here from Montessori schools and they're all tense, they're having nightmares at night. They have a fear of doing the wrong thing. They worry about making a mistake. A few weeks with us and, hey, they're kids again. You have to be careful, you know. There's such a thing as too much order.'

That night Frances was unable to sleep. She lay in bed and thought back to an abandoned Diploma of Education she had begun some years before, and her rudimentary study of child development. She knew of the German visionary Friedrich Froebel who had developed the idea of the *Kindergarten*. As part of his philosophy of Universal Harmony he had repudiated the idea of children as miniature adults who could usefully be put to work. Instead, he thought they should begin by spending their time in a children's garden, a haven of creative play where children could grow like flowers unfolding. Froebel set up a network of these kindergartens, some of which were closed down for a time by the Prussian government as too revolutionary. She thought of Froebel now as one of Sadie's forebears.

Tomorrow she and Tony were booked to look at the Montessori school, the San Diego Montessaurus, and she also knew something of Dr. Maria Montessori's pioneering work in the slums of Rome. Here the great innovator had worked with so-called backward children to develop a highly structured method that demonstrated how any child in the right environment could learn. Montessori believed firmly that freedom was not to be confused with anarchy; on the contrary, inner order was necessary to enable the child to see meaning in his or her existence. Chaos was not stimulating but oppressive. But this did not mean that inner order could be achieved through rigid external discipline of the old-fashioned kind. And so on. All Frances could recall were a few general principles but almost nothing of the detail of Montessori's method. What she did recall was how Montessori had an illegitimate son who was sent to the country to be looked after by a family there, and how she would visit occasionally to bring a toy and to observe him at play.

The following morning, they drove uptown to the Montessori school. It was a large property that took up a whole block, with a high fence all around that might well have belonged to a fort. They parked the car and walked to the tall wooden gates, which were unlocked. When, tentatively, they pushed one half of the gates open they found themselves in a peaceful yard. Here was a picture of perfect calm, of manicured order and low-key Californian charm. Several rustic, cedar-framed classrooms stood within a high-walled compound, almost obscured by trees and ranged in a semi-circle around a bitumen courtyard with a large oak at its centre. A number of red flowering bushes, planted at random intervals, softened the contours of the swings, the climbing tower and the slide. The only discordant note was a scruffy old tyre that hung by a thick rope from the oak tree.

The courtyard was empty. School was already in session.

They found their way to the office of the school administrator with whom they had made an appointment. Nancy was a tall, middle-aged woman with short, stylish grey hair. In her silk print dress and high heels she looked every inch the competent executive. She was also welcoming and cheerful, and she led them without much preamble to the first of the cedar huts. Inside, the hut was one large open space, warm and filled with natural light.

'We often have observers,' Nancy smiled, 'and the children are accustomed to it.' She gestured to a line of chairs at the back of the room and handed them a portfolio of printed sheets. Dutifully they sat on the small chairs and Frances was reminded that Montessori was the first to introduce child-size furniture. She opened the cardboard file that Nancy had given her and began to read her way through the notes. 'The goal of Maria Montessori's educational method was world peace' (yeah, right) 'and we agree with Dr. Montessori that each generation of children has the opportunity to remake the world it inherits.' Suddenly Frances was irritated by this high-minded sentiment, almost as sceptical as she was of children blooming like flowers under a free sun, and she began to skim until she came to a page headed 'Observations':

> The presence of visitors always has an effect on the children and the classroom atmosphere. In order that you may observe as natural and typical a classroom as possible, we ask that you please follow these suggestions:
> 1. Do not smoke.
> 2. Please remain seated.
> 3. Do not initiate any conversations during the work period.
> 4. If a child approaches you and asks a question, please answer briefly.
> 5. Do not talk to other adults who may also be observing.

Well, that was clear; they had their riding instructions. They were not being invited to wander about and become anyone's best friend, not even for a moment.

Every class has two teachers, Nancy had explained to them as they walked the path between her office and the first cedar hut.

'We're very proud of our staff, and they've been with us a long time, probably because they're not interfered with in their rooms. It's their own space. Joan specialises in art, she's doing an MA on children's painting. Clara is currently doing her Master of Education on children's music and plays several instruments herself. Sophie has a doctorate in children's language difficulties. All the teachers bring a range of their own interests and skills to their work.'

Tony had looked at her sideways and she knew what he was thinking. His irreverent streak was already roused. A doctorate? To teach *preschool*?

They settled on their low wooden chairs at the back of the classroom. Feeling vaguely foolish on the child-size furniture and with their knees almost up to their chins they prepared to 'observe'. Nancy leaned over to whisper that she would leave them to it and they were welcome to return to her office, when they were ready, to discuss what they had observed. At the door, she turned and waved at them encouragingly.

As she waved, Tony leaned across and whispered in Frances's ear. 'This place is so clean and tidy, so organised. It gives me the creeps.'

'For heaven's sake, you work in a lab.'

'That's different.'

'It *is* only the beginning of the day,' she murmured. What did he expect? Chip packets all over the floor?

They counted sixteen children who ranged, according to the notes, from two-and-a-half to six years old, and who sat in a circle on a large mat, quiet and composed. This, it appeared, was Circle Time, the first session of the day. There were two teachers in the room, both women. The first teacher sat at the top of the circle, cross-legged, a young woman in her late twenties, slim with shoulder-length black hair and dressed in baggy black cotton pants, leather sandals and a long, faded aqua shirt in Indian cotton. She looked very serious, and the first thing Frances *observed* was that she chewed her nails. It seemed out of place, an unsightly flaw; an unexpected symptom of anxiety on the sunlit surface of calm and order. The teacher's name was Clara, and she began by asking the children, one at a time and working clockwise, to stand up, walk into the centre of the circle and take a card from the neat stack resting on the carpet. When each child had performed this task (in complete silence) Clara spoke in a low sing-song chant. 'If you have the number five, please stand up.' A child rose, holding a cardboard square. 'Thank you, Jesse. If you have the number two, please stand up.'

And so it went on, until all the children had stood for their numbers. Then they were directed to sit again in their circle.

'Tim, will you go over to the Geometric Solids shelf and bring us back the rectangular prism, please.'

The boy, about four, tip-toed over to where a group of polished wooden shapes were arrayed on a ledge. He lifted the five-inch prism and began his return walk, stepping with exaggerated – almost ritualistic – slowness. Perhaps it was the sing-song tone of Clara's instructions but the children all seemed to be operating in a kind of trance.

'It's good how carefully Jesse is carrying that over to us,' Clara intoned.

The children did not move, fidget, or sigh. Their faces were solemn, or blank. Were they usually this subdued, Frances wondered, or was it because they were under observation?

Tony leaned in his wife's direction and grimaced. 'It's as quiet as a cathedral in here.'

She ignored him.

'Good little guinea-pigs, aren't they?' he persisted.

She felt in her husband his characteristic resistance to authority.

'Maybe it's just a quiet poise that we're not used to seeing in children.'

She sounded sanctimonious. Clara's tone was catching.

After all the shapes were assembled on the mat, Clara placed a white cheesecloth over them and the children were invited to the front, one at a time, to kneel and shut their eyes while they felt under the cloth for a particular shape. This they did in perfect quiet.

Frances glanced again at Nancy's notes. 'In order that your observation may be more meaningful we suggest noting the following. *Order in the classroom*: physical order; the order in the design of the materials; order in the sequence in which the exercises are accomplished; order in a child's use of materials ...'

Yea, verily, there was a love of order here.

'This has a horrible fascination,' muttered Tony.

'Don't be such a cynic.'

Clara stood and smoothed her long shirt over her thighs. Circle Time, it appeared, was over and after Circle Time it was off to 'work'. Several projects and resources were laid out around the room, some already begun on previous days. The notes informed Frances that each child was required to work in his or her own clearly defined space and for this a small mat was used. No other child was permitted to trespass on the mat without permission from the mat's 'worker'. A child might leave his or her mat in any state he or she wished but must, on completion of the project, tidy both project and mat away. 'Please note that completion of the project may take weeks, and for this period the mat must be left undisturbed and in the state the child wishes it to be.'

Frances was beginning to catch on. There was an ordered classroom and within this, each child could have a space of free play, her or his own little backyard in miniature; a balance of structure and routine with impulse and spontaneity. There could be apparent chaos on the mat, but order all around. Yet despite the mat being an area of 'free' activity, surely there must be a subtle pressure to do something 'useful' or 'constructive' on that mat?

She looked up. All was proceeding with uncanny decorum. She watched a small boy in a red jumpsuit who had begun to paint at an easel. He wielded his brush with unblinking concentration, painting for much longer than any other child of comparable age that she had observed in other schools. When he was satisfied, he laid down his brush, unclipped his painting and hung it on a wooden rack to dry. Then, without hesitation, he walked across the room to the sink and turned on the tap. With great ceremony he proceeded to carry a yellow bucket of water and a yellow sponge back to the paint corner, where he began to clean his easel.

'Yellow is our cleaning colour,' said a sign on the wall above the sink.

The second teacher, Joan, a fair, freckled woman in jeans and sandals, had sat to one side of the room for the duration of Circle Time. She began now to circulate among the children, commenting, in a low-key way, on their work. One four-year-old girl was doing a giant jigsaw on her grey felt 'territory' mat, and already she was advanced enough for it to be apparent that this was a map of the continents of the world in bright poster colours. Above her on the wall was a display of autumn leaves, pressed flat.

Another child was building a complex series of towers in blocks. 'Some Montessori schools allow children only to use blocks and other project shapes to categorise, not for free play,' said the notes, 'but we've modified this practice in accordance with the philosophy of the staff. We find that free play in no way hinders learning. Familiarisation with the look, and more importantly, the feel of the Montessori wooden letters is the beginning of literacy. Most of our children, with no forced effort or strain, can read by the time they begin primary school.'

So this was a local version of Montessori. A little looser, a little more laid back. But not laid back enough for some.

Tony was restless and wriggling on his child-size chair. 'This is unreal,' he said. 'These kids are like little lab technicians. The only things missing are the rats in mazes and the white coats.'

Frances ignored him. She was mesmerised.

At ten-thirty, the children sat at the small table in the kitchen alcove and ate their snack of raisins and carrot wedges. Then Frances and Tony rose to follow the children outside for their morning play. Out on the warm timber deck they leaned over the rail and observed that the children seemed to play like other children; careening around on tricycles, falling off onto the bitumen and scraping their knees, climbing rope ladders, swinging on the rubber tyre. No-one threw sand.

'I'm just going inside,' said Frances to Tony, who seemed more relaxed now, leaning back against the cedar wall and closing his eyes to the sun. 'I want to look at the learning materials.'

He opened his eyes and fixed her with a stare. 'I don't like this place, Fran.' She ignored him.

Inside she began to wander about the perimeter of the empty room. She wanted to look at the specially designed project materials, up close. These were the famous 'manipulatives', also known as the 'didactic apparatus', designed to be 'self-correcting'. They were arrayed on a wide wooden shelf at child height and all were neatly labelled. These were the Sound Boxes. This was the Pink Tower. This was the Brown Stair, a set of ten prisms. These were the Red Rods and these were the Smelling Jars. These were the Bells and the Temperature Jugs and the Baric Tablets and the Golden Bead Material. And there was even one called the Time Line. And she was thinking: *the names are wonderful.* They sounded like words from a secret code or ritual, like something belonging to the Rosicrucians, or the Masons, something that might admit you to a better world, one where there were no beggars on the streets, where no-one moaned and wailed in the toilets or stared at you with hatred in their eyes. She picked up a soft felt container labelled the Object Bag and looked it up in her notes. This, the notes explained, was for 'exploring the art of feeling'. She opened it, peered inside and was disappointed. There was just a cup, a lid, a pin, some string, a ball. So much promise, so mundane a reality.

More satisfying was the Golden Bead Material, an exquisitely constructed cube of a thousand glittering beads. Though you would never have guessed from looking at it, the Golden Bead was a mathematical toy, designed to teach the decimal system. The beads were made of translucent gold acrylic strung on copper wire.

They sat in a cedar box on top of the shelf beside the open window and when the sunlight caught them they glinted. Each bead was perfect, and each sat in perfect relation to the others: perfect proportion, perfect balance, perfect harmony. They had a mystery to them, as if each bead was a magical object and belonged in that novel by Hermann Hesse, *The Glass Bead Game*. She had read that book as a student (it had won Hesse the Nobel Prize) and had found it wholly absorbing. For several nights she had been transported to life in the twenty-fifth century, to the utopian province of Castalia where an elite priesthood studied to master an immensely complex game that sought to integrate the whole of human knowledge into a harmonious system. The Glass Bead Game was the game of life itself, and these 'didactic' toys on the shelf beside her (they would not, it occurred to her now, be out of place in a Harry Potter novel) seemed like stray fragments from the great game; alluring and enigmatic miniatures of the whole; apparently simple tools with which you could build a series of other, and better, worlds.

Outside, as they walked back to the car, she knew that she and Tony were at odds. 'Well, how many out of ten?' he asked.

'Search me.'

'The teacher in the black pants didn't smile very much.'

'I saw her smile.'

'It's all too organised.'

'So you keep saying. That's better than a shambles.'

'The kids were too subdued.'

'We'd have to observe them over a longer period to tell if that's really the case.'

'I take it this meets with Madame's approval, then.'

'No, there *was* something missing there, but I can't put my finger on it.'

They left the school grounds by the same high wooden gates where, every morning, the teachers stood to welcome the pupils and, even more importantly, to farewell them in the afternoons. This way they could see who was entering, and who collected the children. Nothing was left to chance.

Out on the pavement Tony stopped and looked back at the high walls. 'Did you check out the security devices? The alarmed walls. The cameras.'

She shrugged. 'Well, wouldn't you want your child to be safe?'

'Castle Keep,' he said, intent on having the last word.

Afterwards they had lunch at a café nearby. Tony ate a large, ropey pastry filled with custard and when he had finished he licked his fingers. He had icing sugar around his mouth. He looked silly. She found herself staring out into the street where a young man was begging. Though it was a warm day he wore an army greatcoat with the collar turned up and his eyes had a wild, desperate glaze. The café jukebox was playing old Rolling Stones hits and she was thinking: It wasn't that the Montessaurus was too organised, or too quiet. It was that there was too much responsibility. Yes, that was it, too much of a burden of choice, day after day, to do something constructive, something *sensible*. She saw her son in invisible fetters.

For the next few days she debated with Tony the merits of the two schools. The Montessaurus was almost unnervingly calm.

Some vital spark seemed to be missing. But at The Free School some of the kids were bored, or raced around on the edge of manic distraction. Frances returned to have another look and came home in two minds.

'It was too dirty, too disorganised,' she said over dinner. 'The stuff they were making was junk.'

'Yeah, but they're only three years old,' he said, 'maybe four. Boys need their freedom.' And she felt like a prig.

Another sleepless night followed in which she lay awake and ran the arguments through her head, over and over: the Montessori method was unduly mechanical, formal and restricting; there was not enough free play of the imagination, not enough 'creative expression'; there was too much emphasis on individual rather than group work, on the development of individual skills and disciplines rather than social adjustment to the group. In the constant struggle to balance the needs of self and other – to find meaning for the self *in* the other – it veered too far into elitist individualism. In the dark of their cramped little bedroom she saw the unnaturally quiet classroom, she saw her son in a straightjacket. On the other hand, what was the point of undisciplined, unskilled 'creative play' that went nowhere? And there could be too much emphasis on the social, which only made children slaves to the peer group. Your best friend is away for the day and you're at a loss. Eventually she fell asleep and into a vivid dream. She was in a yard somewhere and all of the Golden Bead Material had escaped its box and was strewn about her feet so that the ground was a carpet of golden beads. 'Look,' she said, to no-one who was present, 'see how the beads lie freely on the ground and still they retain their beauty.'

In the morning, somewhat dejectedly, she and Tony agreed that – The Free School or Montessori – no one system was ever going to be just right.

That evening she made a snap decision, and surprised herself. In the end, she realised, we resist that which has shaped us for the worse, and as the product of stiflingly conservative education systems, she and Tony agreed to go with the spirit of '68 and send their son to The Free School.

At first Mattie was happy enough, and made friends with another boy his age, Jordan. But Jordan only came on certain days and the rest of the time Mattie was restless and bored. He especially hated the compulsory rest period after lunch, and could never drop off to sleep. They knew this because the ageing hippie, Dean, who used to strum the guitar and sing folk songs to lull the fidgeting children into a nap, would sometimes let Mattie 'play' with one of the guitars when he wouldn't settle. He even gave Mattie some strumming lessons and taught him a simple chord that he could get his chubby fingers across. 'You should have him taught lessons,' Dean said one day. 'Mattie has a natural feel for the instrument.' But when she came to collect Mattie, often he would be waiting for her and ready to scoot through the gate. He seemed bored, and she began to dwell on Maria Montessori's dictum that there is often a fine line between freedom and chaos, and chaos is not stimulating but oppressive. Now she began to fret about his eager little face that was almost too happy to see her. While it might be gratifying for her, it was not in other ways a good sign. There were many nights of talking over her fears with Tony, and at last, despite the additional expense, they decided to take Mattie away from The Free School and enrol him at the Montessaurus.

Maria Montessori had designed her didactic toys to be self-correcting, and now they were about to become self-correcting parents.

From the first day Mattie settled in happily, and soon requested that he be allowed to stay on for aftercare activities with a sweet young woman named Missy. Whenever Frances arrived to collect him he would plead with her to stay with Missy for just a bit longer. There was always some exciting and well-organised game about to start, or some ingenious piece of craft being undertaken, and after that he would run to swing, just one more time, on the old tyre that hung from the great oak at the centre of the court-yard. Here they all were, safe within their idyllic high-walled space with its cedar chalets, its sunny decks and its courtyard of leafy Californian shade.

One afternoon, as she was walking Mattie home from his enlightened but fortified school, they paused beside a wide road and waited for the traffic to pass. She remembers looking both ways and seeing no car at all, but then, as they began to cross, a white jalopy appeared on the horizon, hurtling at speed straight towards them. With terror in her heart she yanked her son towards the median strip and stood fuming on the grass as the jeering teenage driver and his two accomplices gave her the finger on their way past.

'*You bastards!*' she screamed, as the car went racing, recklessly, on down the wide, tree-lined boulevard. It was broad daylight, at three in the afternoon, and they had just played chicken with a woman and a child.

All the way home she wanted to bellow her outrage, her impotent anger. How dare they! *How dare they!* But she could have screamed as much as she liked. They were outside the castle gates.

By the time they returned to Sydney they were sold on the Montessori method. Mattie had been happy there and, almost incidentally, had learned to read within six months, with no coaching at home. They sought out the nearest Montessori school and discovered that some things were not portable. They had been given a rare glimpse of the ideal and were unlikely to find it again. This local Montessori was intensely competitive. Information night seemed to be full of ambitious parents who wanted their children to get a jump on the rest; to get out of the blocks fast and get ahead in the game of life. Frances sat next to one handsome father in his late thirties, a solicitor, who explained his concern that his young son of seven was not showing much form in his studies. 'All he seems interested in is Rugby League,' he said, with genial intensity. 'He won't get into law or medicine that way.' And he explained that to combat any early slide into mediocrity he had enrolled his son in a Saturday-afternoon coaching class in maths.

Reluctantly, they gave up on the Montessori idea.

Years later, she asked Mattie what he remembered about the San Diego Montessori school. Not much, he replied, except that he'd been happy there. Did he remember the didactic toys? No. Not even the Golden Bead Material? No. Did he remember Clara and Joan, or Missy? No. All he remembered, he said, was swinging in the sun on a big tyre that hung from the oak tree in the yard.

Perfect

When we first moved into the house

When we first moved into the house overlooking the blue hills we were comfortable but not inspired. It was a contemporary two-storey brick house with a large sundeck. Inside it had beige carpet with mushroom tints, heavy curtains in a bold pattern and bland, expensive furniture from David Jones. When my friend Chris first came to visit she said the place had an impersonal feel, like an upmarket motel. There were conventional watercolour landscapes on the wall and lots of expensive cookware that hung from hooks in the kitchen. The kitchen had everything except charm. It, too, was oddly impersonal.

Yes, we were comfortable in this house. We felt safe. We'd always lived in the inner city, in a claustrophobic terrace on the flat with no aspect and a redbrick factory wall opposite. The kids loved this new house – the 'motel'. They liked to sit out on the redwood sundeck and eat pizza for supper and do their homework from books nestled in their laps. You could gaze out at the hazy blue hills and listen to the bird sounds at dusk, and watch the fiery red sky over the purple scrub. At night I dreamed calm, reassuring dreams in which the light was bright and the land, the plains beyond, breathed with the sense of an immanent and joyful future.

It was a suburb built on steep hills

It was a suburb built on steep hills and the houses had high foundations and split levels and cantilevered sundecks and rambling bush gardens that fell away into gullies. For the children it was a climb from the bus stop to the house and I was nervous parking the car on the narrow woodchip drive, so steep was it, so sharply angled. This was a suburb where walking the dog was a strenuous hike; where you had to have two cars per family if one of you wasn't going to be exhausted from walking up the asphalt slopes. Not that we made serious complaint: it was the leafy, rearing hills that gave the place its character.

The children were intrigued with all the gadgets in the kitchen: the lemon press, the sugar thermometer, the lobster cracker, the boat moulds. 'What's this, Mum?' they'd ask, holding up some oddly shaped or corkscrew implement that, for all they knew, might have belonged in a Guatemalan torture chamber. 'A whisk,' I'd say, 'an apple slicer ... no, they're ice tongs.' And if we couldn't work out what it was, we'd call it an egg scrambler. We were easily amused.

I'd known her slightly

I'd known her slightly, the way you know a lot of people in a city you've lived in all your life. She wasn't conventionally pretty but there was something about her that men found attractive. Something hungry. When she was young, I'd heard, she'd been much admired; the girl most sought after; the girl who always had her choice of lovers.

She was very slim, with high cheekbones and such a strong bony chin that she looked almost wolfish, and sometimes even haggard. She had the kind of dusky skin that brings with it a darkness under the eyes. Once I saw her in an expensive boutique in the mall, and although she was short she somehow dominated the place. There were three assistants and they were all attending on her. They seemed very familiar, in a respectful way. Her small, smartly dressed daughter hovered near her hip with the same deferential air as the salesgirls. She had just finished trying on some clothes and was sorting through what she wanted. Within seconds she had decided on four complete outfits. I got the impression she shopped there often, that she was a regular. I was in awe of the casual ease with which she bought four outfits at a time.

She had this air about her – she was arrogant and smug but at the same time she had an intense, even haunted look. Don't ask me how someone can be smug and haunted at the same time, she just was. And there was that defiant quality, like an insolent schoolgirl. I was envious of her spending power, not of the fact that she could afford it – I suppose *I* could, in a way – but of the fact that she felt comfortable being able to buy so much at once, regarded it as her right. I imagined her as a woman with wardrobes full of clothes.

When first we saw the house advertised for rent I must admit that I wanted to look it over not only because we needed somewhere temporary to live but also because I was curious to see how many wardrobes she had. In fact she had only two, in the master bedroom, and when she went she left them empty. She couldn't possibly have taken all her clothes on the trip with her; she must have packed them away, perhaps in the cellar.

But now they were devoted to their children

They had left their books on the shelves, though, and for educated people they had surprisingly few – and very predictable ones. Again, as with the furniture, there was that peculiar lack of anything idiosyncratic or out of the ordinary. And interestingly, where there was something angst-ridden, like White's *Riders in the Chariot* or Camus' *The Plague*, it seemed to take on the character of its situation and become complacent, just another complacent book on a complacent bookshelf. I should mention that *he* was the deputy director of the local TAFE college, so perhaps he kept his books at work. I knew him to be a handsome man, flirtatious. It was obvious he fancied himself with women but whether he went any further than flaunting it I've never heard, although a friend of mine said he goosed her once at a party. She'd known the two of them when they were engaged and she said they were intensely sexual together, narcissistic. But now they were devoted to their children, a boy and a girl, always ferrying them to drama classes, or tennis lessons, or pottery group, or something.

That sundeck

That sundeck became a seductive space in our lives. As the weather warmed we seemed to spend more and more time on it. It was where I read the papers in the morning. The children had their breakfast there. Our dog, Percy, lolled about in the sun. I moved my sewing out, set up a coffee table permanently in the corner and worked on my files. There was hardly ever any wind. At night we took the radio out and listened to Triple J. We were conducting an experiment: living without television. I'd yearned to try it for a while and living in a temporary place had seemed a good time to spring it on the kids. They were resistant at first but I managed to effect some trade-offs, like more pizza for supper and permission to go to a friend's to watch favourite programmes. It meant that occasionally, in the evening, they became restless and bored. Nine o'clock was a critical time, with the homework finished but one hour to go before bed-time. Sometimes they'd sit happily on the sundeck and talk to me.

But on this particular night

But on this particular night Carla was cranky. She decided suddenly that she wanted to move her room around and completely change the look of it. She persuaded Ben to help her with the furniture and they grunted and puffed their way around for half an hour. Then she was seized with the idea of using an old batik tablecloth as a wall-hanging. It was a favourite piece of mine that I'd bought in the '70s when I was a student, backpacking in Java. Its faded reds and yellows had brightened up our sleazy flat in the city after Brian and I were married.

Carla began to search for it noisily, rummaging impatiently in the huge linen cupboard in the upstairs hallway. And then suddenly, everything went quiet. After ten minutes had passed without even a rustle of sound I rose lazily from the sundeck and called out through the sliding doors: 'Carla?'

No reply.

'*Carla!*'

She came into the wide, spacious living room holding up a small book. 'Look what I found, Mum. I think it's her diary.' And before I could make any sanctimonious adult protestations she began to read aloud. 'Listen to this. *Tuesday, July 16. Left work early to make sure I wasn't held up in the traffic. Got to the gym at 4. Worked out for two hours. Really starting to push myself. Steve is away, kids ate at Mum's. Skipped dinner. Wednesday, July 17. Scott has worked out a new set of bridging exercises on the 5 kg weights for me. Said I'll be ready to go on to the advanced programme soon. Can't wait. Cooked steamed spinach and new potatoes and lean steak with pureed apple sauce and rosemary for dinner. Stewed apricots with ricotta and brandy for dessert. The kids didn't like the ricotta and wanted ice-cream. I ate just spinach because I'd had a large salad sandwich for lunch (a mistake). Ran 2 Ks after dinner. Feel very tired.*'

Carla looked up at me, her eyes glinting. Ben hovered in the doorway. He seemed as bemused by this recitation as I was. '*July 18. Started work on the bench press. Wonderful feeling of stretching. Up to 20 leg extensions. Broccoli and cheese pie for dinner. High in calcium. Low-chol cheese. So tired. July 19. Couldn't get to gym until 5.30. So frustrating. Had to get takeaway. Tired again. Why do I always feel so tired?*'

There was something mesmeric about Carla's reading. I ought to have stopped her then but I hesitated and she read on. '*July 20. Used flex-time to work out from 8.00 to 9.30 this morning. This evening swam 12 laps of the Superlife pool. Felt drained, probably because of period, though flow has been light. Ran 3 Ks after dinner. Promised myself a 10 K run on Saturday afternoon when children at tennis. A treat. Steve said he thought I might be overdoing it. I am tired, but I think it was just the fact that Juliet was up last night with a stomach ache.'*

At last Carla paused, looking at me as if to say: The woman's a lunatic! 'It just goes on and on and on,' she said, and then she began to jog up and down on the spot, in a satiric mincing action, chanting. 'Ran City to Surf, climbed Mt. Kosciusko, played six sets at Wimbledon, *sooooooo tired!'*

Then she tossed the diary into the air and Ben caught it, gawping at it like the clumsy schoolboy he is. 'No way!' he exclaimed. 'She ran three Ks up and down these hills after a workout in the gym! No wonder she's tired. The woman's crazy!' And the two of them fell about in an exaggerated shrieking. Carla went backwards over the beige leather couch, flinging her legs in the air and squealing. Then, as if she'd had a sudden thought, she straightened up, retrieved the book and opened it, ready to declaim the next fraught entry.

Give it to me

'Give it to me,' I said, hearing my self-righteous mother's tone, a little too loud. 'Give it here, Carla.' And taking the book from her limp, reluctant hand: 'This is her private diary. I'm going to put it away. We've no right to read it.'

'Why not? She was silly enough to leave it where we'd find it!'

'Why argue?' This from Ben to Carla. 'It's boring anyway.' And he staggered around the room, legs giving way at the knees, clutching at his throat in mock exhaustion and gurgling hoarsely, 'So tired, so tired …'

Later that night

Later that night, when they were in bed, I sat out on the sundeck with the floodlights on and, of course, read the diary. I'd hoped, I confess, for some account of her sexual exploits, but after a while I realised that the diary was a relentless if cryptic account of her exercise and diet regimen.

Tuesday, July 22. Worked out for an hour at Superlife. Ran into Suzy in the sauna. Cooked steamed vegetables and ocean perch with flambé bananas. Ran 2 Ks after dinner. Feel very fatigued. Wednesday, July 23. Moved up a notch on the bench press and the pec dec. Up to 30 on the leg extensions. Swam 10 lengths of the Superlife pool. Ran 2½ Ks after dinner. So tired.

Almost every entry was this impersonal chronicle of weights lifted, laps swum, time in the sauna or kilometres run. And always a description of what she cooked for dinner and her anxiety that the children were not eating enough. I had visions of her in her immaculate over-endowed kitchen, whipping up blueberry mousse or cheese soufflé or salmon pie, and eating cottage cheese and lettuce herself, pleading a large business lunch that day when in fact she'd had a small fruit salad with the excuse that there would be a huge evening meal with the family that night. I could see her sitting at her desk at work, all the while daydreaming about her pulleys and her weights and her treadmill and of the time, promised soon, when Scott would put her on to the advanced programme, the badge of the initiate. Was her sweaty wolfish concentration broken for even a second by the sight of Scott's oiled and muscular thighs, his skimpy silk gym shorts, his obvious endowment around the groin? Did she sit in the sauna and stretch out her brown legs and feel a narcissistic glow at her own fineness, an impulse to lie on her stomach and writhe against the towel? Or was she saving it up for him, Steve? What happened after dinner? Did he put the kids to bed while she, in natty headband and fluorescent aerobic gear, pounded her small feet against the bitumen paths of those punishing hills? Did her stomach rise up with nausea as, poised on the brow, she contemplated the steep gradient of the descent, or was her mind an endorphin white-out, nothing but the steady thump of her heartbeat, the pumping of blood, the panting of breath …

Then, late at night, in a last methodical attention to self, the entry in the red, leather-bound diary. *So tired*. And often, in the margin, a small, elegant doodle, the drawing of a dolphin.

She was, of course, a compulsive weigher. I'd noted the smart new state-of-the-art bathroom scales when we first looked around the house. 'What are these?' I asked.

'You can't buy them here,' she said. 'Steve brought them back from the US after a conference. They're incredibly precise.' It was the way she said 'precise' with that bony chin jutting forward and the mouth widening and the teeth coming together like a vice. It seemed from the diary that she weighed herself every Thursday evening at the same time, after her shower. At the right-hand side of each diary entry there'd be a neatly written figure, underlined in red. *44 kg*.

Forty-four kilograms was a magical figure. Anything over this would be rebuked by a red exclamation mark.

44.341 kg!

I couldn't resist

When my friend Chris came to dinner I couldn't resist telling her about the diary. We sat out on the sundeck (of course) while the children took Percy for his evening constitutional, and I told her of our find.

'Fear of death,' she said, flatly.

'You think so?' It seemed plausible, for a moment anyway. But no, there had to be more to it. 'I'm afraid of death,' I said, 'but I don't put myself through all that.'

'Her mother died young, you know, of a heart attack. I'm not sure how old she was but I gather she was only in her early forties. Somewhere around there. You'd have to wonder whether it was hereditary, wouldn't you?'

Perhaps. Perhaps that was it. Though something told me there was still more to it, that in some way it was more subtle, more complex, though quite how I couldn't explain.

Chris was gazing out at the purple trees and the dusky red sky. 'It really is beautiful here,' she said. 'You could almost be at peace with yourself.' And laughed her dry, mocking laugh. 'However will you stand going back to the city?'

Just then, Carla came out onto the deck. Although it was after nine it was still hot, and she wore, I remember, a pair of pale-pink shorts and a white halter-neck top.

Chris gave me a knowing look. 'Lovely girl,' she murmured.

'Isn't she?'

Carla was standing in the corner of the deck furthest away from us, far enough away for me to be able to stare at her unself-consciously. She was leaning on her hands, pressed up against the timber rail and gazing out at the dusky purple scrub with that dreamy, expectant look in her eye that only a fifteen-year-old can hold, in good faith, for any length of time. She seemed to me that night, even more than usual, to be a figure of exquisite loveliness; the silky hair, the swan-like neck, the delicate wrists and ankles, all enfolded in an ineffable grace. My dearest girl! It was as if she wore an invisible cloak of promise that would protect her, now and forever, from all harm. It was as if nothing could touch her, and yet of course, everything could, and it was the fragility of this promise, of this moment, that made some passionate, protective breath catch in my chest so that when Chris turned to me with a question, I could barely speak.

'Have you ever thought of going to a gym?' she asked.

'What?'

'I said, have you ever thought of going to a gym?'

'Never. I did yoga once. More my speed.'

'I hear you don't lose weight with yoga.'

'Not really. You become more flexible. You don't lose weight at the gym, either, you just turn it into muscle.'

'If God had wanted women to have muscles he'd have ...' She seemed unable to complete the sentence.

'He'd have what?'

'Nothing. I was just looking at Carla. No matter what we do for ourselves, none of us is ever going to be that lovely again.'

Superlife

I knew something about the gym *she* visited. It was a plush and expensive one on the bay, 'beautifully appointed' as they say. In the early days of the fitness craze it had been started up with great fanfare by some of the smart young businessmen about town, one of whom was a fashionable hair stylist I'd once patronised. The annual membership fee was high and it boasted of its celebrity patrons. It was a beautiful white building near the yacht club, with blue glass and a wide, white sundeck. It had a striking blue dolphin logo painted on one side, and blue and yellow stripes under the eaves. But then, after three years, there had been rumours of financial mismanagement, talk that it might have to close down. She seemed so fond of this place, insofar as these impersonal diary entries conveyed any feeling, so positively to yearn for it, that I wondered how she had reacted to the threat of closure. I got out the diary, looked up the approximate date of the bad publicity and skimmed a few pages. My eye stopped at this.

Had a dream last night. Made me feel sick. Woke in a panic and sweaty. Dreamed that Superlife had closed down. That I drove there in the daylight and everything looked normal, but when I walked through the door the place was stripped bare. Empty. I looked for the mirrors and they were gone. Just white walls. Felt nausea, panic. I ran out of the place screaming. Woke up in a sweat with my heart pounding. Felt as if I'd just run 50 Ks. What will I do if they close? <u>What will I do?</u>

This last question was heavily underlined. It must have been preying on her mind all day. It was a Thursday night and she had forgotten to weigh herself.

In the entries that documented the next three weeks there were constant references to the financial state of the club and the uncertainty about its future. She was obsessed with it. She ceased to note what she cooked, what the children ate or what she ate. The question *What will I do if they close?* was repeated again and again. At this time, as I recall, there was a sudden election, but no mention was made of that, even though she and her husband were party members. But then why should there be? It would be out of character. This was (only) a diary of her body, nothing more.

Finally the traces of anxiety disappeared

Finally the traces of anxiety disappeared. The entries return to their cool methodical formula. This, I recall, is about the time that a wealthy businessman and his socialite wife stepped in and backed the losses of the gym, staging a new publicity campaign and launching a membership drive with a huge subscription party. I assume she was invited. I can imagine her, in that boutique in the mall, trying on several dresses, finding it hard to make up her mind, posing her skeletal body with its lean muscle in front of the asymmetric mirrors, holding her shoulders back, tilting her chin up, gazing into the silver space of reflection: a dolphin in rehearsal.

One night, after dinner

One night, after dinner, I excused the children from walking the dog.

It wasn't so difficult, the climb up the first hill, but the ascent of the second was punishing. My calf muscles ached, my hamstrings strained, my breathing was rapid and short. Percy tugged unmercifully on the short lead, tripping me forward. In new jogging shoes my feet were hot and rubbed at the heel. I thought of her diminutive body pounding the asphalt.

Back home the dog slurped at the water bowl while I collapsed on the sundeck, gazing out in a haze of exhaustion at the red sky above the purple brush, the far-off hills, enigmatic. After a while I plucked a cone from the yellow banksia that crowded my corner of the sundeck and brushed it against my hot cheek. My face was livid, my hair limp with sweat. I was a fool.

Other women

Other women who know her say she was a meticulous mother. That the children were always immaculately and fashionably dressed, that they had every opportunity and dance class going, that she interrogated teachers on parent nights with an unrelenting fierceness of demand, that she was hungry, always, for whatever was the right thing, the right circumstance; hungry for opportunity.

At work she was a stickler for deadlines and protocols. For the correct format. Simple, clean, immaculate grooming. At night she cooked carefully considered, balanced meals. Her dinner parties had a clinical propriety about them: all the right linen, the right silver, the right porcelain; the candelabra just the right size and the flowers set just so; the food cooked to look like the glossy illustrations in her *Cordon Bleu* series. She herself, of course, ate little, making excuses about eating the children's leftovers beforehand ('Can't bear waste'). Yet she was, I imagine, too fastidious a woman to eat even a lover's leftovers.

When our lease expired

When our lease expired and our time was up we wandered about the house, flat-footed, doleful. The interior of the house became repugnant to us; its bland department-store style which had once amused us and we had so comfortably patronised now provoked us. We sneered at those complacent books in the bookshelves. We were grumpy and scornful. We were mourning in advance for the loss of the sundeck.

The morning we left we were querulous and accident-prone. Ben grazed his shins badly when he fell on the steep drive, loading his bike onto the roof-rack; in the kitchen, Carla cut her thumb on a broken glass that had smashed in the packing. As we drove off, Ben slouched down as far as he could into a corner of the back seat, staring ahead. 'Goodbye suburbia!' exclaimed Carla theatrically, but as we drove away down the steep winding drive I could see her in the rear-vision mirror, casting a last look back at the redwood sundeck.

In just under an hour we had returned to our inner-city ter-race. The mould grew in smoky green smudges on the wallpaper; the small courtyard, now more claustrophobic than ever, was clut-tered with dried leaves. We hauled our suitcases, our boxes and our jumble into the dark hallway, turned the lights on in every room of the house, locked the car (no off-street parking) and then walked up the hill, exhausted, to our local Italian restaurant, Rugatini's. Ben said (too emphatically) that thank God he didn't have to eat any more frozen pizza and could get the real thing, and I drank a toast to smog, cigarettes and good coffee.

Carla didn't say anything.

At night, sometimes

At night, sometimes, I lie awake and try to recall her living room or her kitchen. And the odd thing is, it's all become a blur. I can barely recall a single object; I know there were copper saucepans and leather couches and tapestry cushions but I can't see them in my mind's eye. The outlines merge and blur. Even the sundeck recedes into the native bushes that encroach on it, the banksia, the wattle and the fern. And yet I can visualise, with the utmost precision, that little book in the dark cupboard. The diary of her body. Her fine handwriting, neat and precise; the catalogue of her weights; her mileage in the pool and on the road; the Thursday evening ritual with the scales and the clinical notation of her weight underlined in red; the repetition of that one phrase, like a mantra, *So tired*. The strict format, day after day; no deviation, except, now and then, in the margin, the drawing of a dolphin.

It's then, near to sleep, that I close my eyes on the headline. WOMAN TURNS INTO DOLPHIN. SWIMS AWAY AND LEAVES FAMILY DISCONSOLATE ON THE SHORE, WAVING. And there she is, streamlining through the dark water; sleek, poised and perfect.

The Art of Convalescence

They told her to be at the hospital by seven in the morning, so she set the alarm for five-thirty. Greg got up and dressed Annie, who was already awake and calling from her cot. While the two of them munched on toast she packed her bag and tried to ignore the feeling of dread.

They drove first to her mother's house to drop off Annie, who sang all the way. Her mother was in the kitchen in her red Chinese dressing-gown, sipping from a mug of tea. As they left she put her weathered gardener's hand on Toni's arm and said: 'Ring me as soon as you know anything.'

Greg dropped her at the entrance to the public wing of the big private hospital. 'I'll see you up there,' he said, and went off to park. It was a hospital in the east of the city made up of a motley complex of buildings from different eras and built in different styles, some newer than others but none that was attractive. The public wing was an old building, ten storeys high, and uninviting. She made enquiries in the foyer with an elderly nun and then walked the length of the main corridor until she found the lifts.

The eighth floor was shabby. The air was stale. In the middle of the floor was a circular desk-station where three women sat at computer screens. Corridors and rooms led away from them in all directions. When she presented herself to a middle-aged woman whom she took to be a receptionist, the woman was offhand. 'Sit over there,' she said, 'and someone will bring you the forms.'

She carried her bag over to the waiting area, which faced the reception desk. There were old vinyl chairs pressed against the walls and a small coffee table of scuffed wood. She had brought a book with her but was not yet in a mood to settle to it so she looked at the magazines on the coffee table and counted them. There were five: three yachting magazines that were four years out of date and two golfing magazines that were even older.

Greg emerged from the lift looking ill at ease and anxious. He sat beside her on a chair that had a rip in the vinyl and the stuffing let out a sigh of escaped air. He put his hand on her knee and rested it there. Neither of them felt like talking. There was an old portable TV perched high on a shelf and they could see the presenters of the breakfast show mouthing away but there was no sound. After a while Greg got up and went over to the reception desk.

'Is it possible to adjust the sound on the TV?' he asked.

The woman looked up. 'Someone stole the remote,' she said, and went back to her keyboarding.

Greg came back to his chair and they exchanged a look. He reached across and picked up a magazine, glanced at the cover and tossed it back on the table. 'Nineteen ninety-eight,' he said, almost wheezing in disgust. 'Can't they do better than that?'

She tried to make a joke of it. 'I'm sure there are a lot of yachties in the public wards of hospitals. We're an affluent country.' It wasn't helping that he was jittery.

After about forty minutes a young nurse presented herself with a clipboard and forms. 'My, you're here early,' she said.

'They told me to be here by seven.'

'Oh, no, I don't know why they would have said that. You needn't have got here until nine-thirty. You're not scheduled until noon.'

Noon. That was a five-hour wait.

'Well, they told her *seven*,' said Greg, with irritable emphasis, and she could tell he was beginning to burn a fuse.

An old man sitting opposite got up and shuffled over to the reception desk and they heard him ask for a toilet. With a curt gesture the woman pointed back to where he had come from and they realised that the toilet was a small room, like a broom cupboard, in the middle wall of the waiting area. My God, she thought, no privacy. The door of the toilet was only a metre away from where she was sitting and the smallness of the waiting room, and its drabness, seemed to enlarge the awkward intimacy of its nearness. The old man looked embarrassed and glanced at no-one as he opened the door. They could hear the sound of urine trickling into the bowl. Greg leaned back into his chair, folded his arms and sighed.

She realised that she didn't want Greg to wait with her. Bad enough that *she* had to sit here all this time. She turned to him. 'You go,' she said.

'What about you?'

'I'll be fine. I brought a book. And I'm tired. I might doze a bit.' This was a lie. She had never in her life managed to sleep while sitting upright in a chair.

'Will you be okay?'

'Of course.'

He was reluctant to leave but she insisted, even if, as she watched him disappear into the lift, she felt a pang. He was so worried about her, she could tell, but she knew he hated hospitals and it didn't help to have the place inflicted on them both.

At around ten-thirty a brisk young nurse appeared and told her she was to get up and go into an office across the way to see Dr. White. The doctor was a gangly young intern who rose from his seat, introduced himself and shook her hand. For the next ten minutes he proceeded to take her details and he was so polite, so considerate that he made her feel vaguely tearful. She had been in the building over three hours and he was the first person who had been nice to her. Perhaps, because he was new here, he had yet to take on the institutionalised brusqueness of the others, although she saw in his manners the kind of shy, well-brought-up young man, earnestly academic and well-intentioned, that she recognised from her days as a teacher.

Although it must all have been in her file, to her surprise he asked her to tell him why she was there. Perhaps it was a first-line precaution, a way of checking that they had the right person. She told him about the pain, and the slight breakthrough bleeding, and was as matter-of-fact as she could be. She did not say that she had gone to work on one of those radiant mornings that make her feel glad to be alive, a morning when the light glitters on the river and the birds warble beside the deck of her apartment and the young water dragons scamper insouciantly along the drive in a way that makes her laugh out loud. She had gone to work and gone to the loo and found the blood there, and thought, 'Shit!'

Her doctor, Pamela Kerr, was thorough. Two years before, she'd had a patient die of ovarian cancer, diagnosed too late, and she wasn't going to let it happen again. She had dispatched Toni, without delay, for an ultrasound and sure enough that ghostly picture had revealed some kind of growth inside her left ovary. The ultrasound specialist was perplexed. He had not seen one like that before. He could not say whether it meant trouble.

She did not have private health cover but she was busy at work and did not want to spend a long time waiting in the corridors of a public hospital so she booked into a specialist as a private patient just to get a quick diagnosis. She did not want it to be preying on her mind. She was thirty-nine, and while in her own mind she was still young she knew that she had moved now into that bracket where women begin to die. She did not want Death to be shadowing her every move; she did not want grey areas; she wanted clarity and results.

The gynaecologist's name was Neil McCormack and he was a young man, she guessed around her own age. He said it would be best to open her up and have a look.

'And then what?' she asked.

Well, he said, he would begin with a laparoscopy. If the ovary looked 'dodgy' he'd snip it out and have it tested. Couldn't he tell by looking? she asked. No, he said, only by taking it to the pathology lab. And if he found 'something else' in the abdomen, if it looked 'ugly', he might have to 'remove the lot', by which he meant a complete hysterectomy. If there were 'other signs' – if *it* had spread – he would call in an oncologist who would take over. 'It's impossible to say', he said, while her mind reeled at the open-ended scenario he was constructing here. She knew doctors were nervous now, that they feared litigation, that they made no promises, offered no assurances; they must cover themselves against every eventuality. But the prospect of going into surgery where there might be nothing at all wrong, or there might be everything wrong, unnerved her. How do you prepare mentally for the unknown?

She thought of the second child she was desperate to have. There was nothing she wanted more. She even had dreams about this child, this child as yet unborn. She thought of what it might mean to die in early middle age, with Annie left behind. Who would look after her?

'Aren't ovarian cysts common?' she asked. She had of course Googled them. 'And I gather most are benign and you can't take all of them out or thousands of women would be in surgery.'

He shrugged, and reached for a tissue to wipe his nose. He had a cold. She glanced across at the tissue box, which sat beside a photograph of three small children. His abundance, she thought, his own sweet fruit.

'I don't have private health insurance,' she said. 'I take it I'll have to get a referral to see a surgeon at a public hospital.'

He mentioned the name of a big hospital. 'I could see you there as an intermediate patient. In that category you pay just for the hospital facilities,' he said, meaning he would bulk bill her for his own services.

'How much?' she asked.

'Around three thousand dollars.'

They had cut to the chase quickly. It was a business. She shook her head. 'I couldn't manage that.'

'I also do a public list there,' he said, 'and I could arrange for you to be put on it, but this is your choice, it's up to you.'

It wasn't until she got home that she realised he was offering to do her a favour, and she wondered why. It wasn't as if she were manifestly poor. She wished she could like him more, but he was cold. He had pale skin, pale-blond hair and a wart on his forehead. He wore austere rimless glasses that made him look like a lab scientist.

After she had signed yet more forms for the intern, Dr. White, she returned to the waiting area and rummaged in her overnight bag for the book she had brought with her. But it was no good. It wasn't that she read the same sentence over and over again – she managed to get through three pages – but that the words were transparent; meaning leached out of them, and the more she tried to concentrate the more they floated off the page.

'Toni?'

She looked up and saw her friend Cathy leaning over her.

'What are *you* doing here?'

'I had to deliver some parcels to Jackson's and I thought I'd pop in and see how you were going.'

She smiled. Cathy worked nearby, but still, she was touched.

'Won't you get into trouble?'

'It's alright. I've got flex-time owing. It must be awful just sitting here.'

She knew that Cathy was referring to the uncertainty of the outcome, of not knowing what to expect, rather than the dullness of being in this shabby space. But she was relieved to see her. At a time like this it was good to have the company of another woman.

Cathy began to fossick among the magazines. '*A new take on the winged hull,*' she read, and rolled her eyes. 'These magazines are *off.*'

'Tragic.'

'Want me to get you some from the kiosk?'

'I brought a book.' She retrieved it from her bag and held it up like a flag.

They talked for a while, a little gossip, a new movie that Toni must see when she was – here Cathy hesitated. What was the right word? When she was out? When she was better? And the question hovered between them: what if she were not better?

After a while Cathy stood up and said, in the muted, confidential voice that people use in hospitals, 'I'd better get back to work.' They kissed lightly and for a moment the waterworks threatened to return. Cathy had been a welcome distraction, concerned for her but not stricken with anxiety like Greg. None of that angry masculine fuming that sent up smoke in an attempt to conceal the fear. It was bad enough dealing with her own dread. Did she have to read that article last week about a woman in Sydney, not much older, who had gone into surgery for a facelift only to die unexpectedly of a stroke on the operating table? When she was in her twenties the idea of a general anaesthetic hadn't fazed her. Why now did she hate the idea of going under? She was older, that's why, and her youthful sense of invincibility had been mislaid, somewhere in the vicinity of thirty-five. Or was it thirty? These things crept up on you while you were busy filling in your diary and planning your next holiday. A week on the south coast in November? Sure. Oh, and by the way, suddenly I'm aware of being mortal, a body in decline.

She could smell Death in the corridors of this place. In this place, this big public institution, there was no attempt made to camouflage it. No vases of fresh flowers, no elegant artwork, no pastel drapery at the windows, no coffee and basket of muffins and latest *Vogue*, all of which were in the private wing across the way where she had visited a friend last year. Here there were only the bare essentials: a chair, a bed, a surgeon, a knife.

At their second consultation, McCormack had repeated to her that it was 'her choice'. The blood samples he had sent off for cancer analysis had been 'inconclusive'. The growth might be benign. It might be that it could sit there for years with no ill effects. 'It's your choice,' he said again. She went away and thought about this, but once the idea is planted in your head, the idea of Death, it becomes impossible to rid yourself of it. It begins to stalk you like a shadow that has no body of its own and is seeking to attach itself to yours. In the weeks before her admission to hospital she was unable to shake free of it, and at night her dreams were lurid. There was one where she was lost in a series of dark alleys and searching, with sick terror, for a child in old-fashioned swaddling clothes, a child who ran ahead of her and disappeared into the crowd. She woke in a sweat, and groaned aloud so that Greg rolled over and put his arm around her. Then there was the dream where she was trapped in a damp, dark room with walls of spongy tissue that breathed and bled.

The brisk nurse came over again. 'Sorry, but we've had an emergency admission and we've had to put you back until two-thirty.'

Two-thirty. Nothing to eat, and only water to drink. I can't stay here in this ghastly room, she said to herself, and got up suddenly and walked to the lifts, leaving her overnight bag behind on the vinyl chair.

For the next hour she walked around the industrial area that surrounded the hospital: warehouses, tyre depots, trucking companies.

It was all grey and gritty. She went into a small shop that printed slogans onto T-shirts. Yes, they did one-offs, said the swarthy young man behind the counter. What did she have in mind? She thought of a souvenir shirt she might commission, some words of black humour, but her wits were dulled by fear and nothing came to mind.

'I'll get back to you,' she said, and walked out.

Some time after she returned to the hospital a nurse appeared and guided her into a four-bed ward that was empty. The nurse handed her a worn surgical gown and ordered her to undress. She was hungry, her stomach was rumbling. She always did have a healthy appetite, even under duress. She folded her clothes neatly into her bag and sat with her legs crossed on the bed, waiting, a piece of meat ready for the abattoir. What a grim room it was, and the corridors so worn. The paint was scratched, the grey metal trolleys lined up in the corridor were old and creaked. She felt like a dumb cow corralled into a gate-room.

At last the orderly came and asked her to get up on the trolley. Bovine, she obeyed, thinking: why couldn't she walk into the theatre, why did she have to be pushed? It only heightened her feeling of being powerless. The wheels of the trolley grated and stalled and there was a harsh echoing sound coming from somewhere at the end of the corridor. When they arrived the orderly turned and walked off without a word. She could see through the door of the theatre, a swinging door propped open with some heavy object. Nearby, a male doctor in a theatre-gown was standing in an untidy alcove and he asked her for her name. At first she didn't hear him because she was looking past him, looking at the metallic surfaces within, shiny but worn, like an old kitchen in a former boys' reformatory she had once visited. In her heightened state of anxiety even the floors looked metallic and there was the abrasive sound of a radio blaring out into the theatre.

She did not want to go into the abattoir in a conscious state, not just because she was afraid but because if it was like the rest of the building it would be an ugly room. She did not want to see its scratched and discoloured walls.

'Do I get a knockout injection?' she asked the young assistant.

'Do you want one?' he said, in mild surprise, as if this were unusual. She found him offensively casual. Surely he should have asked her first? While she gaped in frozen incredulity, he turned to the small steel trolley in the alcove, turned back and without preamble stuck a short needle into a vein on the back of her left hand. One, two, three, four …

When she woke she was back in the same room and the other beds were still empty. She was cold and shaking uncontrollably. She felt encased in ice, as if she were now a carcass and hanging in the cool room. She was shaking so violently that the young Filipina nurse ran to her with a pale-blue cotton blanket.

'Do you have any more?' she rasped.

Greg was there beside her bed, gazing down at her with a pained expression.

She was woozy, she couldn't think, she was still shaking, but she managed to lift the covers awkwardly and look down at her abdomen. There were four puncture holes smeared with brown disinfectant, one directly on the navel and three just above the pubic line. Whatever had transpired in the cutting room, no big

177

incision had been made. She took this as a sign that the oncologist had not been called in and thought she might remark on this to Greg. Instead she laid her head down on the pillow and closed her eyes.

When she woke, Greg was still there. 'What happened?' she asked.

'I don't know.' He was angry. 'I can't get any sense out of any-one. There's no bloody doctor you can talk to here. That frigid woman at the reception desk treats me like I'm a potential terrorist and says I'll have to wait for the registrar to come tomorrow on his rounds and he'll tell us then.'

'I'm hungry.' She hadn't eaten for twenty-four hours. No-one had offered her food or drink. Greg went off to see the charge nurse, who returned an hour later with a cheese sandwich.

Overnight her blood pressure plummeted and the night nurse kept coming in to wind the pump around her arm and check it again. She seemed worried. 'It shouldn't be this low,' she kept saying, irritably. 'It shouldn't be this down.' As if it were somehow the patient's fault. She was brusque, like all of them. Only the young Filipina nurse who came on in the morning had anything resem-bling a bedside manner.

In the late morning the registrar turned up. He was short with a dark suntan and trim dark hair, handsome in a smarmy kind of way. Beside him was a young intern, a stolid girl with soft, pale features. The registrar stood at the end of her bed and looked at her chart.

'What happened with my surgery?' she asked him.

He gave an inane smile. 'You had your left ovary removed.'

'What was the outcome?'

'I can't say,' he said.

'When will I have a test result?'

'Oh, you can go home today and then ring up in a month or six weeks and get the result.'

She was speechless. *A month or six weeks!* He couldn't be serious. Did she or did she not have a cancerous ovary? She opened her mouth to protest but already he was walking out the door, his assistant trailing behind him. He had not introduced himself, he had not addressed her by name, he had not extended even the most common courtesy. Why had he bothered to visit? So he could tick off the ward sheet? Oh, and to check if she was still breathing?

Meat, she told herself again. Piece of meat.

Her mother rang. 'Annie is fine,' she said. 'She's not fretting, don't worry about her.'

After she put down the phone she hoisted herself onto the edge of the bed and reached gingerly for her dressing-gown. Then she walked painfully down the corridor to the central reception station. The woman looked up from her screen, looked at her as if she were a nuisance. 'Yes?'

'I've just seen the registrar and he says I can't get a result for six weeks. This isn't acceptable. It must be possible to get a test result before then.'

'These services are in great demand,' said the woman coldly. 'There are long waiting times.'

'Who can I talk to about this?'

'You can ask the registrar.'

'I've just seen the registrar and he said six weeks.' They were going around in an endless, deadening circle.

*

When she got home she was sore. Overnight her four wounds opened up. They had not been stitched but smeared with some kind of gel that was meant to hold them together. It didn't. She wondered if they would get infected. How should she dress them? She hadn't a clue. She rang a friend who had once been a nurse. 'They should have given you a discharge sheet,' said the friend, 'with instructions on how to care for them.' They hadn't. One more thing to add to the bitter letter of complaint that she was drafting in her head.

'Ring your GP,' said her friend.

'I can't. It's the weekend.'

Around ten that morning her younger sister came in. 'What's the result?' Jody asked.

'I don't know.'

'*You don't know?*' She almost yelped. She was incredulous. 'Don't they tell you?'

She no longer wanted to talk about it. 'Put the radio on,' she said. Somehow the bedside radio had become unplugged and it hurt to reach across. Jody knelt on the floor to find the power point and the cheerful banter of talk radio broke abruptly into the room. But after Jody had gone she realised that she didn't feel like listening to that. Normally, yes, but she was not her normal self. She was her anxious, angry, humiliated and powerless self; her piece-of-meat self and I-have-had-to-think-about-Death self, and whatever she wanted to listen to, it wasn't this. For a while she lay there in irritable passivity, and then, wearied by her own thoughts, she leaned over to the radio and a stabbing pain shot through her guts. She tried to ignore it. Greg had driven off to the shops so she persisted with the dial, fiddling blindly with the small tuning wheel.

There was some race-caller with the usual nasal twang, then a programme about new car design, an interview with a politician and, finally, music. Not music she was accustomed to but classical piano music, a tumultuous wave of it, rippling across her bed, rippling across her body like a sonic tide, so powerful that she subsided again into her pillows and surrendered to it, allowing the tidal surge of notes to flow through her veins. It seemed to go on and on for a long time, and yet for no time at all, until after a while she became aware of how her body had gone loose and she was breathing more easily, more deeply.

'What's this?' asked Greg when he came in with some tea in a mug.

'I don't know,' she said, 'but leave it on, I like it.'

'It sounds romantic.'

It's not, she thought, it's more complicated than that, but she didn't want to talk about it now, didn't want to analyse anything, just wanted to let the sound wash over her. After a time it created a field, and she was in the field, and in the field nothing else mattered.

Later in the afternoon she learned that she was listening to the Sydney Piano Competition. The competition was held every two years and contested by thirty-six young virtuosos who auditioned from around the world. She had missed the first day but there were several days to come, and all of it broadcast live, every note. All she had to do was to keep the radio permanently tuned to Classic FM and lie there in her bed, or sit out on the deck with headphones, in a trance. It was a force, a whirlwind of notes that filled the abyss. She had come home to a pit of uncertainty: was she ill or was she not? Was she a woman who'd had a benign cyst removed – perhaps unnecessary surgery – or was she about to face up to the worst?

And what if the right ovary did not work – had never worked, for all she knew – and she would now be unable to have another child? How could she brush and comb her responses? What was this absurd state of unknowing, this vacuum of meaning? It was an affront to the plans she had made for herself, an affront to her rational mind, and into this vacuum, to which she was unaccustomed and for which she was unprepared, stole the beauty of the piano music. Better still, it was a competition, a human drama. Players would lose, players would make mistakes, players would be hurt.

After the first day she found that she began to develop an ear. The austerity of her bedroom, its bare walls, seemed to hone the sensitivity of her hearing. There was nothing to look at – she still didn't feel like reading – but there was this miraculous sound. At night she was restless, like a fragile barque on a sinister pantomime stage set, tossed on a sea of rope. She woke, and gasped, so that Greg rolled over, half-awake, and mumbled, 'Pain?'

'It's okay,' she said, because it wasn't, at least not physical pain.

But in daylight the music was there to soothe her. When she woke she found that, before long, she was waiting impatiently for the broadcast of the recitals to begin. First there were the introductory remarks from the presenters and then a sequence of special category performances: sonatas and preludes today, Mozart concerti tomorrow. The entrants had already been refined into a long shortlist: Russian, Japanese, Chinese, American, Australian, Korean, French and Italian. They were young, they were forceful, they were single-minded. They practised seven hours a day. They were obsessed and their obsession fed her. She was hooked up to them, as if on a musical drip. They were her daily nourishment, her milk and honey.

On the Monday morning she rang her GP, Pamela, and found that Pamela was herself unwell and not in the surgery. She had hoped that Pamela could somehow find a way to expedite her test results and with this news she felt another implosion of powerlessness. But within an hour the music had drawn her again into its own benign dream. By the third day she found she was beginning to identify and respond to the different sensibilities of the performers. There were the two young Russians who were, according to the presenters, the popular favourites, but she preferred the Japanese woman who played with a rare irony, a kind of cool feminine candour (if only she had the musical literacy to describe this). And then there was the Chinese prodigy from Kuala Lumpur. Though only eighteen he had a magisterial quality. Unlike the romantic Russians with their tempestuous sentiment, he played with a kind of Apollonian detachment. He, especially, created a kind of sound balm for her body. She bathed in it.

Each day she swabbed her wounds and hoped for the best. One in particular kept opening up and seeping until it formed a crust, which would dislodge in the night and ooze again in the morning, but she did all that she needed to do, knowing that each day almost the entire air-time of Classic FM would be given over to the piano competition. She felt it as a gift, a gift of timing that her personal dilemma should coincide with this festival of lyrical power, and she taped over her oozing incisions, ate breakfast for the first time in days and sat out on the deck to listen to the Mozart concerti. It was in listening to Mozart that she began to hear even more acutely. One work seemed to suggest a bleak gaiety, another spoke of a hectic contentment, while the concerto that followed sounded like the most extravagant parody, a masterly joke. Passages were vaguely familiar but she did not want to see a programme list. She did not want to *see* anything. She wanted to listen.

In the mornings and afternoons there were times when the responses of other listeners were broadcast: a farmer's wife on a remote property in the north, an accountant in Sydney's western suburbs, a piano teacher in Adelaide, a merchant seaman in Darwin; all conducting a proxy debate as to the merits of the performers but all united in their gratitude for the event. And this was not the least satisfying aspect of it; that here, prone on her back, or propped up on the deck, she was absorbed into a live community of listening. As she listened, so too did all these others. Mentally she argued with their responses, just as she hung on every word of the leading presenter, himself a piano virtuoso, a man she had never set eyes on but whose voice was inflected with such warmth, such judicious sympathy that she was already half in love with him. In his taste he seemed to lean ever so slightly towards the romantic, to the Russians, but this only made him seem a warmer and more appealing auditory presence. By now she was confirmed in her own favouritism and it was the young Chinese performer. With no trace of the romantic colouring so loved by the paying crowd and the presenters alike, he played like a young god, pulling it all together, the latent chaos of the notes, commanding it into order.

For a time she became so engrossed in the competition that she would no longer join Greg in front of the television at night or, if she did, she would sit with the headphones on, lost to the intensity, to the beauty of what she now thought of as 'the comp'.

On the Wednesday morning she again rang the office of her GP and found her in. She told Pamela about the six-week wait for the results of the test on her ovary and, despite herself, said nothing more; no complaints, no whingeing. It was enough. 'Leave it with me,' said Pamela.

Later that day, around five in the evening, Pamela rang back.

'I've spoken to the pathology unit at the hospital. They did that test on the ovary three days ago and the results are clear.'

'Why did the registrar tell me I would have to wait six weeks?'

'I haven't the faintest idea.' It was clear from Pamela's tone that she was not impressed, but was not prepared to comment further, except to say, 'If there had been something wrong, Neil McCormack would have come around and seen you himself.' But how was I to know that? she thought. No-one, at any level, had communicated anything. She put down the phone and went back to the Sydney Piano Competition where there was enough communication going on to sustain a universe.

When Greg came home he was both drained and relieved. 'Thank God,' he kept saying, 'Thank God.' And then, 'Why didn't you ring me at the office and tell me straight away?'

Why hadn't she? Well, it had been late, and she knew he might already have left the office and be on the freeway. But also, she wanted to listen to her favourite competitor play his Mozart concerto, and he was the last that afternoon to perform.

On the night of the final programme, at the end of which the winner was to be announced, Greg was at a meeting and she had the house to herself. Once again she entered into the familiar trance, and found herself in thrall again to the playing of the Chinese finalist. When at the end of the evening he was proclaimed the surprise winner she was so excited she hauled herself out of her chair and paced around the living room in a state of elation. She knew nothing about piano technique and she had picked the winner! How was this possible? Energised by a kind of electric current coursing through her, she continued for some time to pace around the room, around and around, almost hypnotically. When, finally, she came to a halt, something in her head and chest had shifted and there was clarity in her thought. She had emerged from the week-long coma of her self-absorption. Tomorrow her mother would bring Annie home. She walked into her daughter's room and began to strip the cot.

The next afternoon, while Annie had her nap, she sat at the kitchen table and began to draft a letter of complaint to the hospital, but after the first few sentences she was inhibited by a sudden thought. The discharge sheet that they had neglected to give her, with instructions for surgical aftercare – this would most likely have been the responsibility of the young Filipina nurse, the only person in that awful place to show her any kindness. What if she lost her job? She screwed up the piece of paper. She would wait until she had her follow-up appointment with McCormack and complain then about the registrar. She would not mention the discharge sheet. She wondered if the registrar had operated on her under McCormack's supervision. They had to learn, didn't they, and how else but to practise on public patients?

Today, four weeks on, she has an appointment to see Neil McCormack in his little consulting room in the public wing of the hospital. This is well away from the waiting room where she sat, frozen, on the day of her surgery; the corridors here are even more narrow, crowded and stuffy. But now she is less absorbed in herself and thinks that it can't be pleasant for him to work in this environment, or any of those doctors who haven't yet abandoned the public system. Still, she has things to say; grievances to air. He is running late, and when at last she is called in, he looks tired. In her head she cuts back on her list of complaints but is determined to tell him about the registrar. She will wait until he asks her if she has any questions and then she will say, politely, 'Well, I have a few suggestions.' (She will try and phrase this as constructively as possible.)

'Registrars vary a lot,' he says. 'I can't comment on this one, it's not my place.' Then he adds, 'He was a first-year registrar,' and this, she knows, is a kind of coded apology.

'But what about the test results?'

'In a public hospital there is no way we can access a histology report at an early stage.'

She opens her mouth. She is about to say, 'But my GP got her hands on it a week later,' but changes her mind.

'If it had looked serious I would have come around and seen you myself,' he says.

'Nobody told me that.'

He holds his hands open and gives an ever-so-slight shrug, a gesture that says, 'That's the way it is.'

'Who operated on me?'

'I did.' He says it bluntly. And she is relieved.

She thanks him. She has had immense anxiety but not all that much pain. She is a piece of meat but she has been successfully processed. Somehow he got her onto his public list. She is in his debt. The system had in the end looked out for her, had checked up on her, had been vigilant. Unfeeling but efficient. The feeling part had come from another source; from the airwaves, from the piano comp. When all her other senses were dulled by anxiety, her ears had kept her sane.

She drives home from the hospital in a better frame of mind than she has been in for a long time. She has taken the morning off work and will eat an early lunch out on the balcony of her small apartment, which looks across to a line of full-grown lilly pilly trees and an ornamental pool where two water dragons are basking in the sun. She loves the way their heads rear up, the way they arch their backs, the long curve of their necks with the serrated ridges and the gloating, sardonic expression of their mouth and eyes.

She settles into a deck-chair with half an avocado and a spoon and looks across to the jutting branch of a spreading plane tree. There, only two metres away, is the biggest, fattest kookaburra she has ever seen. So close. So wily and composed. He is the steeliest of birds; a wolf with wings. Definitely not a whinger. She flicks her empty avocado skin at him. He turns his head sharply and looks at it with contempt, jerking his beak as if to say, 'Bring on the meat.' She laughs. 'You'd make a good surgeon,' she says out loud, and thinks of her lopped ovary, but it's alright, she still has one good one. And she takes out her iPod and adjusts the headphones. She has gone back to her habit of listening to talk radio from podcasts and a man's voice is droning across the airwaves, warning of the coming drought. She does not want to hear this. Instead she switches to the final night of the Sydney Piano Comp. Here it is, then, the first bars of Prokofiev's 'No. 3 in C Major'. The bright winter sun beams down onto her head.

The Existence of Other Men

'... despite the horrors of history, the existence of other
men always promises the possibility of purpose ...'

—John Berger

How long have we got? Me? I can stay for around an hour, I'll just
have to answer the pager, that's all. I'll have a whiskey, what about
you? And some sandwiches, they do a decent club sandwich here
and I haven't eaten all day.

Now, why is it that you're here? Public relations? A series of
profiles for your website? I'd better be on my best behaviour then.
Where do you want to start?

Is there a special mystique about brain surgery? You bet your
life there is. I don't know about a young journalist of your generation but when we were growing up 'brain surgeon' was code for
super-smart. Is that what attracted me to it? No, not at all. By the
time you've done your general training you've had the stars
ground out of your eyes. As a matter of fact, my first interest was
in cardiac surgery. In those days that was the glamour field, especially transplants. But soon you learn that the heart is just a pump,
albeit a pretty smart one. The brain is a much more interesting
organ, for obvious reasons. I've never understood all the glamour

about transplants. It doesn't come from insiders, from the surgeons. To people not actually involved it looks glamorous to take something out of somebody, even if they're dead, and put it in somebody else, but in fact it's one of the less complex procedures that top-level surgeons do.

A simple analogy would be fixing car engines. If you've got a major problem, the easiest thing to do would be to take the car down and ask the mechanic to put a whole new engine in. That only involves bolting in one or two things whereas, say, if you take the head off and repair the valves, well, they'll say, thank you, we'll keep it for a week or two. It's the same thing: if you want to cut a heart out and throw it away and then put a new one in, you've just got four big holes to sew the thing back to, it slots into four places and that's all you have to do.

I shouldn't say this, I'll get into trouble. *(Laughs)* You'd better cut that bit out of the tape. But look, it's the same with the brain, except we don't have as clear a picture of it yet because it's more complex than the cardio pump. But if we think of the brain as a television set, a complicated piece of technology that's transmitting stuff from elsewhere, inputs from the environment and so on, then we're just the TV technicians.

As a young resident I did some work in cardiac surgery but it didn't grab me. I had a friend in training with me at the same hospital and he went on to become a cardiologist. 'Why do you want to do neurosurgery?' he'd say. 'You're working with zombies. Too many of them don't wake up.' There's a better rate of recovery in heart cases and people with heart disease tend to be cheerful. Did you know that? And my friend liked the fact that within days the men would be experiencing better blood flow and they would joke with him about the return of their early morning erections. He loved that. But I decided that cardiology wasn't, well, to put it bluntly, the heart isn't interesting enough, not enough of a puzzle. Mind you I may have been influenced by one of the neurosurgeons I worked under. He was famously eccentric, a bit mad, and he seemed to be able to do exactly what he liked. He had an aura about him. I think I was drawn to that.

Do you have to be obsessive? It helps. Even more than in other specialties you need to have an obsession with detail. One of my colleagues is a dedicated fly fisherman and he took me trout fishing with him once. He hadn't long taken it up and his casting wasn't what it might have been and on the first day his line got badly tangled. So he just sat there on the bank of the river and oh so patiently and carefully untangled it. Took him forever. One of the other guys in the party couldn't get over it. Why doesn't he just cut the bloody thing and rig up a new line? he said. He didn't get it.

Technique? Oh, technique is very important. If you're no good, you're out. Brains and technique don't necessarily go together but it's like anything, aptitude comes into it, there are people who are gifted at doing certain things. You know, Mozart at the age of four was doing things that I wouldn't be able to do if you gave me a hundred years – there are people like that I've seen in surgery as well.

But a surgeon doesn't have to be very bright intellectually. The brightest people don't do medicine. Let's not kid ourselves. It's not intellectually stimulating enough; I mean, it's just on a different planet compared to things like quantum physics or complex mathematics, it's not in the same ball park. There's nothing hard about it intellectually. There's nothing in medicine I couldn't explain to you in words, very simple words, in an hour. It's not that hard. But technique is essential. My father was a suburban bank manager but his hobby was wood-turning and cabinet-making. Perhaps I got my dexterity from him.

So it's like fixing your car, all the fun is in doing it. If you want to get excited, what you do is you take on progressively harder cases, the ones that are harder to get someone through alive. That's what you do so you can raise the ante each time. As you feel yourself getting better you keep raising the ante, making it harder.

(Sound of pager beeping) Oh, that's just some bit of nonsense.

Where were we? Why did I choose the brain? Well, I suppose the fact that the brain is still a bit of a mystery, that had to come into it. I mean, what is this thing we call consciousness? How does it work? We're much more sentimental about the heart – love and romance, and all that – but if your brain isn't functioning as it should then romance goes out the window. What are you feeling then? If you've got a clot on your brain you won't be feeling very romantic, I can assure you. That's one thing. And I suppose you'd have to say that, as a resident, neuro appeared to me to be the most difficult area of surgery. As I said, a lot of people don't wake up. Some wake up straight away but many of them lie there for months and never wake up. You get a fair share of zombies. And you want to see people get better. You don't want disasters to hang around to haunt you. No-one wants to sit around and watch people dying. It's hard enough for me when it happens, anyway, and in neurosurgery it happens more than in any other field. You need pretty good nerves. You have to stay detached.

But as for intellectual stimulation, no, I don't get enough of that. There are no secrets to the brain that are going to tell you how the universe works. I only went into medicine because of my father's insistence. I wanted to study pure maths, that was my real love, but he said I couldn't do that. He said I wouldn't be able to support myself on it. And also, he had an agenda of his own. Dad was a fitness nut who believed in vitamin therapy long before it was fashionable. We had a huge bowl of vitamin pills on the table at every meal and if someone dropped in unexpectedly my mother would rush to hide them. She didn't want people to think we were cranks. And my father berated her if she didn't have fresh home-made yoghurt prepared every morning. It was a strict regimen. Do I still eat yoghurt? No, can't stand the stuff. Anyway, it was always assumed by him that I would study medicine and set the unbeliev-ers right. And look, in a way he was right, at least about the maths bit. When I went through university I saw there were maths graduates who ended up driving taxis. And I'm not sure I would have been good as a research mathematician. Those guys are very, very bright. Guys like von Neumann, Turing, Feynman, there's just no comparison to what we do. They solve the problems of the universe while everyone else is asleep.

What's that? Isn't that what I do? You mean put them under and solve their problems while they're knocked out? Well, sort of, but not in terms of the big picture. When they wake up they're alive, sure, but they've still got to go away and figure out the mean-ing of life. I can't do it for them.

But I've changed a lot since then. I was interested in maths because I thought there were ultimate formulas out there that would provide the answers to life and death. The big Theory of Everything. That was my true interest, really, not so much the maths as finding the answers. I wanted answers as to *why* – why this useless life, where you sort of, you know, you grow up and then you die. It seemed to me so pointless. When I was sixteen I thought about death a lot, it was an affront to me, something that I took personally, like I was one of the few who had been singled out for it. It's very hard to function with that sort of attitude. So I thought mathematical models of the universe would provide the answer.

But not religion. I studied quite a number of religions, but I think Western religion, in particular Christianity, is a religion for kiddies. I mean this Santa Claus business, you know, the old man up there, it's got about as much reality as the tooth fairy and the Easter bunny. I mean it's great when you're a kid but I'm afraid it doesn't fit the bill.

No, I don't have superstitions. You mean when I'm operating? No. That's a poor man's consolation, superstition.

(Pager beeps) Excuse me a minute.

Am I grateful to my father for talking me out of becoming a mathematician? Yeah, probably. Although it didn't quite turn out as he hoped. Not with the vitamins anyway. *(Laughs)* But look, adolescence is a dangerous period. You could easily just opt out. Some kids do, and some of the brightest. A friend of mine jumped off the top of the fire escape at his boarding school when he was seventeen. You get frustrated when things go wrong, but no, I didn't do anything silly. Life is a game, isn't it? I talked to my parents a bit about the meaning of it all but they didn't have any answers. No, they weren't religious people. Were they rationalists? Yes, that would be the right definition. So was I, intensely so, which was why it annoyed me greatly that I could not, you know, could not solve the problem of life and death logically. You can't solve it logically, I defy anyone to solve death logically. You can only move beyond it with something else. And Western philosophy's so bankrupt it doesn't help you.

I suspect most people carry death with them. Obviously I'm not trained to generalise on that matter but I can speak personally and say that for me that would be correct.

What do I mean: trained to generalise? Well, because in logical thought, if you venture generalisations broadly, you end up in a mess. I mean, you just get lost, you have to backtrack through that mess again. Better to stick with what seems reasonable, I think. But whether it's everybody or most people's experience, I wouldn't know. Have you heard of the neuroscientist V.S. Ramachandran? He was here recently giving a lecture. He made the point that we're not angels, we're just sophisticated apes, yet we think we're angels trapped inside the bodies of beasts, trying to spread our wings and fly off. That's the way the brain seems to work, to foster that delusion, and it's a pretty weird predicament to be in, if you think about it.

Am I interested in consciousness? Well, yes, who isn't? It's what neuroscience is all about. Oh, you mean in the cosmic sense? Do we have a soul and all that stuff? Not my field. But if you ask me if I'm interested in consciousness in the wake up, get up, get on with life sense, then yes. That's difficult enough, especially when you're dealing with someone who's been thrown out of a moving motor vehicle and ended up with nineteen blood clots on his brain. Quite frankly in a case like that I won't have a clue what the outcome will be. In that particular case all I could do was try and restore his brain as close as possible to what it had looked like before the prang and hope for the best. But I was as in the dark as the next person as to what the outcome might be. As it happened, that particular patient made a remarkable physical and mental recovery. He did have delusions for several weeks after and then gradually he settled back into who he had been before. Was I surprised? No. On one level I'm never surprised – with the brain, anything can happen – and on another level I'm constantly surprised. As branches of medicine go, it can be very unpredictable.

(Pager beeps) I'll just take this around the corner where it's quieter.

Yeah, I've got time for another drink. I've got another half hour, forty minutes. What makes a good neurosurgeon? Well, technique would be ninety per cent of it, technique and judgement. It's not just technique because judgement comes into it as well. You have to know how far you can go; you have to know when to stop. There's a lot of judgement about when to back out. Some surgeons end up killing people and blowing their careers because they don't realise the importance of discretion, doing the things that have to be done and not doing the other things – and that to get out when something is too hard is often very smart.

Most neurosurgeons are pretty ordinary people, sometimes less than. You shouldn't glamorise them. Some of them are pricks, absolute pricks. Why? Well, why wouldn't they be? If you look at people in positions of great power and authority, or positions where they have great skills, many of them still suffer from self-doubt. And most of them put a lot of time and effort into getting where they are so that they can prove themselves. And the trouble unfortunately, as you would expect, is that if you are really driven to show how good you are, just making it with money, or making it to positions of power and influence, doesn't fix your self-doubt, so even the apparently successful ones remain frustrated people who are still trying to prove themselves every day. They've got to be told how good they are, they're constantly exerting their authority in an arbitrary way, which is not necessary, and this is the sort of nonsense that goes on. I'm sure, from my limited understanding of human psychology, that just proving, just achieving something doesn't stop you feeling on the edge. You're always on the edge of getting to where you want to go but you're never quite there. You can't fix the basic problem; you have to be either psychoanalysed or grow beyond it. Look, I speak as someone who's got the same problem, that's why I'm in neurosurgery. I had to go out and prove myself. And in proving yourself, sometimes you do something useful and people think you're brave and wonderful. Take the guy who developed cardiac catheterisation, Werner Forssmann. He was a German who developed the technique in 1929. First he practised on corpses and then to make his point he threaded a catheter through a vein in the front of his right elbow and threaded it for sixty-five centimetres along into his own right atrium. He did this alone in his lab because no-one would help him, they thought it was too risky. Then with the catheter inserted he walked all the way along the corridor to the X-ray department and persuaded two nurses to help him examine himself through a fluoroscope to confirm the catheter was in his heart. One of the nurses couldn't handle it and passed out. Forssmann survived and won a Nobel Prize. Would I do that? Who knows? Probably not, though it's amazing what you will do when you get caught up in your research. You can get a bit obsessive, especially when you're convinced that you're right and everyone else is wrong.

(Pager beeps) Uh, oh. There it is again. The pager runs my life.

No, it's okay, I've got plenty of time, as long as I answer this thing. What were you saying? Does what I do ever seem routine? Well, there is a degree of repetition. Any manual skill, if you want to be good at it, you've got to repeat it a thousand times, and regularly, so it then gets to a stage where it moves out of the thinking mind and into somewhere deeper than that. Then if you're someone who's goal oriented, who's out to prove themselves, you become bored, because you're not doing something different or hard. Whereas I suspect – and this is conjecture – that if you have, say, a mind trained in Eastern philosophy, in fact you can move into this higher state when doing whatever it is you're doing, whether you're chopping wood or just preparing your daily meal – this is not another repetitive, mechanical task, this is expressing one's unity with the universe. *(Laughs)* I've got a sister who's studied Zen Buddhism, and that's what she tells me. This is what operating should be, but it rarely is because none of us are masters of Zen. Not to my knowledge, anyway.

The downside of our job is that you're flat out so you cut corners and the first corner to go is significant interaction with the patient. Which means that for us, most of us, it's not work on people, it's work on … on objects. I think people are transformed in the process of becoming doctors, and the transformation is that a lot of the humanity within you is destroyed or pushed away. And that has to happen. Well, it doesn't have to happen, it happens because it helps you cope, because it's very hard to watch people die and look after people who are dying all the time if you're close to them, so you tend to push them away and lock them out. I think that's what we all do. We have a shield.

People talk about burnout but I think that's nonsense. I think that what happens instead is that sometimes we get dehumanised. In fact a lot of my day's work is boring, the paperwork and so on, and that's partly because I don't know the people I'm operating on. I think it would be much better if I knew them and cared for them as people, not just as a day's work.

But people are often referred very soon before their operation. They might come in the night before and you might see them around eight or nine o'clock in the evening. They're scared, you're buggered, and it's not an ideal situation for a friendly chat. And they're just the ones that are conscious. As soon as anyone arrives everything's stripped off them and they're stuck in a white gown and a sterile bed. They've got nothing around them that even makes them look human and if they're compos, you know, you have to ask them all the questions related to the disease. You might ask them a few personal questions, like what do they do. But that's the way the government wants it. It used to be people came in two days ahead but everything is cost-cutting now and that's expensive. And then there's all the emergency cases where they've suffered major trauma and they're already unconscious on arrival.

As for afterwards, so often, you know, they don't want to sit down and tell you about their life until they're feeling a bit better. By the time they're prepared to do that, and they want to tell you about what makes them who they are, it's time to kick them out because you want their bed for someone else. And they want to go anyway. It's pretty horrible living in hospitals.

And then there's the pressure of keeping the job turning over. See if you're not doing enough cases a week, you're not going to remain good enough. And every case, even though it only takes, say, two to three hours to operate on, maybe four, there is a lot of follow-up before and afterwards. They take six or seven hours out of your day. Say, six; multiply that by six cases every week, there's thirty-six hours, minimum. And then there's the research you're meant to be doing and all the paperwork, and everything, you know, goes back and forth – there isn't a lot of time.

So you don't end up operating on human beings. I mean, I think some of my colleagues would say that I'm misleading you, but I put it to you that they do not operate on human beings, they operate on objects. But in the end they, the patients, get up out of their beds and go home and their lives are better than when they came in. So in terms of the success of the actual surgery, the result for the patient is the same whether they get to know the surgeon or not. But the point here is the result for you, the surgeon. I mean, if you want to live a meaningful life, then you have to get meaning out of what you do, *more* meaning than I just did something harder than I did a week ago and hence I feel temporarily inflated by it – which is about all most of us get out of what we do.

How do we deal with that? Well, society rewards hard-working, wealthy, inferiority-complex-prone people. They are in fact held up as the people to emulate. Obviously in your job the adrenalin must be flowing a lot of the time and that keeps you going, in a fairly unthinking way. That helps a lot, yeah – when you're operating, it's certainly adrenalin-driven, there's no doubt about that. I mean, it's like flying planes, that sort of thing.

But look, don't get me wrong, doing the cases and getting them right does provide some satisfaction, because they all … they all have the potential to turn around and kick you in the teeth. And they do, regularly, no doubt about that. So having a couple of cases that go well, or solving a couple of disasters, that's good. I certainly don't get *blasé*. If you've got nothing else to do, then it becomes a test against the clock; to say, well, you know, I've done this in two hours and next time I'll do it in less. So that's pretty important.

(Sound of pager) Hang on a minute. No, no, that's okay. Ring me at home about nine.

Where was I? Not many people get into neurosurgery. It's very hard to get into, because you have to achieve a certain level of technical excellence, otherwise you're out, they just throw you out. There are thirty-year-olds who've trained and they're unemployable because they're not considered good enough. And it's hard, hard to go back into other specialties. They won't have you. Even in general practice they say: What do we want a neurosurgeon in general practice for? What do you know about diphtheria, what do you know about treating children? It's a one-way street. You can blow your career. I mean you can set up a general practice in the country, I suppose. So a lot of people say, hey, do I want to be thirty-five before I'm finished – that's if I do well – and only then start to earn a big income, or a sensible income, and have a reasonable life? I mean, most people want to have a family.

Death? I thought I'd covered that. Well, part of the solution comes from this shielding mechanism, which makes you inhuman, so that you don't see it as death. You don't see it for what it is. And if you get involved with the psychology of how a unit coheres – medical staff, nursing staff, physiotherapists, the whole team – it's always us and them, so to speak. And the most horrible thing that can happen is for one of *us* to get sick; then the illness takes on a more interesting, a more worrying perspective. As long as it's one of *them*, the patients, then it's, well that's not us, is it? As for me, I hardly ever get sick. I would have had one day's sick leave in my life. You do get tired, and then … as I say, when you're operating it's okay because the adrenalin flows and you can operate. It's in between you feel terrible. So the biggest impact is actually felt in the home life – where, you know, you're away all day, and your family might or might not be interested in seeing you when you come home a zombie. Then there are the little things, like sometimes my wife complains about the smell of bone dust.

Bone dust? Yeah, well you have to drill through the skull to reach the brain and the dust that comes off the drilling has a distinctive smell. Doesn't bother me, but it seems to upset her.

The other point, of course, is the fact that a lot of my work is very technical, and the only people you can talk to about it are your colleagues. So you may come home and say nothing to your wife and kids for hours, because you don't really want to bring up the trouble of the day, and then a colleague rings and so then you might talk to them for a whole hour about the difficulties of the day and how they could have been avoided, and what they would think, and so forth, and that can cause great displeasure to those at home.

Is there a debriefing after each case? Oh no, certainly not. If there's a disaster, there is, you know, we talk a bit about what happened there, sure. And, you know, if you've had a number of disasters then it starts. There's a serious inquiry into what you're doing, like if you had, say, out of the last ten, three or four stuff-ups then they'd want to know why something's up. And that's where your career is really only as good as your last few cases because if things start going wrong you'll be out.

You just keep trying to get better, that's all you can do. And if you don't like the place you're in, you look at working elsewhere in the longer term. I don't even know if I'll be doing this in ten years' time. I may get out of it one day. I've got into the property market a lot now and one day I might go into it full-time. The property market's just a game, like anything else, and you test yourself against it. Can you make money out of it? Can you do better than the market itself? I suppose it could pall, yeah, but not if I made a *lot* of money. It would be fun to make a couple of million a year.

What would I do with it? Well, I'd just invest it, what else can you do with it? It may sound like going around in circles but it's the same as becoming a surgeon; the fact is, the more money you've got the more important you are, I mean, it satisfies your drive to prove yourself. I was discussing this with my sister recently and she was shocked. She said to me, oh, but at least in the process of proving how good you are you're keeping people alive. I told her: that's just a side effect. *(Laughs)*

Most of the professional aura you get from medical staff is the outer view of the shield, and it's obviously cold and sterile. One sees less of it in those who've had major illness and been operated on themselves, because that forces you, it breaks down the barrier between us and them. They've become patients, they've crossed over to the other side. When they come back there's far more empathy between them and the patients, far more. You can see it in their daily immediate interaction with the people, you know, they treat them much more as people, even as friends, particularly if they've known them as patients for a little while.

Can you programme yourself to do this? To have empathy? Look, what we're describing is protective behaviour that covers difficult situations, like superstition or magic or Christianity.

If you grow up enough you can put that aside but for most of us who are still secretly afraid of death and have other problems, we use these simple tools, which are insidious, they're crippling because they take away all the joy of the job. There's very little pleasure operating on objects.

But listen, one day this will all seem as quaint as applying leeches. One day you might even be able to cosmeticise your brain. How? Well, you might want to get an edge on the person at work, have a more retentive memory. You'll go along to a surgeon and ask for some cognitive enhancement instead of breast implants. *(Laughs)* Look, my job will probably just get more interesting, from the novelty point of view. Neuroscientists are like cryptographers trying to crack an alien code, and bits of the code keep coming in. It means you always have some new challenge to wake up to in the mornings, something new to prove. Maybe I'll postpone that career in investment for a few years yet.

John Lennon's Gardener

We set out on a warm but overcast Sunday morning. At the bottom of the hill the ocean looked flat and grey, and clouds sat low over the headland. The old gate at the end of the drive was stiff and Mick had to hoist it out of a rut in the sandy soil and swing it across to where a stand of ragged banksias dropped their cones onto the dry verge.

'Time you fixed that gate up,' he puffed as he climbed back into the car. 'I'll have a look at it for you before I leave.'

'The place is neglected. I'm never here. I keep thinking I'll get away for the weekend but it never happens.'

'You could sell it.' I gave him a look and he shook his head. 'Sorry. Old memories, I guess.'

Yes, old memories.

It was on my way to the shack, as a young wife, that I'd first met Mick. He was hitchhiking along the coastal road and my husband, Bill, stopped and we gave him a lift.

'Where you headed?' Bill asked.

'Hoffmanns Valley. You know it?'

'Never heard of it.'

'There's a commune there, Yudhikara, or some funny name. Got a mate who's building a house in it.'

'I didn't know there was a commune in this area,' said Bill. 'Bit cold for it. I thought communes sprang up north of Sydney where you can get your gear off all year round.'

Mick grinned. He was an easy presence and we struck up an instant rapport.

We dropped Mick outside the pub in Tandarra, a tacky little seaside town then, and thought no more of it until the following Friday when we ran into him in the main street.

'How's whatsitsname?' asked Bill.

'Yudhikara. Yeah, good, I'm thinking of maybe propping there for a while. Why don't you come out and visit?' He turned to me. 'Chick out there reckons she knows you.'

'Knows *me*?'

'Yeah, chick called Miranda someone.'

I gaped at him. 'Miranda Meacham?'

'Dunno. They don't use second names. Miranda someone who said she went to school with you.'

'Miranda Meacham is living in a commune? You're kidding.'

Mick shrugged.

Now my interest was really piqued. Miranda Meacham had been school captain at my high school and girl most likely to succeed. Last I heard she was working for a law firm in the city; now she was evidently some kind of hippie. 'How do we get there?' I asked.

Mick drew a rough map on the back of my shopping list.

'I'll ring first,' I said.

'No phones allowed. It's a rule. Just front up. People come and go all the time.'

From that moment I felt an urge to visit the valley. As a child and later as an adolescent you measure yourself by certain people, those among you who seem more blessed: smarter, wittier, better looking, wealthier and, above all, more cool. Miranda Meacham had been one of my measuring rods; I envied her more than I could ever have confessed to anyone.

I don't recall exactly when Bill and I made our first visit to the valley but I do remember that it was hot. We drove a long way into the area known as Bell's Country, past the hills where the tin mines were worked out and the Chinese labourers had long since packed up their joss house and moved on; past the fertile dairy farms that supplied the famous butter and cheese; on and on over a rough unsealed road that ran through towering bush of giant mountain ash and peppermint gum. Before long we felt disoriented; we might have been anywhere. Then, suddenly, the road emerged out of a blur of state forest into a small valley. The densely wooded hills sloped down into a lush green clearing where rustic stone houses with roofs of slate tile stood in a cluster on either side of a narrow dirt road. The road was not much more than a track, though it ran right through the middle of the valley. Along the edge of the surrounding grasslands stood a scattering of wooden cottages, timbers faded to grey, their broken guttering and derelict verandas giving notice that they were uninhabited. Two Jersey cows grazed languidly and there was a fenced-off enclosure with four elegant goats and a goat house painted in limewash. Puffs of white cloud hung suspended from a blue sky and a soft, filtered sunlight bathed the stonework in mellow tones so that the entire valley seemed suffused with summer haze. I almost gasped at its beauty.

We parked the car outside one of the stone houses that Mick

had marked on our map with an 'X'. It was a two-storey cottage with a pitched roof and would have looked quaintly English were it not for a narrow front veranda. A man lay in a hammock strung between two poles of this veranda, a dusty bare foot dangling from one end of the striped canvas and a broad straw hat rising just above the rim of the other. He looked up as we slammed the car doors shut and we told him we were looking for Mick.

'You've come to the right place,' he said. We knocked on the open door and Mick appeared, along with a big golden labrador that leapt up onto Bill.

'Down, Gandalf!' Mick growled. 'Bloody dog.' He had a proprietorial air which surprised me; he'd only been there a few weeks. He ushered us into a big open living area where another man was seated at a rough pine table eating his lunch. There was a cob of homemade bread on the table, a ceramic dish of curd and the remains of a green salad.

'This is Dave,' said Mick, 'and this is Ariel,' gesturing to a woman attending to the wood-fired stove with a toddler on her hip. 'And this is little Gracie.' Mick patted the child's head.

Dave stood up with a welcoming grin and shook Bill's hand. He was tall and lanky with black shoulder-length hair and traces of a Welsh accent. I liked him instantly. He was obviously smart, not some dozey drop-out, and Mick had told us that he was something of a leader in the commune. Of course the members of the commune didn't believe in leaders but Dave had a natural authority. Later we discovered that he was the one who had found the valley and negotiated the sale, along with Miranda Meacham who had vetted the contract and handled the conveyancing.

Dave invited us to sit on bush chairs he had made himself and when we declined lunch Ariel brewed some tea made from mint grown in her garden. It was watery and weak.

We asked Dave about the commune, only to be rebuked gently. 'We don't call it a commune,' he said, in his sonorous Welsh drawl. 'It's a settlement.' There was an important difference, he explained; the word commune gave out the wrong message and encouraged spongers and dopeheads. So far there were eight families who had bought in to the valley, and three more were planning to move there and build over the autumn when it wasn't so hot. Right now they were fixing up one of the derelict timber cottages as a guesthouse for itinerant workers who wanted to make a contribution. In October it would be their three-year anniversary and they were having a special celebration, a weekend festival. We were welcome to come.

Ariel had made no attempt to join us and seemed absorbed in her task beside the stove, cradling her daughter on her hip like a young earth mother. She had one of those enviable hourglass figures of fine-boned shoulders and full breasts, a slender waist and curvy hips that give shape to a long skirt. Her silky brown hair hung to her waist and when she passed beneath the skylight on her way to the sink the sun caught it so that it shone with silvery highlights. I wanted to talk to her, to draw her into the conversation, but she was one of those women who are still and contained, as if surrounded by an invisible ring of silence.

'We're not drop-outs,' Dave was saying. 'We're not here because we're afraid of the world, and we're not anarchists.' He gestured towards a bundle of leaflets on the kitchen table and told us that he was about to distribute fliers for a 'good man' in the town who was running for the local council on a platform of conserving the forests. I asked Dave what he had done before he moved to the valley and he said he had been a history teacher in a high school in the city. After he found the valley he applied for a transfer to the school at Tandarra and worked there for two years while he built his house. Now he was on call as a relief teacher and the money was enough since they lived frugally. The other settlers did various kinds of work: each house had its own vegetable allotment and some people sold vegetables and homemade cheeses at the local markets; others worked as deckhands on the coast or nursed at the local hospital. A few were living off savings while they 'looked around'. I knew some must be on the dole, though we didn't mention it.

'I think I know one of your people,' I said, feeling awkward with that word 'people'. They were not communards, they were not exactly pioneers or settlers, so what were they? 'Mick said there's a Miranda Meacham living here and she said she knew me. I think it must be the Miranda Meacham I went to school with.'

'Miranda's away just now.' There was no warmth in Dave's voice and his manner cooled. I sensed that he and Miranda didn't get on, that Dave was one of the few men she couldn't twist around her finger. I didn't press it, though I was disappointed and made a mental note to ask Mick to be sure to let me know when Miranda returned.

'What about the old cabins?' Bill said. Someone had obviously lived here before the commune.

'This area was settled by German families who came out in the 1860s. The local folklore is that they came from villages around Frankfurt to escape having their sons conscripted under Bismarck, so of course we like that idea, that they were anti-war.'

'Perhaps they just wanted to protect their children,' I said.

'Same thing in the end, isn't it?' He pushed his plate away and stood up. 'Would you like to look around? I can take you on a tour if you like.'

All this time Ariel hadn't said a word. I had waited for an opening, a way to bring her into the conversation but she hovered at a distance beside the stove, and Dave was such a compelling presence. He drew you towards him.

We left our half-drunk tea on the rough pine table and headed towards the door. Dave strode out onto the veranda and Bill and I followed. Mick stayed seated at the table. 'Catch you later,' he said. 'I'll just groove around here for a while.'

I looked across at Ariel. 'Goodbye,' I said, and she smiled shyly.

We strolled out into the sun, aware suddenly that the stone house was dark inside, as if built against extreme heat, or snow and sleet. The houses were picturesque, in a Hansel and Gretel kind of way, but I wondered how suited they were to this temperate valley. Bill asked about their construction while Gandalf padded along beside us and I confess my mind wandered. I was trying to picture Miranda lolling about here in hippie braids and a peasant skirt. The image didn't fit.

'How big was the original settlement?' I heard Bill ask. 'The Germans, I mean.'

'Well, in this valley it was just one extended family, the Hoffmanns. Two brothers with eight sons and five daughters between them. To get to Australia they had to offer themselves as indentured labour, which meant working for the local squatter south of Tandarra on the big sheep run. They kept gardens and sold vegetables, and pooled their money until they had enough to buy land. Then they hacked their way through the bush with axes and cross-cut saws until they found this place. They were Lutherans of course and they built a little chapel.' He pointed towards the north-western corner of the valley. 'We can walk there if you like. I'll show you the graveyard. Some of the headstones are still upright.'

As we walked, I looked around at the little village of stone houses, all of different designs but each impressive in its finish. Mick had said something about it being a rule that you had to build your own shelter out of the local stone but these places looked too, well, solid. Surely they had employed stonemasons?

By this time the men were ahead of me and I could hear Dave explaining the property entitlements to Bill.

'There are eleven owners, tenants in common, but a lot of people come for a short stay.'

'Don't you have rules about that?'

'It's up to the shareholders how many people they want to have living with them at any one time. But if anyone causes any kind of trouble they have to go.'

We had already heard from Mick about 'trouble'. One afternoon a mob of bikies had driven into the valley in full leathers and florid tatts. They had pulled up on the edge of the settlement, revving their powerful engines, and Dave had gone out to meet them, had stood for some time talking to them in a low-key way. No-one knew what he said but after forty minutes or so they had driven off with a friendly backward wave, never to reappear. It was an episode that had greatly enhanced Dave's authority. He seemed to have a gift for dissolving tension.

Ahead of us I could see what looked like a miniature church, too small to enter and almost ornamental. It was made of orange-red brick and some kind of plaster and it had a white column on either side and a domed bell tower. Dave saw me looking perplexed.

'That's our bread oven,' he said with pride. 'That's where the real worship goes on around here.' He paused in front of the oven's cast-iron door and launched into a detailed account of its construction, which was of great interest to Bill, though I found the oven repellent, absurd even. They had gone to so much trouble and the end result was grandiose. Too much of a statement.

The real church sat at the far end of the valley on a low rise. It was clad in weatherboard on a stone foundation with a pitched roof of rusted iron and a faded wooden finial. As we approached I could see four worn steps leading up to the door, and both steps and door looked like they might collapse at any moment.

'Is the church used now?'

'We show movies there on a projector, once a week. This week it's *The Conversation*. Come if you like.'

'Seen it,' said Bill.

'So have I,' said Dave, 'and it's a long way to travel for a movie.' He laughed, and gestured at the church. 'Pity it's not big enough to hold a dance in.' Then he opened the door and we looked inside. It was bare except for some green plastic chairs ranged along one wall. It might have been an old schoolhouse. There were dead blowflies on every windowsill and cobwebs high in the corners of the ceiling. Outside again, we followed Dave to the rear of the building which was unkempt, and in among the tall grass there were headstones encrusted with lichen.

'Have to cut that bloody grass again soon,' he said. 'We should preserve these headstones. Graveyard maintenance is on the roster but you know what happens to rosters.'

'I suppose a pastor came and visited,' said Bill.

'Apparently not. It was too far for the nearest pastor to travel in a buggy. And that didn't matter because they didn't believe much in priests. Every man is responsible for his own salvation and all that. I imagine they met on Sundays and took it in turns to read the lesson.'

'They must have been lonely.'

'Well, they were hard workers, a legend in the district. The librarian in Tandarra – she comes from around here – she told me the old men were great characters. They hated having to rest on the Sabbath. After their Sunday dinner they'd go for a walk and knock the heads off thistles with their walking sticks, the closest thing to sacrilegious work they'd allow themselves.'

'What did they farm?'

'They were potters originally, artisan families, but they obviously knew a thing or two about farming and the valley produced enough to support them. As you can see, it's a special place.' He looked around him with an expression of pride. 'They kept pigs and ducks, and cows. Apparently they made cheese and travelled on a horse-drawn wagon to nearby towns to sell it. Cured bacon, grew potatoes. All that.'

'Did they build a kiln?'

'If they did we've never found it.'

We read the names on the headstones. Friedrich Hoffmann, Ada Hoffmann, Heinrich Geller, Ludwig Wolfhagen, Maria and Johannes Hoffmann, Frieda Rubenach. The Johannes Hoffmann headstone had an inscription that I couldn't quite make out. Dave saw me peering at it up close and read it aloud: *'Heaven is my fatherland, Heaven is my home.'*

I liked that inscription. There was something soulful about it, but also defiant.

'Johannes Hoffmann was one of the original brothers. Thanks to the warmongers in Europe he had to renounce his country. Imagine it, he was fifty-three when he arrived in Australia. That was a fair age in those days and he most likely came to the conclusion that from now on the only fatherland that counted was the big H.'

Dave began to walk on and Bill followed but I lingered for a moment, distracted by another headstone. Sophie Hoffmann, wife of Nikolaus, had died in the valley in 1892, aged twenty-seven. Although it was a hot day my skin went cold; twenty-seven, it was my age. At the bottom of Sophie's headstone the names were engraved of the infant son she had left behind, Wilhelm, along with three small daughters, Elise, Bertha and Salome. Dave, who had backtracked, came up behind me. 'I know,' he said, looking over my shoulder. 'It doesn't bear thinking about.'

'So what happened to all the Hoffmanns? In the end, I mean?'

'The young ones eventually moved to the city or towns. Only three spinster sisters were left behind with their widowed brother. The brother's children had no interest in the valley and we bought it from them.'

From that day on Bill and I became regular visitors at the commune. It held a fascination for us. It's easy to mock these things; it was easy at the time and even easier looking back, but that valley was the most beautiful place I had ever seen. It seemed blessed. Bill and I had moved to the coast for a year because Bill was employed with Baird and Markham, a big construction company that had contracted to build a new bridge over the Clarence River. It meant we could live in the family shack for no rent and save money towards a house of our own in the city. Because we had decided to try for a baby I wasn't looking for work; Bill was on a good wage with a generous allowance for working away from home and I expected to fall pregnant soon, so there was no point in starting a new job. This was 1979, when mortgages weren't a killer and everything seemed easier.

Bill was fascinated by the practical problems of the commune and happy to advise on surveying or when a problem arose with the drainage. Dave liked people who were useful and they soon developed a friendship. Bill especially loved the stone houses and spoke for a time about building one himself, but I was more interested in the politics. How on earth were they going to make the place work? What would happen when they couldn't agree? When someone couldn't or wouldn't pay their share of the land tax, or when someone's kids ran riot and rode their bikes through the corn patch, or let the goats out? Perhaps because he had been a schoolteacher Dave was always keen to talk and never seemed to mind my asking a lot of questions. And because we visited often at the weekends we soon learned about the rituals and protocols of the settlement. There was a weekly council for collective decision-making and a roster for chairing the meetings, although the roster was a problem; some people can chair a meeting and some can't and inevitably Dave acted as the council's de facto convenor. Meanwhile Mick had decided to stay on in the valley and was living in the cottage that had been fixed up for itinerant workers. He was a mine of information and was able to tell me that the meetings of the collective went surprisingly smoothly. The last big disagreement among its members had taken place after they built the bread oven. Typically, they had no trouble agreeing on the big item, the design of the oven, but couldn't agree on the small thing, the design of the bread. They had plans to sell it on Saturdays at the local market and wanted to ornament the cob loaf with an emblem of their collective enterprise. But what emblem? Some had favoured the peace sign; it would symbolise their own politics and honour the original settlers, past and present linked together. But Miranda Meacham had been withering in her view that the peace sign was already a cliché. One woman suggested a Y sign for Yudhikara. This had the advantage of being easy to form out of dough, but some of the others felt uneasy about this. After all, they didn't know what Yudhikara meant. It was a name left over from the time of the Hoffmanns but it wasn't German, it didn't belong to the local Indigenous lingo and it wasn't Sanskrit, so who knew what it signified? They could be perpetuating some bad karma. In the end they agreed not to have anything.

Often Mick would arrive at our shack with one of the Yudhikara people known as Dolby. They'd roll up in Dolby's ute to collect Bill and go out fishing on the old couta boat that Dolby's father had left him. It was an easy life. 'I'm glad I took that job with Baird and Markham,' Bill said one night as we lay in bed, reviewing our prospects. He had grown up in the inner city, had spent no time in the country at all and now he was beguiled by it. Between the coast and the valley we seemed to have the best of both worlds.

On one of his visits to collect Bill, Mick announced that Miranda Meacham was soon to return. Immediately my antennae went on high alert; I wanted to know when.

'Dunno,' said Mick, 'but Dave's less than thrilled.' He winked.

'Why?'

'He thinks she's trouble.'

I wasn't surprised to hear this. 'I sensed they didn't get on,' I said.

'That first time we visited and I brought up her name, he went all cold.'

'Well, as I heard it, she nearly scuttled the whole thing.'

'Scuttled? How?'

'Well, they didn't just build those stone houses from scratch. No-one had a clue how to go about it. So Dave sussed out these journeymen dudes that travel around working for people. He organised a couple to come to Yudhikara for a while so they could show everyone how to build in stone.'

'Journeymen?'

'Yeah, wanderers. Haven't you seen 'em? I saw one hitching outside Tandarra a few months back. Didn't come near us though. Probably warned off.'

'Yes, but who are they?'

'Tradesmen. Just out of their apprenticeship, usually. Mostly Krauts. You can't miss 'em. They wear waistcoats with little pearl buttons and top hats. And they have big walking sticks. They do their apprenticeship back home and then they travel around the world looking for work to finish off their training. And there are strict rules. They have to carry their tools on their back and walk, or hitch. If they work for you, you give 'em a bed and feed 'em.'

'So some of them worked at Yudhikara.'

'It was Dave's idea. He heard of two stonemasons hitching around the south and he drove down and found them and brought them back to the valley. So they could teach him and the others how to build in stone.'

'Where did everyone live while they were building?'

'Some were in tents, some rented shacks in the town, or on the coast.'

'That explains it,' said Bill. 'I thought those houses looked professional.'

'Yeah, but they nearly didn't get built.' Mick paused with the knowing look of one who has gossip to impart. 'Your mate, Miranda what's-her-name, shacks up straightaway with one of the journeymen and soon he's building her house at a great rate. Then suddenly she's fucking the other one on the quiet and when the first one finds out all hell breaks loose. They're big strapping boys and they take to one another with their sticks. Dave had to sort it out and got his jaw broken in the process.'

I think my mouth fell open at this point.

'Luckily, by then everyone had the hang of it, the stonework and all.' Mick gave a high, barking laugh. 'Dave read the riot act to Miranda and she told him his fortune. If you listen to what the others say, it's been a power struggle between those two from the start.'

'He could have asked her to leave,' said Bill.

'He wouldn't do that. She's a tenant in common for one thing, and for another he owes her. When they were negotiating the sale of the valley, the Hoffmann family changed their minds and wanted to back out but Miranda nailed them, some kind of legal technicality. That's what Dolby said, anyway. Without her they wouldn't be there.'

Each time we visited the valley I sought out Miranda, only to receive the same answer from those who were sharing her house. 'Haven't heard. She'll be back before long though.' Meanwhile the commune was immersed in preparations for the winter solstice, its big festival for the year. There would be a feast and circle dancing, local musicians had been invited and a giant bonfire would be lit.

One Saturday in late June we drove over to the valley for the solstice. Miranda Meacham had still not returned. As the sky darkened we gathered at one end of the pasture where the settlers had built a bonfire from a huge pile of wood and old tyres. The night was cold but utterly still, the black sky lit by a swathe of stars. On either side of the dirt road there were big white lanterns moulded from papier mâché in the form of goblins or sprites. They dangled from tall, sinewy poles with the eerie glow of benign ghosts and the effect was magical. We sat on rickety canvas chairs in a half-circle around the fire, nursing our mulled wine, and it was noisy; wood cracked and snapped and sparks sprayed into the winter dark like Roman candles. Mischievous from too much wine, I asked Dave about the journeymen stonemasons, saying Mick had mentioned them, but Dave just looked away, over to where Ariel was assembling the children with their smaller lanterns in readiness for the 'parade of light'. Ariel was often in charge of the children; she had a way with them. They would tug at her skirt for attention and hang on her soft words.

'The kids have been making those lanterns for weeks,' said Dave. 'The local school principal's been a big help, lets them do it in class as a special activity.'

I could imagine. Dave would have approached the school and, in his quietly authoritative way, made it sound like an eminently reasonable proposition.

'The journeymen? Did they stay long?' I wasn't going to let him off the hook.

'Long enough for us to learn from them. As you can see.' He

gestured towards the houses at the other end of the valley. 'They were incredibly well trained, better than in this country. One of them, Manfred his name was, told me his father had worked on the restoration of Cologne Cathedral. I told him my uncles had flown bombing raids over Cologne at the end of the war.'

'Was that tactful, Dave?'

'I told Manfred, the past is the past, we start afresh here. And I apologised for the raids over Cologne.'

'It wasn't your fault.'

'I wanted them to know where we stood on the subject of war. That our valley was a place of peace. And to know we valued them. We were stoked to have them here. We took their coming as a sign, a blessing. My God, they could eat though. They ate enough for a platoon. Ariel never left the kitchen.'

Silently I admitted defeat. With Dave the conversation always ended up on his terms. So what if Miranda had bewitched both journeymen, that wasn't the point; the point was that Dave and Manfred had sorted out the bombing of Cologne. Dave wasn't going to tell me about the scandal; the personal was always subordinate to the big picture. To history.

'You were lucky you found those guys.'

'Luck didn't come into it.' Dave stared into the leaping flames. 'If you look past your nose for long enough, Di, you can always find what you need.'

Five days after the winter solstice, Miranda Meacham returned to the valley. Mick dropped by in Dolby's ute with some fish and a red cabbage sent by Dave. 'Your old schoolfriend's back,' he said. 'Thought you'd like to know.'

I drove into the valley on the Saturday. Bill was on a fishing trip and I was glad; I wanted to reconnect with Miranda on my own. I was eager to see her again, but also nervous. She could be charming, intimate and confiding, but she could also be mocking and dismissive, a bitch. At school you never knew where you stood with her and I didn't imagine she had changed.

With no phones in the valley, I could take her by surprise. I drove in past Dave's house where Ariel was squatting on the veranda with Gracie in a sling on her back; she was peeling potatoes from a vast wooden tub and dropping them into an aluminium jam pot. I waved but she seemed to be in a kind of trance and didn't see me.

I parked the car outside the stone house I knew to be Miranda's and knocked on the door, which was ajar. A small boy pulled open the door and said: 'They're out the back.' Damn, she wasn't on her own. Then again, it seemed that no-one in the valley was ever on their own. I walked back down the stone steps and around the side of the house to the rear where a group of sunburnt smokers lay on the grass getting stoned. At first I couldn't see Miranda but then a woman sat up, waved and beckoned me over. It was her. I hadn't recognised her because she had shaved her head, no longer the well-groomed young prefect who ruled the school. Her naked scalp shone in the sunlight, her neck was festooned with thick ropes of red and brown seedpods, her upper arms encircled with silver bangles in the Indian fashion and she wore a saffron-coloured sarong. She was lying back on an old plastic recliner, her legs wide apart, her thin cotton vest unbuttoned and her ample breasts bare.

'Di!' she cried, 'Di! Over here!'

As I drew near I saw that her feet were ingrained with dirt and her toenails painted black. 'Sit,' she commanded, indicating the grass beside her. 'Somebody get Di a drink.'

And someone obediently did.

On that first afternoon she could not have been nicer. It was the charming Miranda, the I-have-found-my-valley-and-am-at-peace Miranda. Some of this might have been for show, for her entourage, but I was pleased when she suggested we meet in the town for, as she put it, a *tête-à-tête*.

It was a Wednesday and I found her at the Green Goanna, a café favoured by the local hippies. She was sitting by the window looking fresh, almost demure, in a white cotton sun dress. Even with her head shaved she looked good; everyone else had grown their hair long as an emblem of where they were coming from but Miranda had to be different. Over coffee she told me that she and Ariel were first cousins and this surprised me. They could not have been more different, though clearly their mothers had shared a penchant for romantic names. I guessed that it was through Ariel that Miranda had met Dave and heard about his plan for a settlement.

'Dave's a control freak,' she told me. 'He comes from some gloomy Welsh valley, and one of those dour low-church families. You can never get that stuff out of you.'

'How do you mean?'

'He's serious about everything. He has all these rules.'

'Don't people agree to the rules when they buy in?'

'Yes, but you have to be flexible. Give and take. People have to live together. We're mature adults, it's not boarding school.'

Miranda hadn't changed. Everything had to be on her terms, which were of course self-evidently reasonable. Perhaps Dave was a control freak; he did have a flinty quality about him, the sharp nose, the long chin. But I liked him. I liked the interest he took in the valley's history and its German pioneers, the way he looked after their headstones. Miranda was one of those people who had their eyes on the future while looking to finesse the present.

'You've been away,' I said, changing the subject.

'I'm looking into imports. It's time I became a trader.'

'A trader? You?'

'I need an income stream. There's a shit-load of hippies around here and nowhere to buy incense, clothes, non-chemical soaps, that kind of thing. There are two good markets in this district, one on Saturday at Tandarra and one at Northbridge on Sunday. I could make enough to live. Black market, darling. No Mr. Tax Man.'

'Where do you get all that stuff?'

'You have to weasel a good deal out of an importer in the city. Which I have.' She gave a knowing laugh. 'But that's not my big news.' She paused.

'Well?'

'My new man! He wasn't there when you came on Saturday but he's arriving any day. And you won't believe this. He works for John Lennon!'

'John Lennon? *The* John Lennon?'

'That's the one.' Her eyes flashed with triumph. Nothing could be more cool than this.

'What? So he's just visiting then?'

'No, darling, John has bought a big property around here, up in the hills.' She lowered her voice confidingly. 'It's a big secret, none of the locals know and I can't say where.'

'Have you been there?'

'Not yet, but don't worry, I will soon.'

'Why on earth would John Lennon buy land around here?'

'Why not? Privacy, a bolt-hole. Somewhere to escape to when they drop the bomb. Geordie says it's magnificent rainforest country. Used to be a farm but has been neglected for years and is reverting to its natural state. John and Yoko flew out last year from New York and looked it over. Private jet, hush-hush, nobody knew. Then they hired Geordie to look after it.'

'He *knows* them?'

'Not personally. Hasn't met them yet. An agency hired him. The agency put a private detective on him to check him out and everything.'

'You mean they've never met him and they trust him?'

'Well,' she pouted, 'they have to trust someone here if they want the place looked after. And Geordie speaks to John on the phone.' 'John' was now Miranda's intimate, or soon would be.

'It gets better. Geordie says they're coming out in October and I'm going to arrange it so they visit the valley. I'm going to break it to the collective at the next meeting. They'll be *hysterical*!'

'I thought it was supposed to be a secret.'

'It is, but I've had an idea. We'll explain to John how the valley is a peace haven, a symbol of a new age. He and Yoko had that press conference for peace in their hotel bed that time, remember? Well, we can offer them a follow-up in the valley, a small private press conference, just one camera. We'll take the footage and after they fly out they can release it to the press. And we can make a documentary and incorporate their visit. Nobody will know about it at the time, except us, and we'll release the doco later. What better way to start a new decade? Nineteen-eighty here we come.'

'You're nuts.'

Her eyebrows shot up. 'You sound like Dave.'

'He knows about this?'

'Not yet.' It was the way she said it; all I could do was smile. 'Anyway,' she continued, 'come out with Bill and meet Geordie. He's utterly gorgeous. In every way.' She was practically drooling.

'Will he live on the property?'

'He'll live with me, of course. There's an old farm house on John and Yoko's property but it's derelict. And Geordie's going to put in a garden for me. I've been such a slacker in that department.' She rolled her eyes. 'The others are pissed off with me because I never grow anything.'

I could see that even if Geordie turned out to be lying about the John and Yoko connection, Miranda might still come out ahead. All of the stone houses had a thriving vegetable plot, except Miranda's, and the rampant buffalo grass around her foundations had done nothing for her credibility in the valley.

That night I told Bill the big news and he pulled a face. Bill didn't take to Miranda. I once described her as a free spirit and he said: 'Free spirit? That would be another name for wrecker, would it?' But he loosened up when she started to drop in on us, usually on her way back from the city to collect goods for her market stall. She would arrive wearing a flowing dress in some bold tropical print and clutching a bottle of champagne in each hand, and over dinner she would regale us with funny stories. Unlike most women she could tell a joke and she had an eye for the absurd. Bill would chortle despite himself. Then she would fall into our spare bed because she was too drunk to drive back to the valley. It was not beyond Miranda to roll up and greet us effusively as Mr. and Mrs. Boring, but at least she said it to our faces, and because she seemed to have some genuine affection for me I never took offence. That was the thing about Miranda: either you bought the full package or you didn't buy at all. Bill didn't buy. 'She's alright when you get her on her own,' he'd say after she left, but in matters general he was on Dave's side.

By mid-August, Geordie McCausland had moved into the valley. Mick announced his arrival on one of his regular visits to the shack and we asked what he thought of him.

'Is this stuff about John Lennon for real?' Bill asked.

Mick shrugged. 'Seems to be.'

'What's he like, this Geordie?'

'Seems okay. Haven't spoken to him on his own.' He winked. 'You'd have to prise Miranda off him.'

Eager to meet this unlikely steward, we drove into the valley the following Sunday and knocked on Miranda's door.

'Come in,' she called, and her voice had a happy sing-song note. Things were obviously going well.

We walked through the whitewashed passageway and out onto the back veranda where Miranda was lolling on a scruffy day-bed in a see-through sarong, bare-breasted as usual and entwined with a man in skimpy jocks. We took this to be Geordie. He eased himself up into a sitting position and extended his hand to Bill while I looked him over. He was attractive, no doubt about that. He had broad shoulders and long reddish-brown hair that fell in loose curls over a high forehead. His skin was weathered into a dark tan and his full mouth and long scimitar nose made him look like a bush Arab. His legs were strong and muscular and he had a way of holding himself, a relaxed, almost feline slouch of the kind that suggested he knew how to take his time. Miranda gave me a look, a gloatingly possessive see-what-I've-got look. I laughed.

We sat for a long time and drank our way through a cask of wine. No mention was made of 'John'. Geordie talked knowledgeably about the valley's vegetable allotments and his plans for Miranda's patch but there was something odd about him, something creepy and at the same time childlike. He certainly seemed to know a lot about soils, and phrases like 'potassium deficient' and 'seaweed mulch' came and went on the mild afternoon breeze.

*

Weeks passed and it was some time before we returned to Yudhikara. There were problems with the construction of the bridge and Bill was working long hours and coming home spent. In his time off he slept a lot and didn't feel like going anywhere. We hadn't seen Miranda for ages and I imagined her to be preoccupied with Geordie.

Finally Mick turned up one Sunday in Dolby's ute and plonked himself in a chair in the kitchen. He looked like a man who had had a surfeit of something. 'Had to get out of the valley, mate. Major shitfight going on there.'

'Yeah?'

'The three-year anniversary celebration. No-one can agree how to handle it. Dave and Miranda are at each other's throats.

It's getting ugly. Had a meeting of the collective last night, bloody thing went on for five hours. Dave wouldn't let it go and neither would Miranda. Since Dave is usually the one to call stumps I thought we were going to sit there all night.'

'What's the problem?' asked Bill.

'Bloody John Lennon, that's the problem.' Mick grinned. He'd knocked back a double brandy and was starting to relax. 'Miranda wants to phone him, via Geordie, and invite him to the anniversary celebration. Like, to preside over it. A new era of peace and all that bullshit.' He snorted.

'As if.'

'Exactly, mate. As if. Like they'd be able to keep it a secret and it wouldn't leak out. But Miranda's going on about it being a cosmic moment, a gift from the universe. "What better way," she goes, "to see in the '80s?"' And he gave a naff imitation of Miranda's haughty tone.

It wasn't leakage I was thinking about. I was wondering why any of them thought that John Lennon would want to hang out with a bunch of hippies at the bottom of the world. George, yes, maybe, but never John.

'Miranda's gone off her trolley,' said Mick. 'She thinks the sun shines out of Geordie's arse. Full stop.'

'What does Dave think of him?'

'Dave didn't mind him moving in, especially after he put in Miranda's garden. Now she's got the best laid-out patch in the valley. And Dave checked him out and found his father runs a big nursery in the south, so he's a gardener alright. But Dave's got doubts about the John and Yoko thing. For one thing I don't think he believes it, and for another, even if it's true he doesn't want to invite them to the valley. "We're not into celebrity stuff," he says, last night. "That's not what we're about." Then Miranda goes spare. "But the man's a genius!" she goes. "He's a peace warrior! Isn't that why we're here, isn't that what we believe in?" She was spitting chips from the word go, like she's made her mind up and Dave's just getting in the way. The more wound-up she gets the quieter Dave goes. You know what he's like. He just lets her go on and on until she's said her piece. And then he says, very calmly, "That's all very well, Miranda, but you can get burnt by this stuff." And he tells this story about when Dylan came on his first tour of Australia and sang at The Black Swan folk club in the city. A friend of Dave's called Okie used to make guitars and he took his best one along and offered it to Dylan, who strummed a few chords on it and said: "This guitar's shit, man." Okie never got over it.'

Bill laughed derisively. 'What did the others say? Was there a vote?'

'No, no vote. Dave said we'd leave it "in abeyance", whatever that means. He knew Miranda had got to a lot of people and he might lose a vote.'

Sometimes Mick surprised me: he didn't miss much.

'Miranda stormed out in a state. Fit to burst. Now she's working her way round the valley, talking down Dave.'

I could picture the scene all too vividly. 'What did Geordie say?'

'He wasn't there.'

'Isn't it a rule that everyone comes to the collective meetings?'

'Supposed to be. Ariel wasn't there either. Little Gracie's crook. Everyone else turned up, not that they got much of a word in.'

'Nothing serious with Gracie?'

'Don't think so.'

'Wise of Geordie to stay away,' said Bill. 'Leave it to the power-brokers.' He shot me a fleeting glance.

'So, Mick, is Geordie up for all this,' I asked, 'or is it just Miranda's idea?'

'Dunno. He's hard to read, is Geordie. But he knows a lot about rainforest restoration and he showed me the draft plan he's drawn up for John. He also seems to be pretty cashed up. Heaps of dope. Someone's paying him, even if it's not the Beatleman himself.'

'He probably grows the dope on John's plantation,' said Bill.

'If it exists,' I added.

Mick shrugged. 'Any more of that brandy?'

Mick stayed with us that night and he and Bill got up at four to go fishing off the beach. They clumped about so noisily that I couldn't get back to sleep so I lay there until sunrise wondering why I hadn't yet conceived. In the seven months since Bill and I arrived on the coast, two women in the valley had got pregnant. Dave maintained that the valley was on a ley line and had a rare fertility, so perhaps Bill and I should spend a night at Yudhikara. But I wasn't worried. There was plenty of time.

The men returned with perch for breakfast and we fried it up and ate it with a cob of the Yudhikara bread that Mick had brought. Then I left them drinking on the veranda and drove off to do the weekly food shop in the town. It was a bright spring morning and I was in the best of moods. This really is the life, I thought, as I parked the car in the pretty little car park behind the beach and its crumbling pre-war promenade.

After I had worked through my shopping list I sought out Dave at the market where he and Ariel ran a weekly stall and sold their vegetables. He was carrying Gracie in a backpack and had dark rings under his eyes.

'You look wiped,' I said.

'Ariel's got a fever.' He frowned. 'I've been worried about her. She's been off colour for weeks now. No appetite, nothing.' He looked dejected, kind of hollowed out, which was unlike him.

'Can you take a break?'

'I certainly feel like one.' He called to a teenage boy whom I recognised and who lived in the valley. 'Jamie, can you mind the stall for a bit?'

We sat at the Green Goanna and I thought I had never seen him so deflated. I asked him about the meeting of the collective, and then confessed that Mick had already given us an account of it. There was no point in hiding anything from Dave; he had a nose for where you were coming from.

'Oh, that,' he said, as if it had been a minor difference of opinion. He knew Miranda was a friend of mine. But I prodded him gently until at last he gave in to his exasperation. 'It was a bit much,' he drawled, 'when Miranda started on about the old German settlers, and how we needed to keep the peace tradition going, and how Lennon was a link to all that. A modern peace pioneer, she called him.' He sniffed. 'Holding a press conference in bed in a luxury hotel, I'd hardly compare that to packing up and leaving your home to sail across the world.'

I didn't know what to say. I didn't want to take sides. We sat for a minute in silence while Dave pushed the orange Smartie in his saucer around and around the base of his cup until the chemical dye began to run in blotches on the white porcelain. 'History repeats itself as farce,' he sighed. Gracie began to wail.

We parted in the car park beside the beach. 'Don't worry, Dave,' I said, lamely. 'It will work itself out.'

And it did, though not in the way we expected. Later that afternoon Dave would pack up his stall as usual and drive home to the valley with Gracie asleep on his lap, back to the haven of peace he had so patiently husbanded. When he arrived at the door of his stone castle, the one he had built with his own hands, the princess Ariel was gone. She had run off with Geordie McCausland.

*

And now here we were, Mick and I, driving towards the valley after a gap of fourteen years, speeding along the coastal road where the sea-changers and their money had moved in and the old fibro shacks had been demolished in favour of over-designed palaces of wall-to-wall glass and vaulting decks. None of this was new to me. Since my father retired to the shack I had been coming to visit him for years, but Mick had been long gone and, as he told me now, living of late in a commune in New Mexico. That he should turn up out of the blue when I was at the shack for just a few days to pack up my father's things was beyond belief. When I opened the door and saw him there on that dusty, windswept porch – unchanged but for grey hair and a thickness around the middle – I could have wept.

'Had to come this way to see Dolby,' he said. 'Remember him? Thought I'd drive out to the valley while I was in the area and see how the old place was going. Then I thought I might as well drop by here on the off chance you still owned the shack.'

I had never owned the place but now that my father was dead I did. At last. When I no longer wanted it.

Seeing Mick, so unexpectedly, had the effect on me of walking through an open door, back into the past. Mick especially. To begin with he had been more Bill's friend than mine, one of those innocuous-seeming men who grew on you. Soon they were eating your food, sleeping on your couch, doing odd jobs about the place and maybe even sleeping in your bed. But my own deep affection for him derived from the time of Bill's death. It had been a violent spring, the wettest on record. In a week of storms and gale-force winds the scaffolding at one end of the construction works had collapsed and Bill and another man had been swept into the flood-swollen river.

Exactly one week after the funeral, when my parents had departed at my insistence and I was on my own again, Mick turned up. He cut the grass, chopped the wood, mended the pump and casually looked after the place for a whole summer while I grieved silently. There were days when we scarcely said a word to one another, when I made sandwiches and we sat outside under the shadecloth that Bill had tacked up, and we smoked and stared across to the hills. Friends came to see me and offered to stay but I didn't want anyone else around. Only Mick. Mick understood about silence; he was comfortable with it. One night we slept together but it didn't work, and in the morning nothing was said. With that instinctive tact that had enabled him to lead the life of an amiable nomad, Mick behaved as if nothing had happened. Eventually, when he thought I was ready, he packed up and hit the road.

Now he was back, with a yen to see the valley again, and he wanted me to come with him. But I had avoided the valley for years. After Bill's death I couldn't bear to go there; it was a site of too many promises that remained unfulfilled. Yet here I was, driving Mick along the coast beside the eroded sandhills. Each year the tides rose higher and the drop from the spiky grass to the beach below grew more and more steep. It was a windy day and a big sea was blowing in from the south-east, scattering a fine mist up over the sandbanks and across the road. 'Wouldn't have recognised the place,' said Mick as we slowed into the outskirts of Tandarra. The town was flashier now, with a new beach promenade and ten-storey holiday apartments lined up along the foreshore. There were powerboats at the marina and talk of a canal development. But we still had an hour's journey ahead of us so we drove through the town without pause.

When at last we arrived at the turn-off to the valley there was a woman there, sitting idly by the roadside at a stall of home-grown blueberries. She looked vaguely familiar.

'Do you recognise her?'

Mick shook his head. 'You?'

'No.' But I felt unnerved. Soon we would be in that lush clearing with the steep wooded hills and the filtered sunlight, that paradise of youth, and I could feel myself beginning to choke. It was too much. I could never have driven here alone.

We swung into the turn-off and began the steep ascent, up the narrow winding pass and through a passage of dense forest until, suddenly, we were gazing down into the sunlit open. At first glance the valley looked exactly as it did before: the cluster of stone houses, the old timber cabins, the rich grasslands. But there was no-one in sight. We drove on further, along the dusty unsealed track, and saw a man standing in what had been the goat enclosure. He seemed absorbed in the act of tying up a grey donkey and didn't look up, though he must have heard us drive in.

I parked beside the fence and we got out. 'I hope you don't mind us driving in,' I said. 'We used to have friends who lived here and we wondered if they still did.'

He was young, no more than twenty. He began to fill a wooden trough with water from a hose, then looked up from under his broad-brimmed hat and said: 'What friends?' I thought him not so much blunt as shy.

'Name of Eyenon,' said Mick. 'You know 'em?'

'No.'

'Live here, mate?' asked Mick.

'Nah, just keep an eye on the donkeys. Nobody lives here. People come weekends, but.'

'Alright if we look around for a bit?'

'Yeah,' he said, flatly, like it wasn't his place to give anyone permission to do anything.

We began walking in the direction of Miranda's old house. 'She was bloody shattered,' said Mick, as if Geordie's abandonment had occurred only last week. 'Drank herself stupid for a year.'

I looked around. 'He left her a wonderful garden. Look, the orchard is still here.' There were apricot, apple and peach trees, ragged and in need of pruning.

Mick began to pull at some tall shoots of buffalo grass. 'Yeah,' he murmured, 'lots of fruit.' He yanked hard at a clump of the stubborn weed and suddenly it came away. 'But no Geordie,' he said, casting the weed to one side. 'And no John Lennon, either.'

I walked on ahead to where the oven had been. It was gone, completely dismantled, though you could see the concrete square where they had cemented it into the turf. The church, too, was gone. 'Probably blew off its foundations,' said Mick, who had

236

caught up to me. 'They would have carted it away.' We could see, though, that some of the headstones remained upright, and the grass around them had recently been cut.

The stone houses, so sturdily built, looked just as before; if anything they seemed even more imposing. Only the wooden window frames were worn. 'They're as pretty as ever,' I said. 'Indestructible.'

'You'd have to put a stick of gelignite under *them*.'

'Dave still owns his.' I had kept this piece of information from Mick until now. I wanted to surprise him.

'*Dave?* Still comes *here?*'

I nodded.

'I thought the old crowd had all gone.'

'They have, except for Dave. He comes here sometimes, at Easter, and school holidays.'

'You're a dark horse. I didn't know you'd stayed in touch.'

'I didn't.' And I told him of how, when I went to enrol my son in high school in the city, I had looked at the school's prospectus. There, towards the top of the staff list, was a David Eyenon. It was an unusual name and I thought there couldn't be two of them. And there weren't. It was him. 'He's the deputy principal,' I said.

Mick laughed. I could see he was pleased. 'That'd be right,' he grinned. 'Dave would be running something, you could back that in.'

'You know, he doesn't look any different. Still the same Dave, but in a collar and tie. Still a beanpole. Even wears his hair a bit longer than everyone else. He told us they'd stuck it out in the valley for two more years but the work dried up. They couldn't grow enough produce to sustain the lifestyle, and some of the women got restless. They wanted to move into the town, or back to the city.'

'Got a new woman, did he?'

'I think so. He said something in passing about his children, how they used to love the valley but now they're older they don't want to come. I've sometimes wondered if Ariel ever came back for Gracie but I didn't like to ask.'

Mick gave me a look. 'Always fancied Ariel,' he said.

'I know.' I knew what he was thinking: if it hadn't been Geordie it might have been him.

'Look at this place,' I said. 'It … it feels so empty. It all went wrong, didn't it?'

Mick put his arm around my shoulder and gave it a squeeze. 'Yeah, mate, something usually does.' But his voice lacked conviction. He was gazing in the direction of Dave's house and his eyes had gone all misty. 'I loved this placed, just loved it. It was so good while it lasted.'

Letter to the Romans

He wakes at the usual time, around dawn. He needs no alarm clock; it's as if his body had been programmed to respond at first light. It has always been his habit to lie in bed, reviewing his dreams. Sometimes he recalls nothing, but this is rare; on most mornings there is a vivid hangover of false memory, false because nothing in the dream world really happens, does it? And yet his dreams can produce such intense feeling, either of fear or rapture, that he feels compelled to conjure a meaning out of them. Why this? Why now?

On the morning that he first met her he had just had one of the most profound dreams of his life. He had been walking beside an expanse of water in the English Lake District, treading on a carpet of dry acorns in a quaint village lined with oak trees, and all that separated him from a precipice that fell away into the lake's dark surface was a dry stone wall. The stones were oval and flat and when he touched one he found it dislodged easily, as if this barrier wall were fragile. He stopped walking, the better to contemplate the relationship of the stones to one another, their surreal equilibrium, a quality even more affecting than the grandeur of the lake. In their un-mortared state of grace they seemed to embody an invitation, and perhaps even a promise. And what did all this mean?

Well, nothing; it meant nothing, and yet it was so *there*, even though he knew there was no 'there'. Some of his most vivid experiences occurred in a place that was nowhere.

When he woke he lay in bed and walked beside that stone wall again, in his mind's eye, and already the dream was vapid, had lost its potent aura. All the details were recoverable but not its mysterious charge, in this case a feeling of peace, of coming home. When his wife was alive he would sometimes describe one of his dreams, or listen to one of hers, and this was a condition of marriage, part of the unwritten contract; you had the right to bore each other with these disjointed night hauntings in the hope that someone who knew you well might decipher the code. Your dreams must mean something or why would the brain bother? Everything in biology has a function.

He got out of bed and raised the blind to let the light in. *One day I will dive into that lake, but not yet.*

After he had showered and dressed he went downstairs and already it was eight. On the table was a note he had left for himself the night before. *Milk, tomatoes, chorizo.* When his wife died he and his daughter, Alice, agreed they would take it in turns to prepare dinner and since he passed the shops on his walk to and from the university it was easier for him to do the shopping. But that was Alice's first year in the confinement of an office and the claustrophobia of her ten-hour days as a junior solicitor. More often than not it was he who had a meal waiting when she came home and the preparation of it yielded a quiet satisfaction. Alice is the love of his life. She is such a good girl; she has always done the right thing. But now she has met Adam and moved to live with him in Adelaide, only eight months after her mother's death.

'I feel that I'm abandoning you,' she had said.

'No, no,' he had protested. 'You have to live your life. Your mother would want that.'

Now he lives under the weight of a double loss.

His walk to work is a necessary ritual; it loosens the stiffness in his 59-year-old body and brings him down to earth, if one could describe the raffish energy of King Street as earthy. Still, there is the avenue of plane trees along City Road, the glinting silver surface of the public swimming pool and the haze of smog that hovers over the city's glassy towers. He likes the smog; it reminds him that he has escaped the rural tedium of his child-hood. He turns in through the university gates and walks beside a sloping expanse of parched lawn that no amount of academic privilege can save from drought and water restrictions. When he reaches the Underwood Building he bounds up the main stairs to the second floor (yes, he can still bound) and collects his mail from its pigeon-hole. His heart rate is steady and he breathes easy: not bad for fifty-nine.

On that first morning, in the corridor outside his office, he had observed a woman, waiting. She was, he assumed, the mother of one of his students who had rung the day before to make an appointment. This woman had sounded irate, and recognising an edge of hysteria in her voice he had tried to put her off. But she had insisted it was urgent, even as she declined to say what she wanted.

He paused at the door and introduced himself. 'John Garde.'

'I'm Inez Charlton,' she said, 'Daniel Charlton's mother. I rang yesterday.' She was agitated; she had black, glittering eyes.

Oh, dear, he thought, I am not in the mood for this, and turned his key in the lock of the door.

She entered his room with an air of nervous entitlement, sat without being invited and immediately began to rummage in her large, black-leather handbag for something she meant to show him. He watched her from behind his desk and he saw that she was a handsome woman with a shock of black hair, swept back, and small, fine features. He noted that she wore an expensively tailored business suit and seemed a woman of means. Despite her nervousness she had a certain presence.

Every now and then, maybe once a year, a parent materialised in his room to excoriate his influence over their child. What, he wondered, was it to be this time? Libertarianism? Nihilism? Anarchism? It certainly wouldn't be Marxism, not anymore.

He put on his polite but solemn face and waited for her opening sally. He heard himself utter the appalling words: 'How can I help you?'

Without preamble she leaned across and thrust a cluster of printed sheets at him, some stapled-together text on A4 paper, which she dropped onto his desk with no comment other than a look of withering scepticism.

When he glanced at the top sheet, expecting to see notes from his own lectures, he could not have been more surprised. He was looking at an extract from the New Testament. The Letter of Paul the Apostle to the Romans.

'*This* is my son's current reading,' she began, the first of her words issuing forth as a prolonged hiss.

'It's not prescribed on my course.'

'I know it's not. Maybe it would be better if it were.' There was a certain theatricality in her delivery and she had a fine trick of raising one perfectly pencilled eyebrow into an expressive interrogation of everything in the room. 'I mean,' she went on, not waiting for his prompt, 'that if you included this in one of your courses you would at least be able to expose it for what it is.'

He frowned. 'I'm sorry, but isn't this a personal matter?'

'Personal in what way?'

'In the sense that this has nothing to do with any of my courses. It's something Daniel has undertaken to study elsewhere. Perhaps you should talk to one of the student counsellors.'

'Read it. Read chapter 7, verses 18–28.'

He picked up the top sheet and held it out in front of him at arm's length. He did not bother to put on his reading glasses. He would not enter into her game. '*O wretched man that I am!*' he read. '*Who shall deliver me from the body of this death? For I know that in my flesh there dwelleth no good thing …*' But she could not contain herself even for this long.

'*You* are supposed to be teaching him to think rationally and analytically!'

'That's part of what we're here to do,' – was there safety in that 'we'? – 'but in the end students must make their own choices.'

'That's all very well but my son has turned into a zealot. As soon as we get in the car or the house he starts to preach at me. And sometimes he prays aloud in the living room or reads aloud from the Bible. *O wretched man that I am! Who shall deliver me from the body of this death?*' She paused for a moment, and glared at him. 'He calls it crying out to the Lord! And he insists on saying Grace at the table, very loudly, like he's in a stadium.' She lowered her voice. 'I can't bear it, Dr. Garde.'

He felt uncomfortable. It was something to do with the way she used his name, a dark intimacy, as if already they were colluding against the boy. He sensed that she was one of those women for whom there were no half measures; but that was her problem, not his. She needed to deal with this analytically and it was up to him to steer them both onto neutral ground.

'Are you a Christian, Mrs. Charlton?'

'No, I am not. I hope I would have the courage to live without facile consolation—' She stopped suddenly, as if a thought had just occurred to her. She was looking at him shrewdly. 'And what about you, Dr. Garde? Are you by any chance a Christian?' She was probing him. It had no doubt occurred to her, long before she walked through his door, that he might be a proselytising peda-gogue, a Pied Piper who ran scripture classes on the side and had led her son astray.

'No.' He looked at her coldly.

'I'm sorry. That really is none of my business. I do apologise. But the thing is ...' She sighed, almost entreatingly. He saw that some old-fashioned notion of good manners had begun to exert a check on her confrontational mood and this visible effort to rein in her passion disarmed him. 'Have you read this stuff?' she asked, and her tone was more conciliatory. 'It's a rant, it's all over the place. I wouldn't mind if it made any sense but it doesn't. It's unhealthy.'

'How long has Daniel been an evangelical?'

'I'm not sure. Three months, maybe four.'

'It could be worse, Mrs. Charlton.'

'Inez.'

'It could be worse. He could be shooting up in a back lane. He could be hanging from manacles at the Hellfire Club.'

'You think that's funny?'

'I'm perfectly serious.'

'I've raised my son to be sceptical and above all tolerant of others and now he's a Bible basher, a religious nutter! If he has to save his soul, why can't he be a vegetarian and a Buddhist like all the rest? Isn't that the fashion now?'

He couldn't help it. He laughed out loud.

'I know, I know.' For the first time since entering his room she smiled, and with a hint of self-consciousness placed her right hand over her chest in a protective gesture, as if the rapid beating of her heart was too much for her. In that moment she looked like a demure madonna in a painting. 'No doubt you think I'm a monster and I've driven the poor boy to it.' Now she was rueful, but had relaxed a little. She leaned back in her chair and crossed her legs so that her skirt rode up to mid-thigh and he could observe the perfectly moulded shape of her knees, neither bony nor fleshy.

What could he say? He liked her; she had a frankness and a sardonic edge that he warmed to.

'He gives me things to read, you know. He puts extracts from The Book in my briefcase. Folds little bites from scripture into my filofax. And I can't help myself, I have to speak my mind. Have you read this stuff?' She nodded in the direction of the stapled extract that lay on his desk. '*Their throat is an opened grave; with their tongues they have used deceit; the poison of asps is under their lips.* Charming isn't it? All sin and righteousness, and more sin, and the evils of the flesh and talk about how we should all become the slaves of God. *For I know that nothing good dwells within me?* I ask you, is that healthy?'

Yes, she was vivid. There was a current in her that surged around the room.

'Tell me, Dr. Garde, what impression do *you* have of my son?'

'He seems perfectly normal to me.' He recalled Daniel sitting at the seminar table and droning through a lacklustre paper. Tall with a loping gait and lank, unruly brown hair pushed behind his ears; conventionally dressed; a private-school boy but not the bland, complaisant type. There was a diffidence there, a modest reserve, with a strange, abstracted insolence just beneath the surface.

'Does he say much in class?'

'Not a lot. But that's not unusual.'

'What is he studying with you? I can't get any sense out of him.'

'He's enrolled in II B, Option A.'

'He told me he's writing a paper on whether animals have souls.'

'I haven't seen it yet.'

'Would that be considered a major question in this department?'

'You could say, from the point of view of the study of philosophy, that every question is a major question.'

She gave him a look, as if to say, 'You're playing games with me.'

Then something occurred to him. 'Tell me, does Daniel's father have a position on this?' He ought to have raised this earlier.

'His father is not in the picture.' She said this coldly, and then: 'Will *you* speak to my son?'

'I'm sorry, Inez, this is none of my business. It's a private matter. I really can't help you.'

At that point, he recalls, her mobile rang, a soft discreet *brrrrr*. Without missing a beat she extracted it from the outer pocket of her handbag and cupped it to her ear with a heavily ringed hand. Lowering her voice she said, almost furtively, 'I can't talk now.' She looked up. 'It's *him*,' she mouthed.

He felt he should look at his watch, pretend to have another appointment, but by now he was fascinated by her manoeuvres.

She flipped her mobile shut and dropped it into the gaping hole of her very large handbag. 'You know, Dr. Garde, my generation fought to free itself of all this ... all this *stuff*, and I can't believe my own son is turning into a puritan before my eyes.'

No, not your generation, he thought, *my* generation. We were the baby boomers, we broke the rules first. He guessed that she was ten years younger than him, at least. 'It's probably just a phase,' he said, lamely, and as the words came out of his mouth he was ashamed of them, ashamed because they patronised the boy. Perhaps it was not a phase and Daniel would end up a missionary in Africa, tied to a stake in the desert and eaten alive by ants. 'Adolescence is a time of extreme opinions,' he added. 'Everything is black and white.' And there's a passionate desire for truth which later fades, he might have added, but refrained.

'I hope you're right,' she said, and rose, looking towards the door. It appeared that she was satisfied, her anger discharged, at least for now. Well, that was a relief. He had navigated the tempest for them both, piloted them into the shallows of a nil-all draw. He always was good with women. Politely he rose to escort her to the door and when she turned to offer her hand an impulse took possession of him. 'I'm just on my way to have coffee,' he said. 'Would you care to join me?'

Within days they were lying together in small motel off Parramatta Road. It was a place that was commonly used for visiting scholars and he knew it well.

Thereafter they met every Thursday evening; same place,

same time. Since he was a widower and she was divorced, with no current entanglement, there was no obvious reason for this clandestine arrangement. They never spoke of it but he assumed she did not want him to visit her house because of his pedagogical connection to her son. And he was reluctant to ask her back to his place because the presence of his dead wife was still everywhere; it saturated the house, the garden, the air in every room.

On their first night in that motel room with its flecked beige wallpaper and murky green upholstery, disaster had threatened. At first she removed her skirt and he was delighted to discover a hint of glamorous and no doubt expensive lingerie. Then she surprised him. Still fully clothed above the waist she removed her skimpy lace pants so that his breath caught. Next she unbuttoned her shirt to reveal a deliciously seductive bra, what there was of it, and it suggested that her breasts were small, like those of a young girl. She loosened her hair, which was pulled back with a tortoise-shell clip, and by this time he was fully aroused, entirely without trepidation. In that exquisite flex of the shoulders that women give, she unhooked her bra and removed it in a single gesture, and his eyes went straight to the pinkish-white scar where her left breast should have been. It was long and neat and disappeared under her right armpit. *Mastectomy.* The hideous word captured him; it might just as well have been tattooed on her skin. Caught. He was caught, and he could feel the rush of detumescence, like air escaping from a tyre. Thank God he hadn't undressed yet and she couldn't see.

'Come over here,' he said, to cover his shock, and he sat her on his knee and bent to kiss the scar. But it was no good. He was impotent and he began to stall. 'How is Daniel?' he asked, and she jerked her head back, and looked at him askance as if to say, 'Why ask about that now?' Then her shoulders slumped, and he could see the moment, this moment she had been preparing for with nervous hope, beginning to dim.

'He's still at it,' she sighed, 'still tormenting me.' Her face dissolved in an expression of silent agony and she trembled. 'Last night he shouted at me. *"As it is written, for thy sake we are killed all the day long, we are accounted as sheep for slaughter."*'

And with those words a kind of thrill went through his body, and suddenly he was erect again. 'Sheep for slaughter,' he murmured, nuzzling her collarbone, 'are we now?' And he lay her down against the murky green bedcover, and enclosed her with his hulking middle-aged body. And was himself again.

It was a short session, but satisfying to them both.

The following Thursday they met again, and again he was flaccid when he looked at that pink slit of a scar. Silently he cursed himself, and delayed the moment of undressing by pouring himself another whiskey. He could not again ask after Daniel or she would think him perverse. Instead he eased her down beside him and began languidly to stroke her hip, but it was no good. He was a torpid hulk.

For a time they lay there, side by side in a pantomime of useless caresses, until at last she sat up with her back to him and smoothed her hair. 'I don't think we can manage this,' she said.

He was touched by this 'we'. 'Of course we can manage it,' he said, brusquely. If he did not resolve this impasse, and resolve it quickly, she would be lost to him. He lowered his head and began to mouth at her single breast, which brought from her an instant response, until she began to sigh deeply and rhythmically and it was not a mother's sigh. He lowered his body still further until his lips were brushing against the fine wisps of her pubic hair and he knew then that it would work. *Our mouths are open graves*, he told himself, *the poison of asps is under our lips* and all the while, as the blood began to surge through his arteries, he was spurred on by the thought of the young man, of Daniel. He wished that Daniel were in the room with them, this stuffy, banal motel room, to hear his mother's orgasmic sobbing.

After, when they lay in grateful repose, he felt again that singular peace that can be felt in no other way, never mind that it doesn't last. And it was odd and shameful but he felt that he had triumphed over the son. He had triumphed over the young. He was his old self again.

And so they conspired together. There was a kind of game going on between them and he wondered if her playing of the game was artless. Perhaps, even, unconscious.

'There's something about a bible,' she said one afternoon as they shared their ritual whiskey. 'Just looking at one gives me the horrors.' She took a demure sip; she was not much of a drinker. 'Daniel is making a collection of them,' she added. 'Last night he came home with two, a fresh new one with a pale-green plastic cover and a musty old hardbound monstrosity that he found in a secondhand shop, one of those with the family tree written up inside.' She grimaced. 'On every page there were passages blocked out in thick red crayon.'

He found the image of the red crayon titillating. He imagined a man his own age in a heavy serge suit on the Sabbath, reading aloud to his wife; a man with a large hand and a clumsy grip on his red crayon, pressing hard into the page, a pious vandal. Instantly it made him want to take the glass from her hand and push her back onto the bed, roughly. And did she guess? Did she feed him this stuff with intent? Evidently not, for on that occasion she spoke with genuine revulsion, as if she were describing some cursed or decaying artefact found on an archaeological dig. And then, more plaintively: 'Daniel insists on keeping a bible on the kitchen table. Near the fruit bowl. Sometimes I feel I can't bear to be in the room with it.'

'It's just a book, it won't bite you.'

'It does bite me,' she said, and smiled sheepishly. 'It takes a chunk out of me. I feel like, like … it's hollowing out my heart.'

This was such an arresting image; he hadn't thought of her heart before. He mostly thought of her other parts, her excellent muscle tone, its warmth and elasticity. Amazing that a woman's breast could fail her while the rest of her body went on working magnificently.

'You need to be desensitised,' he said. He leaned across, opened the drawer of the bedside table and got out the Gideon Bible. 'Here,' he said, holding it out to her. 'See, no teeth.'

She stiffened.

'Read to me.'

She made a face. 'What?'

'How about Letter to the Romans?'

She put the book down on the side table. 'You *are* ridiculous,' she said, and gave him a shove. He laughed, and thought they might soon become friends.

'Go on,' he coaxed, 'just a few verses.'

She picked up the book and searched for a moment, a seductive but dutiful schoolgirl. Then she glanced up at him coyly. '*We know that the whole creation has been groaning in labour pains until now; and not only the creation but we ourselves, who have the first fruits of the Spirit, groan inwardly while we wait for adoption, the redemption of our bodies ...*'

He reached out and took the book away. 'The redemption of bodies,' he said. 'I can show you a thing or two about that.'

After his first encounter with Inez he felt the need to talk about her, to use her name in the company of friends. He couldn't, of course, not under the circumstances. Though eating alone no longer bothered him, there were nights when he would sit at the table in the kitchen and say her name out loud: 'Inez.'

One evening in the middle of dinner Alice rang, as she did, faithfully, once a week, and he told her about Daniel, and of Inez's crack about young Buddhists and how it was the fashion now. Alice sounded tired and overworked and he thought it might make her laugh. It didn't.

'He's probably lonely,' she said. 'When you join the Evangelical Union you get instant friends.'

'That doesn't explain why he reads scripture aloud at the dinner table and shouts it out in the car.'

'Come on, Dad. He wants to annoy his mother. He's a boy.'

'Don't be glib,' he said.

'Glib?'

'Smart. Don't be smart.' Sometimes a word would come between them, a word that made him feel old.

'I *am* smart, Dad. Remember? You've told me so often enough.'

And she laughed, and he was relieved that she had taken it in good humour. He had not meant to rebuke her (God forbid) and had surprised himself by wanting to defend Daniel's seriousness. He had been a serious young man himself.

After they had spoken for a half hour he returned to the cold remains of his dinner, one of his wife's specials that he ate at least once a week: chickpeas, tomatoes, garlic and spices, smoked paprika, some rounds of chorizo and rice or bread. His wife hadn't liked to cook; it was too time consuming. There were too many other things to do in life. A quick meal is a good meal, she would say; it allowed more time for her garden. At first he resented this; his mother had cooked for him and he expected his wife would do the same, but he'd soon gotten over *that*.

He carried his plate to the sink and began to rinse it, distracted by an image of Inez, naked but for a pink cotton shirt, and as the water ran wastefully over the plate he happened to glance into the white plastic compost bucket that sat by the sink. It was the bucket into which he and his wife had scraped their leftovers, scraps that were destined for the state-of-the-art compost bin she kept in the yard, a bin that hadn't been attended to since her death. And still he emptied the leftovers into this bin as if any day she might return and resume her favourite activity, and he might glance out the door and see her kneeling on the flagstones beneath her wide-brimmed hat. On weekends he weeded the small patch of front garden and saw to it that the flowering shrubs were pruned, but her built-up vegetable bed at the rear of the house was a labyrinth of weeds. He couldn't bear to look at it.

He knew the presence of the compost bucket was a bad joke, that one day he would have to take it outside and dump it in the wheelie bin, but he was not ready, not yet. Some reminders of his wife unhinged him, others helped to keep him on track and the bucket, oddly, was one of them. For a while he just stood there at the sink and gazed out through the kitchen window that looked onto Camperdown Park, and an old sandstone wall that separated the park from St. Stephen's churchyard. Often on summer evenings after dinner he and his wife would stroll across the park and through the overgrown cemetery there, past the picturesque gatehouse and the enormous Moreton Bay fig tree, its roots like great sleeping pythons. The congregation had long ago shrunk away to nothing and the churchyard was derelict and filled with weeds. Many of the headstones were damaged and leaned askew while dogs roamed through the kangaroo grass and drug deals were transacted in shadowy corners.

One evening he and his wife had been accosted by a young woman, thin and pale with rats' tails of long greasy hair. He remembered the bright orange singlet top she wore and the row of tattooed rosettes across her shoulders. She smiled ingratiatingly and asked for money and his wife smiled back and held out her empty hands. Gestures like this were liable to flare in his head without warning, more vivid than ever they had been in life.

In bed that night he found himself wondering if Inez liked to cook, but pushed the thought away. He had no desire to see her in a domestic setting. But the thought persisted and when at last he fell asleep he had a dream in which she and Daniel were sitting at a polished oak table with plates of food in front of them, food piled into steaming mounds while Daniel declaimed Grace, shouting his holy words across the bare wooden table. The Last Supper:

mother and son. The apostles dismissed; Mary and Jesus, alone at last.

*

There were many things that, by tacit agreement, they didn't mention. He once raised the subject of her missing breast – he felt he ought to – but all she said was, 'Don't ask.' He had always thought of it as missing, as if it fell off her somewhere while she was walking in the bush, not that it had been cut out of her by a surgeon's knife. He was curious, though not very, as to why she didn't have a reconstruction. Somehow it was like Inez not to fake anything, not that he could say he knew her well, but by then he knew her body and there was truth in that. Some women were soft and feminine in their manner but hard between the sheets, grasping and self-centred; others seemed brittle and haughty but were soft in bed, a revelation. Inez was neither. She did not fit into any of his categories. But there was something exotic about her, so unlike his wife, and she exuded what he had once described to himself as a seething sexuality, as if all her desire was forcefully contained in an internal cauldron of anger, a dark, biting resentment that enveloped him in her pain and sharpened all his senses. And she had her idiosyncrasies; after her climax she could not bear to be touched, at least not sexually, but in that phase of peace beyond peace she was willing for him to put his arms around her, though only so long as he was completely still and did not move. That motel room became a cradle in which they lay as newborns.

One evening she told him that Daniel now kept a spiritual journal and that he left it around the house in obvious places, from which she deduced that he wanted her to read it. This intrigued him, and he persuaded her to bring it along the following Thursday.

'Do you want to read it?' she asked.

'No, that would be improper,' he said, archly. 'I'd like *you* to read it to me.'

And she did, though only the once and it was nothing out of the ordinary. 'He is with me always. I feel His presence. I know His love.' The usual, or what he imagined was the usual, though there was one passage that amused him. 'Ralph said tonight that Jesus inhabits me, that he has come to take up residence in the rooms of my body. But I find it hard to visualise these rooms. I see only the attic in my head, full of junk, all my junk thoughts. I am waiting for it to fill with light. Either that or I will have to look for the manhole into my Father's roof.' The bit about the manhole was a joke, he thought; the boy had not lost his sense of humour. But Inez couldn't see it, was anxious for reassurance. 'Do you think he's in danger?' she asked.

'How do you mean?'

'You know … of losing his grip?'

'His grip on what?'

She was exasperated then, as if he were missing the obvious. 'His grip on *reality*.'

Unhappily the diary didn't have the same galvanising effect on him as the Letter to the Romans. The diary was wistful. It did not rouse him to combat. It did not have the gladiatorial ruthlessness of Paul the Apostle. Not that he had ever read any of the Pauline epistles and nor did he intend to. It would not be the same as hearing it from her lips. But he did one evening look up the website of the Evangelical Students Union. It showed a cluster of happy young faces and was emblazoned with the banner, *Faith alone will save us.*

Would it, he wondered? Wasn't it all about their young bodies? For believers in the spirit these Protestant youth were obsessed with the body, just like their great mentor, Paul. In all of their literature on the net there seemed to be scarcely a single reference to the soul. Death was complete, and the body lay mouldering until the moment of the Second Coming, when Jesus would appear, not to liberate the soul but to resurrect the material body. Well, then, he could relate to that bit at least. The body was the all and the everything, and in their motel-room trysts on a Thursday evening he and Inez enacted their own sacred revivalism.

Would Daniel preach at his mother if he had a girlfriend? He thought not. Young evangelicals, he discovered, believed in virginity. They even got engaged before marriage, a quaint old custom that seemed to be making a comeback. He told himself that what Daniel needed was sex, which he desired but which terrified him. Though inexperienced he perhaps already knew from deep instinct that this, the greatest of consolations, was also the most fragile. It was short-lived, and worse, another man could take it away from you. God was abstract but more reliable, and if you could throw the cage of God around your girl and hold her there then so much the better. Except *that* didn't work, as numerous scandals among the devout testified. The terror of sex could not be avoided. You had to put yourself on the line. You had to have faith of another kind.

For seven months his evenings with Inez continued without interruption. Amazingly, the cocoon held. The same room at the same time, and both of them, they discovered, unerringly punctual. In between these assignations they never rang one another. For his part he was tempted, but resisted the urge to a more mundane familiarity because he knew it would break the spell. The uncertainty of their arrangement, the knowledge in any given week that one of them might not turn up, and the other be left stranded, only heightened his sense of anticipation and the thrill of her appearance, each time, since it was he who mostly got there first (having only to walk across the footbridge over Parramatta Road). He never asked if it worked this way for her, because that would have risked analysis and the intrusion of the cerebral into their teasing animal foreplay. They might even have bored one another, and it was too big a risk to take. The tumescent magic of it was too fragile and so it had to remain as it began, like a time capsule or, rather, a capsule out of time. The very mediocrity of their surroundings was conducive: the beige wallpaper, the standard catalogue lamps with chocolate-brown shades, the green quilted bedcover, the electric jug on a tray and the cheap teabags and instant coffee they never used – all perfectly calculated to offer not a single distraction, no trace of the personal, or of fashion. No *statement*.

Some evenings they hardly spoke at all. After the first month she ceased even to mention Daniel and by then the time had passed when he had need of any proxy in the room. Paul the Apostle had served his purpose.

But there were other temptations and he had to be careful, to maintain a constant alertness. One night he dreamed again about the lake, a terrifying dream of falling. He stood on top of the dry stone wall and swayed; at any moment the stones beneath his feet threatened to dislodge and slide into the dark water so that he staggered, and gasped, and scrambled for a foothold, until at last he woke in a cold sweat, mouth agape.

It was a Thursday morning, and all day the dream stayed with him, the sublime, unearthly shadow of it, so that by evening he was tempted to tell Inez, to dissolve the terror of it in her embrace. There was a moment when, staring down into his whiskey, he hovered on the brink of confidences, but something pulled him back. If he spoke to her as he once did to his wife then the spell of their sexual intimacy might shatter. The risk was too great. It was not part of their compact.

Then, one Thursday, she failed to turn up. He waited for a phone message or a note (a note would have been more like Inez) but, nothing. Had she decided to break it off? Had she become bored with his lovemaking?

In the days that followed he felt years older. Every small pleasure became dulled, his coffee tasted bitter, he missed an important deadline. He waited and waited; he would not attempt to contact her. He thought it might be an aberration and he ached for the following Thursday.

Again, an empty room. The hideous quilt cover, the cheerful travel magazines, the tacky brochure on available movies with special rates for 'adult viewing'. This time he felt hollowed out with rage. Now the blandness of the room mocked him, recast him into an impotent old fool, and he felt an urge to smash his fist through the cloudy grey glass of the television. What an ugly, futile object it was! He wanted to hurl those brown bedside lamps at the discreetly curtained window and bellow out the insult of his aloneness, of her desertion. He flung open the door of the room with a loud crack and strode out into the car park, over the footbridge and back across the campus to his office, where he drank from a bottle of whiskey he kept in a drawer. The department office was closed, the staff gone home. It was too late to access the files but he would do it first thing in the morning; he would look up Daniel's home address and get her number that way. He would ring her at home and tell her what he thought of her.

Her voice at the end of the phone was beyond disconcerting. He could hear himself breathing heavily, like a stalker. 'Well?' he demanded.

'The cancer has returned,' she said, flatly. Her voice was reedy and strained. 'I can't see you. We have to stop now, John.'

'The cancer? Where?'

'What does it matter where?'

There was a silence. For a few deadly moments he had nothing to say.

'Look, John, I've had this conversation too many times already this week.'

'I'm sorry. I'm sorry for blundering around like this.' Yes, he was, blundering that is, which wasn't going to be of any consolation to her. 'It makes no difference to me. I'd still like to see you.' There was silence at the other end of the phone. 'I can help you,' he said feebly.

'No,' she said, and her voice was corrosive. 'No, to be honest with you, John, you can't help me.'

For a moment he thought to say, 'Yes I can, of course I can help you. I can help look after you. I can drive you around, I can cook for you.' But of course this was absurd. He was beyond the pale.

That had been the essence of their arrangement and it was too late now to change it.

'Daniel will look after me,' she said firmly. 'It will be a test of his Christian charity.' She allowed herself a bitter laugh, and that laugh was seductive. It flooded him with muscle memory, flesh to flesh, bone to bone. Letter to the Romans.

'Please ring me,' he said feebly, 'if you change your mind. If there is anything I can do.'

'Yes, John,' she said, dismissing him. 'Thank you for calling.'

Thank you for calling! How could she say this? How could she patronise him in this way, he who had given her hours of pleasure. How dare she? Again he was enraged. He deserved *more*, he deserved better. Unable to sleep he lay rigid on his bed with taut shoulders and a stiff neck. Into the hollow cave of his mind came an image of her chest, not one but two pale-pink scars, wounds of living tissue that he would press down on, the greying hair on his chest, he would smother all this out of reckoning in an hour of lovemaking. In their room. In the cocoon. One more time, at least. And how special it would be, how loaded with portent, like a loaded gun at their heads. The excitement of it! The excitement of death. He had faced it once before and he could face it again!

He must go and remonstrate with her. He must show her, prove to her that her body still had life in it. He had no rights but he was a man possessed. He had never asked her where she lived but of course he knew, because he had looked up Daniel's file.

He sat up abruptly like a puppet in jack-knife and went downstairs, out to where his car was parked on the street. In the driver's seat he looked in his road atlas and it was easy to find her house, right in the bend of Quakers Hat Bay.

There was little traffic at that time of night and within twenty minutes he was there, parked outside an impeccably maintained Californian bungalow with leadlight windows. The large front garden was paved and there were small flowerbeds in curved shapes, bordered by trimmed boxed hedges and trees in terracotta pots. It was all so very neat; hideously so.

He rang her number. It rang and rang and no-one answered, and yet there were lights on inside. He got out of the car, picked up a pebble and threw it at the front window where the light was on. Then he threw another, and looked around quickly to see if he was being observed. He returned to the car and rang again. This time she answered.

'Please go away,' she said curtly.

'No.' He was breathing hard.

She hung up.

He got out of the car again and this time he almost tripped over one of her flowerbeds. The path to the front door was narrow and winding, and although there was a bright moon he was disoriented.

'*Inez!*' he yelled, thumping with his fist on the front door. He waited. '*No,*' he whispered to himself. '*No.*'

For a while he stood there, fuming, waiting for her to open the door. A car shone its headlights directly at him, no doubt some busybody neighbour, and he turned and glared. What now?

It was still early, not yet nine, and he would give her time to think about it, to relent. He would go for a walk and work off some steam and come back in half an hour. On his map it showed a bush reserve at the end of the street and he locked the car and set out down the road to where the bitumen terminated in a clearing. As he drew closer he could see a barbecue stand, some picnic tables and a cluster of moonlit gums that overlooked the water. Without hesitation he strode through the clearing and plunged into the bush, heedless, down a narrow track and into the path of a spider's web that clung to his hair and shoulder. Through the trees he could see the ripple and gleam of water, could hear the swell from a passing ferry as it lapped against the rocks. When he emerged onto the shore he tripped and fell, and steadying himself against a large boulder he grazed his palm and swore. Then, panting and dizzy, he sat on the boulder and pictured himself in her bedroom. It would be upstairs, next to Daniel's, and with thin walls so that sound would travel, and he looked around this room and he saw that it was full of … full of *things*, personal things, little blobs of sentimental meaning, women's things, distractions every one of them; photographs of people he didn't know, knick-knacks, cosmetic creams and perfumes, a basket of sweaty linen. And who would he be in this strange room? Where would he fit in? A rutting ersatz spouse who got up in the morning in his shorts and flip-flops and squeezed orange juice? What sadness would inhere in all this, and how awkward he would be, how out of place.

He got up, and his joints had stiffened and there was an ache in his hand where he had grazed it against the rock. He could see the opening of the path only a few metres away, and began his climb, back up to the level of the bitumen. As he approached the grassy verge a pair of headlights swept the road and he looked up to see an old blue Mitsubishi Magna pull into her drive. The form that emerged from it was unmistakably Daniel's.

*

That night was a long one. By four in the morning he was beyond exhaustion; he felt as if he might never sleep again. I have been abandoned a second time, he told himself. And so soon. For a long time he thought only of their motel room, and relived the act itself, over and over with infinite variation; it had become sacred to him, undefiled. And now she was dying and he didn't even have a picture of her, not even an image on his mobile phone (he had once, like a gauche adolescent, tried to photograph them together naked on the motel bed and she had pushed his hand away). He had nothing to remind him of her, no memento. The nearest thing, perversely, would be the small school Bible that belonged to Alice. It would probably still be in her old room. With this thought he dragged himself off the rumpled bed, feeling as if his body was weighted with lead. He slouched into the small bedroom next door and surveyed Alice's bookshelf. There it was, on the very top shelf, layered in dust.

Back in his own room he sat by the window, the one that looked out to the steeple of St. Stephen's, and settled into the cane chair in which his wife had spent her last day. He opened the Bible and turned the pages until he found the beginning of Romans: *To all God's beloved in Rome, who are called to be saints …* And for a moment he could hear Inez's voice, the rise and fall of its sharp, sardonic inflections. But no, it wouldn't do, the text was too abrasive: *For the wrath of God is revealed from heaven against all ungodliness …* Paul was passionate but he was a scold: full of rage, of grievance and indignation. Still, he was reluctant to put the book down as if, in abandoning it, he was abandoning his last connection with her, so he skimmed ahead, looking for the first verses of Corinthians. Wasn't there something in there, somewhere, about love? But the tone, alas, was the same. *Where is the one who is wise? Where is the scribe? Where is the debater of this age? Has not God made foolish the wisdom of the world?*

Enough. He was too much of an old Roman to endure this stuff and he laid the book on the windowsill and returned to bed. It was almost 5 a.m. He had survived the night. Now he could sleep. And sleep he did, though not for long, and he dreamed again of the lake. The village, the oak trees, the carpet of acorns on the ground, the dry stone wall, everything as before, only this time he wasn't afraid. He hoisted himself onto the top of the wall, dislodging a hail of rock that almost cost him his balance, and he took a deep breath and steadied. Then, with slow deliberation, he extended his arms and dived out over the glassy surface of the water—

He woke. The room was stuffy and he lay there in a sweat, his heart pounding. I am still here, he thought. *I am still here.* He looked at the clock. 5.40 a.m. The light had begun to filter in at the edges of the window and the blind hung like a stiff shroud. Well, he would get up, he would get up and wash this night off his skin.

Inside the shower bay he stood woodenly, feet planted apart, and he allowed the merciful wet to envelop him. When at last the water turned to lukewarm he emerged with a towel to stand at the window and look out over the terraced rooftops, shadowy in the dawn light. The street was deserted; frangipani flowers lay along the gutter and a beady-eyed currawong perched on the iron ledge of his balcony. I will just stand here, he thought. The water dripped from his body but he could not summon the energy to move. Then the phone rang and a car pulled up outside his gate. As he reached for the phone he glanced down into the street and in that moment his heart contracted. The car was Inez's. The passenger door opened and Daniel unfolded himself onto the pavement. He had an envelope in his hand and in a quick, deft movement he slid it into the letterbox and climbed back into his seat.

The car pulled out into the empty road.

He still has the contents of that envelope, propped against the desk lamp in his study. It is a postcard, a painting of Monet's waterlilies. It reads:

Dear John,
Thank you. Thank you for everything.
Love,
Inez

PUBLICATION DETAILS

All stories are previously unpublished apart from the following:

An earlier version of 'Reading *Madame Bovary*' appeared in *The Best Australian Stories 2002*, ed. Peter Craven, Black Inc., Melbourne, 2002.

Two earlier versions of 'Perfect', entitled 'Diary of Her Body', appeared in *Scripsi*, Vol. 6, No. 2, Oxford University Press, Melbourne, 1990; and in *Bodyjamming*, ed. Jenna Mead, Vintage, Sydney, 1997.

An earlier version of 'The Art of Convalescence' appeared in *New Australian Stories*, ed. Aviva Tuffield, Scribe, Melbourne, 2009.

An earlier version of part of 'Ground Zero' appeared in *Overland*, 164, Spring, 2001.